...mily tragedy? Liza Gyllenhaal plumbs the complexity of human emotions in this wonderful novel. With sensitivity and compassion, she creates characters that will pull at your heart on their journey through grief. I loved reading *So Near*, a truly believable and compelling story."

—Katharine Davis, author of *A Slender Thread*

Praise for
Local Knowledge

"This is a book to savor. . . . Selling real estate is the surface story, but as you peel back the layers throughout the chapters you realize it is about family relationships, old friends, and new friends." —*Publishers Weekly*

"A damn fine novel. . . . Gyllenhaal truly makes the Berkshire setting jump to life. And she is terrific with character—I particularly admired the way she wove personality into action—so that the behavior of her characters in her setting seems natural, unforced, and often really compelling. In a way, this is what really makes a novel like *Local Knowledge* exciting—I constantly felt as if I knew the people on the page, so I was captivated by their story. . . . I really look forward to her next novel."

—John Katzenbach, bestselling author of *The Wrong Man*

"Gripping and deeply perceptive, this powerful debut novel reveals the pleasures and struggles of true friendship and the painful decisions we often make for acceptance and love. Small-town life and work are rendered in vivid detail, as are the memorable characters, who come alive in the hands of a gifted new writer."

—Ben Sherwood, author of *Charlie St. Cloud*

continued . . .

Written by today's freshest new talents and selected by New American Library, NAL Accent novels touch on subjects close to a woman's heart, from friendship to family to finding our place in the world. The Conversation Guides included in each book are intended to enrich the individual reading experience, as well as encourage us to explore these topics together—because books, and life, are meant for sharing.

Visit us online at www.penguin.com.

"A powerful and deeply moving novel about the lies we tell ourselves, the moral corners we cut, and the loved ones we betray to get what we want. Gyllenhaal has X-ray vision into the human heart and a sharp eye for contemporary mores and social maneuvering. She knows women and men and children, and pins them to the page with some of the most dazzling prose I've read in a long time."

—Ellen Feldman, author of *Scottsboro*

"Liza Gyllenhaal's new novel invites instant immersion. . . . With insight and sensitivity, Liza Gyllenhaal deftly draws the reader of *Local Knowledge* down through the layers and layers of intimate entanglements her characters have with each other, the land, and the new and old ways of life. I highly recommend *Local Knowledge* to anyone who loves good writing, a good story, and hopes to come away from a book with a deeper understanding of others' lives and choices."

—Tina Welling, author of *Cowboys Never Cry*

"Enjoyable and intriguing. . . . Gyllenhaal has a magnificent grasp of small-town dynamics. . . . Gyllenhaal breaks the mold of expectation by weaving in complex interactions over years of shared economic and emotional struggles. That weaving is both figurative and literal. The alternating story line is far more effective than [the] typical flashback passages of many novels. The background chapters flow beautifully with the present and explain the long-standing tensions among Maddie, Paul, and Luke. . . . [T]hrough Gyllenhaal's superb skill there is an almost poetic quality to how the events of the past tie into the fragile relationships of the present."   —Jody Kordana, *Berkshire Eagle*

"How accomplished this first novel is . . . a rich, authentic read . . . with a tightly focused cast of characters once again proving the old adage that less is more . . . a timely enough message if ever there was one."

—*Berkshire Living*

So Near

LIZA GYLLENHAAL

NAL
ACCENT

NAL ACCENT
Published by New American Library,
a division of Penguin Group (USA) Inc.,
375 Hudson Street, New York, New York 10014, USA
Penguin Group (Canada), 90 Eglinton Avenue East, Suite 700, Toronto,
Ontario M4P 2Y3, Canada (a division of Pearson Penguin Canada Inc.)
Penguin Books Ltd., 80 Strand, London WC2R 0RL, England
Penguin Ireland, 25 St. Stephen's Green, Dublin 2,
Ireland (a division of Penguin Books Ltd.)
Penguin Group (Australia), 250 Camberwell Road, Camberwell,
Victoria 3124, Australia (a division of Pearson Australia Group Pty. Ltd.)
Penguin Books India Pvt. Ltd., 11 Community Centre,
Panchsheel Park, New Delhi - 110 017, India
Penguin Group (NZ), 67 Apollo Drive, Rosedale, Auckland 0632,
New Zealand (a division of Pearson New Zealand Ltd.)
Penguin Books (South Africa) (Pty.) Ltd., 24 Sturdee Avenue,
Rosebank, Johannesburg 2196, South Africa

Penguin Books Ltd., Registered Offices:
80 Strand, London WC2R 0RL, England

First published by NAL Accent, an imprint of New American Library,
a division of Penguin Group (USA) Inc.

First Printing, September 2011
1 3 5 7 9 10 8 6 4 2

LIBRARY OF CONGRESS CATALOGING-IN-PUBLICATION DATA:
Gyllenhaal, Liza.
So near/Liza Gyllenhaal.
p. cm.
ISBN 978-0-451-23457-5
1. Traffic accidents—Fiction. 2. Children—Death—Fiction. 3. Married people—
Fiction. 4. Loss (Psychology)—Fiction. 5. Life change events—Fiction.
6. Psychological fiction. 7. Domestic fiction. I. Title.
PS3607.Y53S6 2011
813'.6—dc22   2011009612

Set in Sabon • Designed by Elke Sigal
Printed in the United States of America

In memory of my mother,
Virginia Childs Gyllenhaal

And for W.E.B.,
as always

Acknowledgments

I am indebted to Michael Lambertus for his insights into the workings of product liability law and to Maurice Sieradzski for explaining the ins and outs of the New York State court system. I am deeply grateful to: Ellen Feldman, mentor, friend, critic, and cheerleader nonpareil; Natalie Lambertus and Patricia Aakre for their thoughtful and extremely helpful early reads of the manuscript; my agent, Susan Cohen, for going beyond the call; my editor, Tracy Bernstein, for being such a wunderkind; and my husband, William Bennett, for once again acting as my toughest critic and staunchest ally.

So Near

Part One

1

Cal

❧

"Horigan Lumber and Hardware?" said the girlish
voice on the other end of the line. Lori Swinson.
She's been answering the main number and handling phone
sales at the store for five or six years now, and it drives me
crazy how she always turns the name of my father's forty-
year-old business operation into a question.

"You sure about that?" I asked.

"What?" Despite the fact that we go through this routine
almost every time I have to call the 800 number, I could
almost hear the wheels creaking in her brain. "I'm sorry, but
I— Oh! It's you, isn't it, Cal?"

"Yeah, Lori, it's me. How're you doing?" But before she
could launch into it—and she always assumes I actually
want to know—I added, "The old man around? He's not
picking up his cell."

"He's over at Deer Creek Bistro with Edmund and
some guy."

"Still?" I looked at my watch. It was closing in on two

thirty. My dad's lunch hour is typically a ten-minute pause over a take-out sandwich from the deli counter at Covington Public Market next door. Even his business lunches tend to clock in at under an hour. Most of us know he's only wasting his time at a sit-down meal because he's hoping to squeeze out another thirty days on the payables schedule or browbeat some poor bastard into a better bulk-discount deal. Any sales rep who thinks he's going to sweet-talk Jay Horigan into some new line of double-hung thermals over dessert and coffee has a thing or two to learn.

"Want me to page him?" Lori asked.

"That's okay. Kurt and I will probably just swing by and surprise him."

"That's got to be some kind of a record," I told Kurt as I hung up the phone. My older brother is an online solitaire addict, and when he finds himself with free time on our office computer, he spends it riffling through a digital stack of cards. Without taking his eyes off the screen, he tilted his head back to let me know he heard me and was primed for my big news. We've been working literally side by side for nearly eight years now, and that, combined with the brother thing, means we could probably communicate on an entirely nonverbal level if we had to.

"Dad's still at lunch."

Kurt swiveled his chair around to face me.

"What's up?"

"Edmund's with him. So I guess everything's okay." The whole family's been in code red since my dad's open-heart surgery last August. They caught the blockages at a routine checkup and were wheeling him into the operating room at Albany Medical by five that afternoon. But the reverberations of a near-miss linger: the seismic activity that you can't feel but still sense continues to shift ominously under the family's tectonic plates.

"Maybe he's finally taking our advice," I told Kurt as he shut down the computer. "Maybe he's just smelling the roses."

"Yeah, maybe," Kurt replied as we hit the lights and headed out the door. But we both know the odds aren't good. Jay Horigan doesn't take advice; he dispenses it. He glad-hands his opinions around to everyone in the vicinity the same way he doles out his beloved bright green Horigan Lumber and Hardware magnetic business cards. The man lives to work. He built the business up from nothing, and his character is practically pressure treated into the main store's floorboards. The day he actually does start to slack off? That's when we begin to worry.

Kurt preceded me down the steps, and I noticed how his scalp was starting to shine through on top. At thirty-three, Kurt's five years older than me, a shorter, stouter, bearded take on your basic Horigan model. He started losing hair and putting on weight at an accelerated pace about the same time our company, Horigan Builders, really began to take off.

We raised this cinder-block outbuilding in the back of Kurt's place two years ago. We store our heavy equipment on the ground floor and have our office space above. It's nothing fancy—just insulated drywall, a couple of electrical space heaters, and furniture and computer systems from the exclusive Office Depot line. We lucked out on the business, I know: right place, time, background, backing. But Dad says you make your own luck. And for both Kurt and me, our father's outsized pride in Horigan Builders means more to us than the six figures we've been routinely pulling down the past few years.

It was only early April, but the sunny Saturday afternoon was as warm and promising as any day in June. The robins were back, performing their little three-hop jig on the hill behind Kurt's contemporary colonial. The trees hadn't greened out yet, but I could see that some of the furry buds on the pussy willows down by the brook were already beginning to flower. Kurt's wife, Tessa, eyes closed, face turned to the sun, was sitting on a folding chair in the backyard with eighteen-month-old Jamie planted next to her on an army blanket. As we approached, the baby wobbled to his feet, took five short steps, teetered briefly, then collapsed onto his well-padded backside.

"Jaybird!" Kurt said, scooping the kid up before he had a chance to cry. "Birdie Bird!" Kurt covered his son's face with kisses, and Jamie kicked his feet with joy—just the way my two-year-old, Betsy, does when I plant raspberries across her belly.

"What's up?" Tessa asked, shielding her eyes against the strong, unfiltered sunlight. Something in our stance seemed to put her on alert. Tessa teaches math and science part-time at the regional high school and has zero tolerance for any sort of male shenanigans.

"We're going down to talk Dad into letting some of the guys go early for a pickup game," Kurt told her as he danced in a little circle with Jamie. "Get a head start on the season."

"It's too nice a day," I said when Tessa just sat there, saying nothing, looking from Kurt to me and back to her husband again. I didn't add "to work," though it was on the tip of my tongue. The whole subject of work, or lack thereof, is one we're all tending to dance around these days as clumsily as Kurt was with the baby. It was fine during the long winter months to complain about how dead things were. Whoever worked in January and February except to cut down trees and make lumber? And that's one thankless job in the often subzero wind chills that regularly sweep across our hills. No, in winters past, Kurt and I were happy to put our feet up for a stretch, bear down on the paperwork, and wait for the ground to thaw and the phones to start ringing again.

But this year we were uneasy even then; two of the three projects we'd lined up for the spring fell through due to financing problems. And we kept hearing about how the roof was collapsing on new housing starts across the region. Kurt and I would sit around and grouse for hours about the fucking banks and the greedy Wall Street bastards who'd sliced and diced those subprime mortgages into pieces of worthless shit. But when the snow began to melt in the middle of March and we still sat for days at a time without a single lead, we began to slowly move away from the economy as a topic of conversation. We talked instead about the Red Sox's chances. How long Giambi had been juicing. Whether we should go ahead and asterisk the whole damned Baseball Hall of Fame.

Just that morning we'd gotten another call from one of our regular crew members, Mike Lerner. He was touching base again about the Ravitch job, the one big piece of new business we still had on the docket. Kurt had put in a call to Philip Ravitch in the city earlier in the week about breaking ground. He hadn't called back yet. This was our second house for the criminal defense lawyer. The first, a hilltop octagonal contemporary, had been ceded to his second wife in a nasty divorce settlement. Some guys never learn—the "cottage-style" megamansion we were going to build that spring for the balding septuagenarian was a wedding present for wife number three. We'd already signed the contract and banked his deposit. Trouble was, for the first time in years, we had a lot more guys counting on us for work than we could use.

"Any day now, I think . . . ," Kurt was telling Mike. I could hear the uncertainty in his voice. I hated to think where all this was heading. Kurt and I hadn't talked about it yet, but very soon we were going to have to go down the roster of our regular guys—many of them lifelong friends—and make some tough decisions.

"Hey!" I called over, interrupting my brother. "Ask Mike if he wants to play ball. Look at this beautiful day! What are we doing inside? Let's get out there and see what we've got."

Between Horigan Lumber and Horigan Builders we've cobbled together a baseball lineup that usually ends the season ranking first in the informal network of teams that crisscross our quadrant of the county. Depending on the year, the five or six teams that make up the league rotate every Saturday, playing on one of the run-down ball fields behind the old Covington or Red River high schools. Both of these brick buildings are abandoned now, windows boarded up, empty since the mid-1980s, when flush state tax coffers underwrote the big new regional complex.

"Yeah, why the hell not?" Kurt had said, and half a dozen phone calls later we had the Horigan Builders team lined up. Now we had to see if Dad would let his guys go.

I was expecting some kind of blowback from Tessa. She

tends to keep Kurt on a short leash, especially since Jamie arrived. And nobody has to tell me that she considers me a bad influence. The pampered, party-boy baby of the family. Tessa can be prickly and judgmental, and I know she feels that I take my good luck way too much for granted. My wife, Jenny. Our business. The old farm as a wedding gift. Then Betsy, without any of the miscarriages I know Tessa and Kurt had to suffer through.

So I was surprised and gratified when she said to Kurt, "Okay, sure. We could all use a break. I'll call Jenny, and we'll pull things together for a cookout after the game. You go with Cal, and I'll pick up Jenny and Betsy on my way down."

The inside of the Jeep was stifling. I rolled down my side window after I started the engine, and Kurt did the same. It must have been almost seventy degrees out by then, dangerously warm for this time of year. The heat could force fruit trees into flower, and then a late frost might come along and wipe out a whole crop. I was feeling both edgy and elated, like the nights during Jenny's senior year when she would sneak out to meet me. The air had that rich, wormy smell of thawing earth. On our left, the land sloped downward into a long valley where rows of winter corn straggled through the mud like a defeated army. Beyond that, the Berkshire hills rolled eastward in huge gray swells.

The only place in Covington that serves a decent sit-down lunch is Deer Creek Bistro. Though Jenny likes it, I think the Frenchified menu is pretentious, and the owner, Larry Bisel, is always first-naming you and announcing the day's specials in hushed, reverent tones. But he was nowhere in sight when Kurt and I came through the door. The only people left in the place were my father, my brother Edmund, and some overweight red-faced guy in a dark blue suit whom I vaguely recognized. The three of them, seated at a banquette in a dark corner of the room, were leaning toward one another over a jumble of coffee cups, half-eaten desserts, and a bottle of wine. My dad and Edmund drink only beer or whiskey, so I thought the wine might account for the high color of the man lunching with them.

"Guys!" Edmund said, half rising from his seat when he saw us winding our way through the tables.

Edmund's the oldest, Dad's right-hand man, the number-crunching end of the operation. Since Kurt and I left the business to go off on our own, he's been heir apparent and increasingly impatient to ascend his coveted throne. People say we resemble each other physically: big framed and lanky with a kind of bowlegged swagger. But there's always been something secretive and judgmental about Edmund that actually makes us about as different as two—or three—brothers can be. What you see is what you get with me. I like to give the other guy the benefit of the doubt. Gullible, Edmund calls it. I think Edmund believes, like Tessa, that my success is the product of dumb luck and Dad's brand of hail-fellow salesmanship, something that doesn't come easily to Edmund. He's more comfortable in his back office with his inventory printouts and aging-receivables reports. Edmund and I, born eight years apart, have been squaring off against each other for as long as I can remember. Kurt, our middle brother, plays mediator.

Dad turned around.

"Hey, boys," he said. "Pull up a chair. You remember

Terrence Kennedy from First Union, don't you?" I worry about the fact that Dad's heart surgery has left him looking so physically diminished. His neck has gotten scrawny, his face pouchy and off-color. There's also something overhearty in his attitude these days, as though he's trying to compensate for some deep-seated exhaustion or sadness that he can't quite name.

I didn't take up Dad's offer to sit down. I could sense a definite uneasiness hovering around the table. Our visit wasn't welcome. Kurt must have picked up on it, too.

"We can't stay," he told Dad as his gaze moved from Terrence to Edmund. "We called around and our crew's meeting for a practice game in half an hour. We were hoping you'd let your guys off a little early, too."

"I mean, look at the day out there," I added.

"Well, I don't think—," Edmund began.

"Sure," Dad said, throwing down his napkin and pushing back from the table. "Good call. Let's go get some of that vitamin D into our bones."

Dad's still as tall as me, but he's lost so much weight he had to hitch up his pants as he rose from the chair. None of his clothes really fit him anymore. He's been backsliding recently, but when he was first recuperating he swore off drinking and cigarettes and started a big regime of herbal supplements and vitamins.

"You go on, Dad," Edmund said. "I'm going to stay and finish up with Terry."

"Right. Thank you, sir," Dad said, leaning over and shaking hands with the banker. "Your insights and advice have been edifying. And keep my boys here in mind if you decide to go ahead and build that new branch office up in Harringdale."

"What was that all about?" Kurt asked Dad when we got outside.

"Who knows?" Dad said as we walked three abreast across the empty parking lot to my Jeep. "Something Eddie has up his sleeve. You'll have to ask him."

But he knew we wouldn't. And I think Dad counts on that for cover. There was never any overt break with Edmund when Kurt and I started Horigan Builders, but there were plenty of bad feelings all around. We hadn't invited Edmund to join us, not that he would ever have left his safe perch with Dad. But he had to act all pissed off anyway, and then turn around and tell Dad that he couldn't advise backing us on a start-up loan. Not that Dad listened to him, but my blood still boils when I think about it. We got the last laugh, though, riding that beautiful long crest of the construction wave. Or the most recent laugh, anyway. No one's laughing much now.

❦

"It's starting to drop off," Jenny said, coming up to where I was standing behind the backstop with a group of the guys around the cooler. As usual, we'd been drinking beer on and off through the game. It felt great to be out there again. We'd divided the players up so that it was basically Horigan Lumber versus Horigan Builders. We were in the top of the ninth and all tied up. My shirt was soaked through with sweat.

"It is?" I said, smiling down at her. She looked so good,

standing there in her jeans and bright red Horigan Builders sweatshirt, Betsy straddling her hip. Jenny's petite but curvy, even more so since our daughter was born. She has a husky voice that catches like an adolescent boy's. No question, she's still the prettiest girl in the room. I must have had something of a buzz on, because I wasn't really thinking about what she'd just told me. Instead, I was contemplating what we'd do later, after the cookout, after we bundled the baby into bed. The other days of the week are optional, bonus days, but Saturday is always our one sure night.

"Yes, it is," she said in a chiding tone, smiling back at me as if she knew exactly what was on my mind. "Tessa and I think it's going to be too chilly for a cookout by the time you guys are done. And besides, we looked at the grills and they're all gunky. I don't think anybody's cleaned them since last summer. Why don't we just have everybody back to our place and you can do the honors?"

"Fine by me," I told her. Since my folks gave Jenny and me the farmhouse as a wedding present, making their long-discussed move to a restored Victorian nearer town, we've felt obliged to throw open our doors as often as possible to the rest of the family. Not that entertaining is any kind of hardship for the two of us. We both love a good party. Kurt and the crew helped me renovate the back of the house so that we now have one long, beamed room that's just right for entertaining. We have speakers mounted inside and out. In warm weather, we open up the row of new French doors and blast music out into the backyard. The yard takes a lot of our spare time. I've been repairing the flagstone patio and Jenny has been trying to rehabilitate the old gardens. We've got one of those Weber Genesis gas grills that's almost professional grade and has a cooking area big enough to feed a small army.

"I'll need to do some shopping," Jenny told me, just as Ivan Gruber struck out swinging. I was up next. The bases were empty.

"Okay, but wait until the game's over," I told her as I picked up a bat and started to walk toward the plate. "I'd hate for you to miss seeing me hit this home run."

Sometimes, when everything's aligned just right, I think wishing can actually make a thing happen. For the last half hour or so, the sun had been caught behind slow-moving cumulus clouds. But as I tapped my bat against the little dirt mound that formed home plate, a fistful of sunbeams burst through the cloud bank and, like God's hand in that Michel-angelo painting, seemed to bless the worn paths and beaten-down winter grass of the playing field.

I kept my thoughts from drifting toward my father, who was somewhere behind me, and how he wasn't coming back from his surgery anywhere near fast enough. I refused to let my mind dwell on Jenny, sitting with Tessa and the babies on the bleachers, and how quickly her moods could shift these days, how I kept catching her staring off into space. I made my mind a blank, erasing Kurt, the business, Ravitch not returning our call, all the guys who were counting on us. Instead I concentrated everything I had on the ball leaving Craig Linaweaver's right hand. I distilled every last damned shapeless worry in my world into one laser-sharp pinpoint of need. *Make it happen,* I told myself. *Just go ahead and make it happen.*

The second my bat connected with the ball I knew that

I'd gotten my wish. The impact went right through my body—a bolt of electricity—and the ball sailed high over the center-field fence, bounced once, then dribbled into the parking lot. And in that moment, when my hands were still twanging, even before the guys started shouting behind me, I felt a sudden letdown of easy victory. *What larger, better thing should I have asked for?* I wondered.

Mike popped up to make it an easy third out, and Horigan Lumber came roaring back with two doubles and a nasty grounder that bounced off Burt Mayer's glove and let the guy on third slide home in a cloud of dust and cheering. So my homer didn't count for much of anything after all.

Both sides gathered around the infield for one last beer before heading home.

"Tessa's going to help me with the shopping," Jenny said, walking up to me with Betsy slung over her shoulder, fast asleep. "But you better take this one back with you. I'm afraid she's coming down with something. Feel how hot her forehead is."

"I can never tell," I said, leaning over and kissing my daughter on her temple. I breathed in her sweet, musty smell. Her thumb drooped in her mouth. "She seems okay to me. Here, let me take her for you—"

"No, I don't want to wake her. I'll carry her to the Jeep. But you'll have to transfer the safety seat from Tessa's car."

We walked with the others toward the parking lot, our shadows fanning out behind us across the ball field. Jenny had canvassed the crowd and figured we should plan for at least twenty people. As we approached the cars, I was surprised to see Edmund, leaning against the hood of his Explorer, parked next to my Jeep, arms crossed, talking to Kurt.

He never comes to our games. His wife, Kristin, was sitting in the passenger seat of the Explorer, reading a book, with the five-year-old twins, Ava and Alan, buckled into their car seats behind her. Edmund and Kristin tend to live a more exalted existence than the rest of us. They've renovated one of those old Victorian-style mansions outside Hudson and usually limit their exposure to the rest of the family to major birthdays and holidays.

"Damn," I said under my breath. "I guess we'll have to invite them, too."

"Now, play nice," Jenny said. Though she's naturally accommodating, I know Jenny finds Kristin, who works as a speech therapist with underprivileged children and has zero sense of humor, pretty heavy lifting socially.

But I didn't have to ask. Thankfully, Edmund and his family were about to take off for a weekend visit with Kristin's folks in Albany. He was just hoping for a quick word with me and Kurt before they left.

"I didn't want you two to worry," Edmund said, following me and Kurt over to Tessa's Subaru. "That meeting was all Terry's idea."

"I wasn't worried," I said. "At least not until right now. Why drive all the way over here to tell us that if nothing's wrong?" Kurt unlocked the car and I leaned in to get Betsy's safety seat. It's anchored by a seat belt that snakes through narrow passages in the back of the bucket. I invariably have a hell of a time getting the damn thing unbuckled.

"Why do you always need to be such a smart-ass?" Edmund said.

"And why do you always have to be such a—," I began,

just as the belt suddenly released and the car seat fell into my arms. I staggered back with it.

"Whoa!" Edmund said, catching my arm. "I guess you guys have been putting away the old brewskies."

If anybody else had made that comment, I might have actually taken stock of myself and wondered if, indeed, I wasn't a little loaded. After all, it had been a long, hot afternoon. And I'd had—how many beers? I couldn't remember clearly now. But Edmund's condescending tone, that fake, folksy "brewskies," just provoked the hell out of me. I shook his arm away and turned to face him, gripping Betsy's car seat in my right hand like a shield.

"What the—?" Edmund said, taking a step back. "What the hell's with you, little brother?"

"Nothing," Kurt said, stepping between us. He slid his arm around my waist and pulled me to him in a rough hug. "Don't be such an asshole," he whispered in my ear. Then he slapped me on the back and said, "We're all good. Right?"

Jenny and Tessa, who were waiting for us by the Jeep, had stopped talking. I never like to walk away from a fight, but I realized that I'd somehow lost the thread of my argument with Edmund. Or, more to the point, that it wound back through so many years and around so many issues that to face off against him now seemed too arbitrary. A waste. *What the hell's the problem here?* That was a question that eventually the two of us were going to have to answer. But I knew that there were bound to be other, better opportunities to do so.

"Sure," I said. "Sorry. Long day."

Betsy woke up and started crying. I took her while Jenny

strapped the car seat into the back of the Jeep. Edmund and his family drove off. Kurt loaded their Subaru wagon with our equipment. I handed Betsy back to Jenny and walked around the parking lot, trying to work out my anger. How could I have let Edmund push all my buttons like that? I felt a little foolish now. Muddled. Something was weighing on my mind, but I couldn't get to it.

I came back to the Jeep and climbed in. I watched in the rearview mirror as Jenny gave Betsy a long kiss on the forehead. She leaned into the front seat and told me, "She seems a lot better. Maybe it was just the heat after all." Then she smiled back at Betsy and waved.

"See you later, little gator," she said.

I took the back way up North Branch. It's not the fastest route, but it's one of the prettiest roads in the area, winding up through long rolling pastureland and a couple of old dairy farms. The last of the sunlight glinted off the top of a silo and blazed across the surface of an old cow pond. We had all the windows down. Something wasn't right. I tried to think back to what Edmund had said. About not wanting Kurt and me to worry. That business with the bank. That the meeting had been Terry's idea. Except, I remembered now, just as we were leaving the restaurant, that my eye fell on the black leather folder Deer Creek Bistro uses to present the check. It had been placed in front of Edmund.

I came to a series of little roller-coaster hills. At the crest of the third one, I heard Betsy behind me. I glanced in the rearview mirror. She was wide-awake. She was giggling as we rode the swells, her hair blowing in the breeze. Just as my gaze turned back to the road, I saw something flash right in front of us. A reddish blur with a white tail. Fox. I braked. I swerved. The fox ran into the woods. I felt the Jeep lift off the ground. We were flying. Betsy was laughing. And I remembered how I felt earlier that afternoon when I hit the home run. The euphoria, so quickly followed by regret. The conviction that I'd wished for the wrong thing. That I'd missed something important. That my luck was running out.

2

Jenny

&

*D*ahlias, I'm thinking, maybe five or six of the big white dinner-plate variety. They'd be just the thing to fill the bald spot between the hostas and the lilies of the valley. I'm visualizing that whole corner of the garden below the porch in cool shades of green, blue, and white. It would contrast nicely with the red trim around the French doors and our green wicker outdoor furniture.

I crosshatched a shape for the dahlias in my sketchbook and sat back on my heels, swatting at the no-see-ums that formed a nimbus around my head. The unseasonably hot April temperatures have forced nature out of its dormancy—insects, robins, even a lone black moth—though there was something wobbly and a little surreal about all the activity.

"Yessa and Yay Yay!" Betsy cried. She had been digging in the grass behind me, but now she dropped her plastic trowel, climbed to her feet, and took off toward the porch steps. *Tessa and Jamie. Oh damn,* I think, clutching the sketchbook to my chest. I'd been looking forward to a long, quiet afternoon of puttering around in my gardens, making notes and plans, breathing in those first tangy scents of spring: mud, grass, sap, chives. Not that I don't love Tessa and dote on Jamie, but I've been yearning for a bright spring day just like this one when I could dig my fingers into the cold and yet finally yielding earth. Another gardener would get it. But Tessa was raised in suburban Niskayuna, and her idea of a garden is a couple of plastic pots of impatiens on the front-porch steps.

This winter has been long and oppressive in ways that I'm still trying to understand. And I've been baffled about feeling down because I'm usually so good at being able to shake off the occasional bout of anxiety or depression. I learned early on how to pick myself up by my emotional bootstraps, how to shun self-pity as a sin. I've always tried to keep on the sunny side because I know what happens when you stray even briefly into the shade. How quickly darkness descends. So I count my blessings every day: Cal, Betsy, this beautiful old farmhouse and property that have been in Cal's family for more than 150 years. And, thanks to the way Horigan Builders has taken off, I was able to stop working when Betsy was born and stay home to raise her with all the love and attention my sister, Jude, and I were never shown. I've been thinking lately that maybe that's it. Maybe Mom's the reason I've been struggling with these densely knotted feelings of unhappiness and unease. And the news about Jude has just intensified the tension. Maybe I never really made that clean break I imagined, and the whole time the past has been steadily and stealthily climbing up through my heart like a rampant vine, trying to reclaim me.

"Here's our little Betsy bee!" I heard Tessa say as she

came through the kitchen. Tessa and I don't knock or ring bells in each other's homes. We were friends before we became sisters-in-law. We were pregnant together. Our babies were born just more than three months apart. We're family; there's nothing to hide. But there's also no escape. That thought would never have occurred to me a couple of months ago. I hardly like to admit it even to myself, and maybe it's just my moodiness, but recently our closeness, the assumed access Tessa has to every part of my life, has begun to chafe a little.

"My Yay Yay!" Betsy cried, climbing the steps. I followed behind her, ready to help, if need be. She's so independent these days. So determined to do everything on her own. At the same time, she's still not all that steady on her feet. She's got a rolling gait and often gets going so fast she can't help but stumble over herself and fall.

"I figured you'd be out here," Tessa said as she pushed open the French door with her hip. She was carrying Jamie in a BabyBjörn that he was rapidly outgrowing; his legs dangled down almost to her knees. "I tried calling you a couple of times before I came down."

"Look at this one," I said, laughing in spite of myself. Betsy had scrambled to her feet at the top of the steps, had grabbed hold of Jamie's right sneaker, and was kissing it. She worships her slightly younger cousin with an uninhibited intensity that's both touching and funny. She calls him "my Jay Jay" as though she owns him, or as though her love is so deep and pure that it feels like he's actually a part of her. Jamie, typical guy that he is, doesn't seem to mind—or even pay much attention to my doting daughter.

"What a day, huh?" I added, grabbing Betsy by the waist and swinging her back onto the grass where she had been playing. Tessa came down the steps, unbuckled Jamie, and set him down next to Betsy. My daughter gravely handed her cousin her plastic trowel, her most prized possession of the moment, and watched adoringly as he put it immediately into his mouth.

"Oh no, Jamie!" I said, bending over to take the toy tool away from him. "That's for digging, not eating, okay? It's dirty."

"We've had a lot worse than that in there lately," Tessa said. "I found him gnawing away on one of Petie's dog chews the other morning. I'm thinking that at least he's got to be immune to most germs and stuff by now, don't you think?"

"I guess," I said. Despite the hell Tessa went through to have Jamie—two early miscarriages that she told me about and I think a couple more she decided to keep to herself—she's a remarkably relaxed, easygoing mother. Unlike Betsy, whom I have on a strict regimen of meal- and bedtimes, Jamie's allowed to follow Tessa's and Kurt's adult schedule, which means he sometimes doesn't get put into his crib until after midnight. I've had to learn almost everything I know about child rearing from the likes of Spock, Leach, and Brazelton, whereas Tessa picked it up naturally as the middle child of five with two fully functional parents.

A part of me longs to emulate Tessa's more freestyle approach to motherhood. But like so many things that look easy at first glance, I believe it takes a lot more experience and inner confidence to pull off than I possess. I know I overthink and worry too much about every little thing when it comes to Betsy. Am I good mother? I keep asking myself. Am I at least good *enough*? The trouble is, I have no established points of reference, no inner barometer, so how can I really judge?

"It seems our husbands have reverted to their boy-hoods," Tessa said, looking out over the meadows, the fallow farmland, and the gray-blue line of rolling hills that make up our view. A lone wood duck honked overhead. Our neighbors the Grubers still keep half a dozen Holsteins, and their little herd dots the field beyond ours. I never tire of looking at this scene, though I suspect that Tessa doesn't really register it. She tends to prefer the indoors and air-conditioning. I doubt she even noticed the crazy quilt of daffodils and hyacinths I planted last November that now blanket the old haying field to the north of our house.

"Kurt's down with Cal and the other guys playing *base-ball*," she added, shaking her head. Though I know how much she loves Kurt, Tessa often talks about her husband as though he were one of her more difficult students.

"I was just getting a jump on spring myself," I said, turning back to the corner of the garden where I'd been working, my gaze resting on the thickly braided clumps of bearded irises. "I'm planning on redoing this whole section. I don't think any of these plants have been divided in at least a generation."

"So they can wait one more day, then, right?" Tessa said. "I told the boys we'd put together a cookout after the game." I know she believes she's liberating me for the afternoon. Giving me permission to have fun. I know she thinks my gardening is a way of making up for the fact that I'm a stay-at-home mom now. She imagines that I'm trying to put my five years of work experience at Pellani's Garden Center to some practical use in my own backyard. In fact, I inherited these overgrown gardens from Cal's family, and they've become as precious to me as heirloom silver or a leather-bound library might be to someone else. I'd rather be here, fingernails grimed with dirt, than anywhere else on earth. But it's hard to explain to someone who thinks that what I'm doing is just another chore. Besides, I can sense how much Tessa herself wants to take off, to do something spur-of-the-moment and carefree.

⚘

"Jude's coming back," I told Tessa after we settled down on the bottom bench of the old bleachers. It was the first time I'd said those words out loud, though I'd been turning them over in my mind ever since my younger sister called me two days ago. I know I'll have to break the news to Cal pretty soon; telling Tessa first, I realize, is my way of practicing. We'd spread a picnic blanket out in front of us for Betsy and Jamie, and they were playing side by side with a bucket of beach toys Tessa carries in the back of her car.

"To stay?" Tessa asked, turning toward me. I nodded, keeping my gaze on the playing field beyond the backstop. Cal's waved to us a few times since we got here, but I can tell he's wrapped up in the action. He's a natural athlete and a born competitor. Sometimes I worry a little how much winning means to him, how much he'd sacrifice to come out ahead.

"Yeah, she's going to move in with my dad. Which could be a good thing, you know? I think he could use the company at this point. And, God knows, she could use a little structure." My father, the Reverend Karl Honegger, still lives in the gingerbread colonial parish house next door to the Lutheran church in the center of town where Jude and I were raised. For the last thirty-plus years, he's been presiding over a congregation that has now dwindled to just a few dozen souls. Neither of his daughters among them.

"I know you told me, but I forget," Tessa said. "Where's she been most recently?"

"With Jude, the more important question is 'who's she been with?'" I replied. "Though I actually had some hopes for this one. He was a part-time teacher at a high school outside of Boston. They were together almost two years."

"What happened?"

"Turns out he was also a part-time drug dealer. Jude claims she had no idea. But the guy was selling to eighth graders, for heaven's sakes! He won't be around for a while. Jude had moved in with him, wasn't really working, and was depending on him for room and board. So it's either here or out on the street at this point."

"And how are you feeling about all this?" Tessa asked. "I mean, have you two ever really talked through, well . . . you know?"

Tessa, who didn't grow up in Covington, never really got to know my sister all that well. Or she wouldn't have had to ask if we'd talked about the fact that I'd caught Jude trying to seduce Cal five years ago last Christmas. The year we got engaged. Jude claimed she'd had too much to drink, that she was feeling jealous and threatened by our up-coming marriage. Up until then, I'd been her protector, her champion, and her best friend. It was Jude's final, flagrant act of rebellion and bad behavior before leaving Covington. But, yes, in her own way, she's never stopped "talking through" what happened. Chapter and verse, ad infinitum. Though I haven't seen her since, she calls me a lot, and we rarely have a phone conversation when she doesn't try to

bring up "that insanity with Cal" and want to analyze and
parse it yet again.

"Sure, we've talked," I told Tessa. "But it's really not the
kind of thing you can 'talk through,' you know? I don't think
it's ever going to go away. But honestly? I have missed her.
It's been way too long. She's a real character. Wild and crazy.
I see her in Betsy sometimes. All that passion for life! I can't
wait for the two of them to meet."

Though, in truth, my feelings are a lot more conflicted
than that. Confused and confusing, like just about everything having to do with my family and upbringing. I wasn't
lying: I *have* been missing Jude, especially since Betsy was
born. But I haven't missed the worry and the constant emotional roller coaster of having my younger sister in my life.
Without her around, I haven't felt quite the same need to be
on guard—for her and myself. I haven't constantly had to
remind myself to stick to the straight and narrow. To never
put a foot wrong, because once you begin to stray—well, my
childhood was an object lesson in what happens then. And
though it was Jude who was born with Mom's wild streak,
I've always been afraid that some of that craziness is buried
within me, too, like a faulty strand of DNA, just waiting to
break loose and spiral out of control.

It started to cool off. Betsy hit Jamie with the bucket by
mistake and they both began to cry. Tessa and I picked them
up and bounce-walked them over to the picnic area to start
setting up for dinner. But all four grills were a mess—coated
with grime, the fireboxes caked with ash and debris. I saw
Cal behind the backstop and walked over to him with Betsy
and suggested that we have everyone back to our place instead. We both really enjoy throwing open the house to

friends and family. Though I'd have to do some shopping first, I told him.

"Okay, but wait until the game's over," he said. He was sweaty and grinning. I haven't seen him this relaxed since before his dad's operation. Whatever prompted him to quit work early now seemed like a good idea. "I'd hate for you to miss seeing me hit this home run."

When he did hit one, we all cheered. But by then Betsy was starting to whine. She felt hot. I kissed her forehead and had Tessa do the same. She told me not to worry, that it was probably nothing. But then Betsy fell asleep in my arms, which she would normally never do with so much going on around her. She loves being in the middle of the action.

"Let Cal take her home after the game and put her to bed," Tessa suggested. "I'll help you shop. We can get it done twice as fast working together."

Despite his homer, Cal's side lost, though nobody seemed to mind very much. The sun was just beginning to set as we made our way across the field and up to the parking lot. Edmund was there, talking to Kurt, and Kristin and the twins were in their car, windows up. Cal groused about how we'd have to invite them back to the house now, too. I tried to be upbeat about it, but I wasn't thrilled by the idea either. Edmund and Cal are like oil and water. And Kristin's such a cold fish.

"So, what are you thinking? Just burgers for everyone?" Tessa asked, coming up to me as I waited next to the Jeep with Betsy. She was carrying Jamie, who was teething on one of the straps on his BabyBjörn. Cal had gone over to the Subaru with Kurt to get Betsy's safety seat. Edmund had followed them, gesturing and talking with some animation. It seemed odd to me that Edmund had come to the game at all; I wondered what was up.

"Let's get some sausages, too," I said, turning back to Tessa. "And maybe some peppers and—" Out of the corner of my eye I saw Cal stumble out of the Subaru with the car seat. Edmund said something, and then Cal turned toward him. No, it was more like Cal turned *on* him. I couldn't hear what they were saying, but I could tell it wasn't good. Nothing's been quite right between Cal and Edmund since Cal started the business, though I think it actually goes back much further and deeper than that. Cal's dad claims he doesn't play favorites. But you'd have to be blind not to see how he dotes on his youngest son.

Betsy woke up and started crying. Cal came back with the seat. He didn't meet my eye when he took Betsy from me, but I could almost feel the anger radiating off of him. Tessa was right there, so we didn't say anything; I knew we'd hash it out later on. Cal waited while I dug around for the belt to hook into the back of the safety seat. When I had the thing locked in, I took Betsy back from him. Cal wandered off by himself across the parking lot. I could tell he was still fuming about whatever had happened between him and Edmund. I started to strap Betsy in, but then something occurred to me. I stood back up. Tessa was resting against the Jeep's hood, waiting for me, her arms forming a sling under Jamie for support. She was bouncing him gently, trying to get him to stop fussing.

"I haven't gotten a chance to tell Cal yet," I told her. "About Jude coming back."

"Enough said," she replied.

I was really dreading talking to Cal about my sister. She's

a subject we usually do our best to avoid. She'd been our first big argument, our only really, really bad one. I'd blamed him initially because I just couldn't believe I had to blame her. I'd raised her, after all, shared that whole first part of my life with her. The same painful memories bound us together, closer than blood. How could she have betrayed me like that? I still don't understand it. Cal came back. I leaned over and kissed Betsy's forehead again.

"She seems a lot better," I told Cal as he climbed into the driver's seat. "Maybe it was just the heat after all." I felt a sudden urge to reach over and kiss him, too. But we're never particularly demonstrative in public, and he'd probably wonder what was up. It's so hard to find the right moment to say the big, important things. And so often it seems that the timing is more critical than what's actually said. I wanted to tell Cal right then how much I loved him, how I could never really doubt him. But I also had to tell him about Jude coming back—and I had to do it soon—and that would only undercut whatever loving things I might have said. No, I realized, it was already too late for that. I gave Betsy one last look, and she smiled drowsily up at me.

"See you later, little gator," I said, leaning over and waving as Cal pulled out of the parking lot.

3

Cal

❧

The Jeep rolled over. We landed upside down in a ditch. It took me a few moments to make sense of what had happened, but I decided I was okay. Nothing broken. I couldn't turn around, but the rearview mirror allowed me to see partially into the backseat. Enough to realize that Betsy wasn't where I thought she ought to be. I couldn't get my bearings. The steering wheel and gearbox had crumpled around me, and I was pinned inside the car.

"Betsy?" I cried. "Betsy? Don't worry, it's going to be okay."

I go over it again and again. That first half hour or so, when I believed I was talking to my daughter. That she could hear my voice. It's the only period of time after the accident that I can think about for very long. Everything seemed dreamlike. The world had been upended and set atilt. The rolling fields rose above us like storm clouds and were lit up by a fire-tinged horizon. I watched the first stars of evening blink on like distant house lights. I felt that Betsy and I were suspended between worlds. Slipping back and forth between waking and sleep. Drifting over a looking-glass surface where everything seemed a little off-kilter—and anything was possible. I thought, if I could just push through the floor of the car, I could grab my daughter's hand and we would be able to float free, like balloons climbing into a magical twilit land.

The guy who stopped and called 911 drove on to try to get immediate help from one of the nearby houses, but the police were there in ten minutes anyway. Chief Tyler and Denny Lockhardt, who had been a grade below me in high school. He'd been at the baseball game, too, until he had to leave for his shift. They knew before I did. Kurt and Mack Carlson, another guy on our crew, are volunteer firemen and EMTs. So they knew before I did, too. I don't know why that hurts so much. I kept asking about Betsy: had they gotten her out okay? How was she doing? I heard more sirens. I remember all the lights circling.

Kurt was right there when they pulled me out of the car. He put his arm around me. He tried to say something, but then he just shook his head. He walked me into the woods, where some paramedics I didn't recognize were crouched around something wrapped in a white blanket. It was Betsy. The earth stopped moving. I staggered a couple of feet into the underbrush and got violently sick.

"Take it easy," Kurt was telling me when there was nothing left to throw up. "Just take it easy." He grabbed hold of my elbow as he said to someone behind me, "Keep him walking. Keep him upright and moving. I'll be right back."

"Where's Kurt going?" I asked as Mack Carlson took my arm and started to guide me back toward the roadway. "I want Kurt." I remember when I was seven or so, falling off the parallel bars behind the elementary school and hitting my head on somebody's skateboard. I was sick and distraught that time, too; crying, not for my parents, but for Kurt, whom I trusted more than anybody else to know instinctively the right thing to do when things go wrong.

"Okay," Mack said as we walked back slowly toward the circling lights. Night had fallen. The temperature was dropping. I felt shivery. Light-headed. Afraid.

"Tell Kurt I need him," I said to Mack.

"Hold it a sec," he replied, stopping a dozen yards from the group of men who were huddled next to the cruisers. Mack put his hand on my shoulder, restraining me.

"And you were there, too, Denny," I heard Kurt say. "How many beers did *you* put away?"

"That's not the point," Chief Tyler said. "I'm sorry, but this is the scene of an accident. There's been a fatality. It's my job to follow certain procedures. You know that."

"Well, to hell with you and your job!" Kurt said. "You are not putting my brother through that right now, okay?"

"Don't make this hard."

"I'm not. I'm making it easy," Kurt told him. "You want to talk about procedures? Why do I think that deputy police chiefs—Denny, for one—should not be chugging back beers half an hour before they go on duty?"

"Now, listen here, Kurt—"

"No, you listen," my brother said, cutting him off. "We were *all* drinking. We *all* had a few. We were playing ball and it was hot. It was totally fucking harmless, okay? You even try to give my brother a Breathalyzer when his little baby is lying over there in the woods and I will personally see that Denny gets thrown off the force, okay?"

"Jesus," the chief said. "I don't know—"

"Sure you do," Kurt said, his tone changing. "We all know the right thing to do here." I'd never heard my brother sound like this before—like my dad. Glad-handing. Hail-fellow. Selling something. "We all know this is a tragedy. You start laying blame where it doesn't belong, and the tragedy just gets a whole lot worse. None of us want that to happen, do we? This is your town, Chief. It's our town. And I think we have the right to decide the best procedure at a time like this. I think everybody understands that, right?"

I don't know what the response would have been if Kurt and I weren't Jay Horigan's boys. If Horigan Lumber and Hardware wasn't one of the bigger businesses in the area. But it's not just that. The Horigans go back a long way in Covington; my great-granddad Harold helped build the town hall and Grange. At this point, I'd say we're related by blood or marriage to at least a third of all the local families. The wealthy weekenders may have more money, but the Horigan name is right up there in the social hierarchy of Covington. We're hardworking, successful, civic-minded. Dad just about underwrites the annual volunteer fire department steak roast every year.

How was Chief Tyler—whom my father, a longtime se-lectman, helped hire away from the Northridge force a dozen years ago—supposed to stand up to someone like Kurt? Someone who, putting everything else aside, the chief surely thinks of as one of the good guys. We all do. And Kurt *is* the best. The straightest arrow. Yet here he was demanding that the rules be bent. No, be broken. And he'd asked, it seemed to me, reflexively, without thinking twice. How quickly the lines blur. I felt sick again. Dizzy. I turned away from Mack, doubled over, and started heaving. The conversation halted as everyone turned around and looked at me.

"We need to get him up to the ER in Harringdale," Kurt said. "He's got a concussion for sure. Don't you think Mack and me should run him right up in the cruiser?"

"Yeah, okay," the chief said, sighing. "You don't want to take any chances with a head injury. But you better get a move on. The state police are on their way."

❧

"I can't leave her there," I said when Kurt tried to pull me toward the Chevy Tahoe.

"I'm sorry," Kurt told me, leaning in close. "But I need to get you away from here—*now*."

"I'm not leaving her," I told him again, turning back to the woods. I could see the little white blanket gleaming through the trees. Kurt grabbed my arm, hard, and wheeled me around. I'm bigger and stronger than he is. We both know I could take him if we ever got into a real fight.

"You want to totally fuck up your life?" Kurt whispered. "Is that what you want, Cal? Because that's what's going to happen if we don't get the hell out of here right now."

"No, Kurt, I just—"

"Listen to me," my brother said, cutting me off abruptly. "There's nothing more you can do for her. I know the guys are going to try everything, but I think they know the score. They'll bring her up to the hospital when they're done here. Whatever happens: I promise you'll get to see her again, okay?"

We both heard the siren approaching from the north. I turned and saw the chief motioning to Cal: *get moving*. I let Cal lead me to the cruiser, open the back door, push me in.

"Go south," Kurt told Mack, climbing in beside me. "That way we can take 206 across and 4 up. It'll be faster."

I sat with my head in my hands, sick and dizzy. When I closed my eyes I saw Betsy lying there, looking up, unseeing, at the starlit sky. Her mouth was slack, in what seemed to me in my confused state a look of wonder. I sat back up, shaking my head, trying to purge the memory. I turned to stare out the window as the fields and farms and woods blurred into a wall of darkness.

"I'm going to call Tessa on my cell," Kurt told me. "I think I should just tell her that there's been an accident. That she should drive Jenny up to the hospital and meet us there."

A sickle moon dangled low in the sky. I felt myself drifting back to those first, hallucinatory moments right after the Jeep rolled.

"Cal? Did you hear me?" Kurt said. "I'm going to call Tessa, but I'm not going to tell her what happened. Okay? You'll want to be the one who tells Jenny, right?"

"Yes," I said. "Yes." I'll want to be the one who tells Jenny. I tried to think about what that actually meant, but my mind skittered away from it. Instead, I listened intently as Kurt made his call. He attempted to keep his voice even and calm. But he was too calm. It was like he was already bracing for hysterics, and Tessa knows him too well not to pick up on it. I could just make out her end of the conversation:

"What do you mean? What kind of accident? We heard sirens on our way back from town. Are you okay?"

"I'm fine. Listen, just forget about supper. Tell everyone to go home. Drive Jenny up to the hospital in Harringdale. We'll meet you there."

"Oh God. What's happened? Who is it? Oh no, don't tell me—is it Cal?"

"Tessa—please."

"Jenny's in the kitchen. She can't hear me. But you've got to tell me. I can't stand it. I'll be able to manage if you tell me. You know I will."

"Okay, but I need you to do this. I need you to drive Jenny up to the hospital. Tell her you don't know the details, you don't know anything. But it's really, really bad, Tess. Do you understand?"

"Yes. Just tell me."

"It's Betsy. She's gone."

The sound of Tessa crying on the other end of the cell phone was muted and distant, but it unleashed something inside me, something that roared right through me, that crashed through every fragile defense I'd tried to construct over the past frantic hour. Kurt knew. And now Tessa knew. I'd had the childish notion that for those who didn't yet know, it hadn't really happened. And that somehow I could contain it, keep the thing from spreading. But that was all swept away now, along with any last hope I'd been harboring that I would wake up from this nightmare. Wake up any moment. Drenched in sweat. But whole. Reprieved.

❧

Kurt was right by my side the whole time I was in the ER. My memory of that hour or so is patchy, but I'll never forget the moment when he told me that the coroner had made it official: Betsy was dead. When I didn't respond right away, he asked me if I understood what he had said. I nodded, but I was lying. How was I supposed to understand? Kurt came with me to the X-ray unit when they took the head scans. But he slipped away after the doctor came by to let us know that I seemed to be checking out okay. No swelling or bleeding that they could detect at that point. I should try to take it easy for a couple of days and be on the lookout for any headaches, dizziness, or nausea.

"Other than that, I'd say you're going to be just fine," the young doctor told me. I stared at him. He looked tired but relaxed. A resident, probably, stuck with weekend duty. A few hours ago, I would have appreciated his affable, easygoing manner. Obviously, no one had told him what had happened. It wasn't his fault. But even knowing all that, I wanted to slam my fist into his face.

"Jenny's here," Kurt said, coming in as the doctor left and closing the door. "I talked to the head nurse. You two can have this room for as long as you want."

"No!" I said. "No. Let me walk out with you." It wasn't until that moment that I realized what a total fucking coward I really am. Jenny and Tessa were waiting at the end of the hall, huddled together. When Jenny saw me, her face lit up, but as we got closer and she saw my expression she began to shake her head.

"No," she said, shaking her head faster. "Please, no—"

"Jenny, listen—," I began. A part of me still wanted to deny it. To allow her to keep hoping for just another moment longer.

A little more than two years ago, she'd given birth to our daughter, three floors up in this very hospital. We'd done Lamaze together to prepare for it. I was Jenny's coach. We were both as nervous as hell, but determined to make it a natural delivery if possible. Jenny was into all that sort of thing and had convinced the maternity ward at Harringdale—not exactly the most forward-thinking place on earth—to let her bring in her own midwife and doula. If things got complicated, we assured them, we'd switch over to the traditional way of doing things. Their way. We put everything in writing; signed waivers. The whole nine yards.

But none of it was necessary. An hour after Jenny's water broke, I had her registered on the maternity floor. By the time the midwife arrived, Jenny was seven inches dilated. I remember standing there, gripping her hand, waiting for the moment when I was supposed to start yelling for her to push. When all the agony we had heard so much about was going to begin. But the midwife just advised me to go down and stand at the foot of the bed.

"This baby's taking the express train," she told Jenny. Within minutes, Betsy came tumbling out: right hand first, uncurling and waving, I swear to God, to all of us assembled there to meet her. The midwife told us it was the fastest, easiest birth she'd ever seen. It had seemed like a miracle to me then, as if something had intervened—cut through all the pain—and handed us this gift.

Now this thing had intervened a second time—with the same speed and finality—and snatched our miracle back again. And the suffering I thought we'd managed to avoid hadn't even really started yet.

"I'm sorry," I told Jenny at last. "God, I'm so, so sorry."

She fell into my arms and began to hit my chest with her fists. We both started crying, openmouthed, uncontrollably. We staggered—in a desperate kind of embrace—like two boxers in the final rounds of a fight. I kept waiting for her to ask me what had happened. How it had happened. How I could be standing there, without a scratch. How I could have let our baby die. But she just kept crying, her whole body convulsing with sobs, defenseless, battered again and again by each new incoming wave of grief. I held on to her for dear life, but it was as though some powerful undertow that I couldn't feel or fight had taken hold of her—and had begun to pull her slowly and steadily down and away.

4

Jenny

❧

I tend to go right to the worst-case scenario. It's my default setting. I learned the hard way when I was growing up that it's always safest to prepare for disaster. That way, you're maybe a little bit braced for impact if those fears materialize —and so relieved if they don't that you can actually make yourself believe that you've come out ahead. So when Tessa told me that Kurt had called to say Cal had gotten into an accident, I went immediately into lockdown mode.

"What happened? Where? Is Betsy okay?" I'd wondered briefly when we got back from shopping why Cal and Betsy weren't there waiting for us. But then I figured that Cal had probably dropped by his folks' place in town to invite them to join us for supper. He's there every other day as it is—the Horigans can never seem to get enough of one another—and loves taking Betsy along with him. Now, though, when I searched Tessa's expression for some kind of instant reading, I felt my panic start to escalate. Her skin looked splotchy, her eyes red rimmed, as though she'd been crying.

"Take it easy, Jen," she told me. "He didn't really tell me much. Just that we're supposed to meet them at the ER in Harringdale. I'm sure everything's fine." She knows I'm an alarmist; we joke about it all the time. But her voice sounded thin and breathy, not her usual no-nonsense tone at all.

"You've been crying," I accused her. "What's happened? What's going on?"

There were a dozen or so people milling around our downstairs at this point, more coming in the door as we spoke. Tessa had tracked me down in the kitchen, where Burt Mayer and his wife, Kaye, were helping set things up for an indoor buffet on the butcher-block counter that separates the kitchen from the great room. I was holding a party-sized jar of pickles and had been about to twist off the lid. Tessa took it away from me and handed it to Kaye.

"I'm going to have to run Jenny up to Harringdale," she told the Mayers. "Cal's been in some kind of an accident. No big deal, but I think we'll have to cancel supper here. Could you let everybody know? And could you guys maybe hang out and keep an eye on Jamie for me until we get back? He's right over there watching cartoons with the other kids."

"You don't want to take him with us?" I asked her. It was still fairly warm out; we had the screen doors open to the patio, but I felt my fingers start to go numb. Tessa would never normally leave Jamie with the Mayers, whom she doesn't know all that well. It was beginning to occur to me that this wasn't a fire drill after all; there was a real possibility that my life was burning down.

"No, that's okay. He loves being with the big kids," she said, taking my elbow. "He'll be fine. Come on, let's go."

Tessa and I didn't say much on the drive up. That right

there was a pretty clear indication that something was seriously wrong; we've been talking basically nonstop for the entire five years that we've known each other. Especially at a time like this, I thought, when words could so easily offer distraction and comfort. But she seemed oddly intent on the road ahead. She leaned forward, her hands gripping the wheel, her body tense. After the uneasy silence had stretched on for several miles, it dawned on me that Tessa knew what had happened. Kurt had told her—and then made her promise to keep it from me until we got to the hospital. It was that terrible.

I wasn't going to ask her what she knew. In fact, I suddenly became frightened that she might change her mind—and decide to tell me. Because if I didn't know then I could almost convince myself it hadn't really happened yet. And if it hadn't happened, there might be something I could do to still prevent it or at least divert it. So I started to bargain with God. Unfortunately, despite my being a minister's daughter, God and I don't communicate all that much anymore. Actually, I think it's probably *because* I'm a minister's daughter that my relationship with the Almighty has always been fraught. From my earliest childhood, I had a tendency to confuse my earthly father with the heavenly one. They both seemed so distant and judgmental, so easily exasperated by the neediness and questions of a nine-year-old girl. *If God is all-seeing, why can't he tell us where Mom has gone? Since the lilies labor not nor spin, why do I have to do so much work around the house* and *take care of Jude?* The answers seemed gruff and dismissive to me, obscuring rather than revealing the larger truth I was hoping to uncover:

"God's not some kind of crystal ball, Jennifer. He works

in mysterious ways we cannot begin to fathom or try to bring down to our own pedestrian level."

So what was the point of him? I wondered. I listened for as long as I could to my father's dry and didactic sermons every Sunday. I sat obediently next to Jude in the front row of the Lutheran church in town as more and more of the pews behind us began to sit empty over the years. I tried my best to be good and obey the word of both my fathers. And for the most part I succeeded, that is, up until my earthly father caught me kissing Cal Horigan one night and forbade me to see him again. At that point, I started breaking commandments right and left: bearing false witness, committing adultery (which meant anything racier than holding hands in Reverend Honegger's lexicon), dishonoring my father, and, though not exactly forgetting the Sabbath day, no longer doing much to keep it holy.

It all started, though, because I broke the first and most severe commandment: *I put another God before his face.* Or, more precisely, *I made for myself an idol from the earth below.* He was tall and big-boned with a macho swagger and a smile that could make ice melt. He was two years ahead of me and one of the high school's superheroes: star athlete, student council president, an easygoing guy's guy whom every girl I knew worshipped. I adored him, too; it seemed silly not to, though I assumed that it would always remain the kind of vague, impossible crush I entertained for Justin Timberlake and Leo DiCaprio, as well.

So when he reached down and plucked me out of the obscurity of the lowly sophomore class to be his date for the senior prom, it seemed to me that a miracle had occurred. There I was, riding next to Cal Horigan in his pickup truck, a wrist corsage he'd given me just about levitating my arm. It made the conjuring of manna from heaven or loaves and fishes from thin air suddenly seem like mere magic tricks. But the true revelation of our first night together—the thing that altered the course of my life and the constitution of my heart forever—was that underneath that cocksure walk and disarming smile was a boy struggling hard to find his way as a man.

"My dad expects me to join the business," he told me. "But I want to be more than what he expects, you know? I want to try to be something better. Something else. I just don't know what it is yet." He talked a lot about his dad that night. It was as though he'd stored up all these important things he'd been waiting to tell someone. I was taken aback by his seriousness. He had a reputation as a party boy, a real heartbreaker. I'd steeled myself against that sort of thing, waiting all night for him to pounce. I wasn't at all prepared to be seduced by his earnestness, his obvious need to have me think well of him. That Cal Horigan was a real person after all—as flawed and uncertain as the rest of us—made him seem all the more perfect to me.

"I've been watching you for a long time, Jenny," he told me at the end of the evening without so much as a peck on the cheek.

I should have known I'd been too lucky. That it had all been far too easy. I should have realized that I'd been blessed, that God had actually been looking after me all these years. I should never have allowed myself to think of Cal as a given; he'd been a gift. *I'm sorry. I'll change.* I was ready to promise God anything as we reached the outskirts of Harringdale, where run-down two-family clapboard houses sit wedged between gas stations and used-car dealerships. *Just don't take Cal away from me.*

Why didn't I think to include Betsy in my prayers? Was it because Tessa had told me that it was *Cal* who had been in an accident? Because she hadn't mentioned my daughter? No, I believe it's because the very idea of losing Betsy is so unthinkable. She still feels like a part of me. Even when she's out of my sight, off with Cal or at the little playgroup in town, I can sense the warmth of her body at my side. I can predict her moods. I know when she wakes up in the middle of the night. I'm able to guess what she wants before she even knows what it is. How could I lose her? It would be like losing myself. Impossible to even contemplate. But then God, as my father says, can do the impossible. If you believe in him. If you submit to his will. And, in the end, I can't deny it. He listened to my prayers. He didn't lay a finger on my husband.

❧

"No," I said when I saw Cal coming down the hall toward me with that look on his face. "Please, no—"

"Jenny, listen—," he started to say. Then he stopped. I could tell he didn't want to say the words out loud. Nobody did. It felt like a bad movie. Maybe it was the glaringly bright overhead lighting. Or the awkward way everyone was standing there: Tessa with her hand over her mouth, Kurt hugging his chest as tears ran unchecked down his cheeks, Cal so pale and stunned looking, his shirt blotched and wrinkled. I smelled beer—and vomit. And something else: fear, I guess. Everyone was waiting for me to react. None of it was real to me, but I understood enough to register the fact that the worst had finally happened. I felt like I was watching myself, all of us, on some kind of a hidden monitor. Except I was looking down on the whole thing, thinking: please, let's just back up. Start again. Rewind the tape. All these thoughts ran through my head in a single instant.

"I'm sorry," my husband told me. "God, I'm so, so sorry."

I felt like I was following someone else's script when I fell into Cal's arms. It didn't feel possible. It was just a terrible sentence, as yet unspoken. I couldn't remember ever seeing Cal cry before. His face was all scrunched up, like a baby's, I thought. No, don't think that. Don't go there. I buried myself in Cal's embrace. We wept together, Cal already with resignation, me just at the very thought. At the very beginning of the very thought.

Then something else took over inside of me. I had to see her. Kurt tried to tell me that it wasn't a good idea, but I wouldn't listen. I think I had some crazy notion, the first of many, that I could somehow fix things. I was her mother. She needed me. How many times had I told her that I would make it all better?

"I have to see her," I told Kurt again.

"Okay," he said, though he was shaking his head. "Give me a minute."

I stopped crying in fits and starts. It was going to be okay. I was going to see her. Cal looked blank, though his grip was tight, almost painful. When I glanced up at him, his gaze was unfocused, staring down the hallway after Kurt. Tessa was the only one weeping now: loudly, openly, wiping her nose on her sleeve like a kid.

Kurt's known at the hospital because of his EMS work, and he was able to talk someone into clearing the chapel for us. It's a small, windowless room, with a stained-glass panel, backlit, built into the far wall. Jewel-like light spilled out over the little nondenominational altar and scattered its bright shards across the darkened floor. It took a moment for my eyes to adjust to the dimness. Later I learned that it was Kurt who helped arrange Betsy on the gurney in front of the altar, the sheet tucked carefully around her body. But as soon as the door closed behind us, I went right over and started to pull her into my arms.

"No, Jenny, don't—," Cal said, though I didn't think to ask why not. And it didn't matter: nothing was going to stop me.

"It's okay," I told him, hugging Betsy to me. I don't think it took more than a few seconds for me to realize that she wasn't really there. That I was cradling something inanimate. Beyond needing or wanting my help. I've never felt that I could get enough of Betsy. When she was first born, just a few floors up in this very hospital, I stared at her for hours on end. But each time I looked at her—it was like seeing her for the first time. And in the months since, though I'd spent endless hours watching her at play, or asleep, I still felt that I could never see the whole of her the way I can Jamie, say, or any other child. It's like looking at my own reflection in a mirror. So familiar, yet also unknowable. Now, though, when I looked down, I was able to take her in at last. I don't think I've ever seen anything so absolutely still.

Cal finally took her from me and laid her back down on the gurney, tucking the sheet around her again, blocking my view of her until he had her just the way he wanted. When he stepped back, I noticed she had some dirt on her forehead. I licked my thumb and tried to smudge it away.

"Don't," Cal said, stopping me. Suddenly my eyes were opened. It wasn't dirt. It was a bruise. How could I have missed that before? Was I losing my mind? It was the first in what would become an endless series of loops: denial, disbelief, confusion, and then a door closing on a windowless room from which there is no escape.

❧

They gave me something to sleep the first night, but I woke up moaning from a nightmare. No, I woke up to the nightmare. Later that morning Chief Tyler stopped by the house. Cal was still asleep upstairs; he'd come up hours after me the night before, an hour or so after the last of his family had left. The Horigan family needs to be together to face disaster. I was beginning to discover that I needed to be alone.

"Cal's not up yet," I told the chief.

"That's okay," he said. "Could I come in for just a minute? Sorry, I tried calling, but something's wrong with the phone."

"I unplugged it," I said, leading him back to the kitchen. "I couldn't talk to another person." There was only one voice I wanted to hear. I kept listening for her singsong babble of nonsense words. Earlier that morning I was convinced I heard her calling *Mama! Mama!* from somewhere downstairs.

"I'm really sorry to intrude," he said, taking the mug of coffee I poured for him and putting it down on the countertop. "I'm sure you have a lot on your mind right now. But I thought you'd want to know about this."

"It's okay," I said, pushing the sugar bowl toward him. The milk carton was already out on the counter along with a coffee cake that Cal's mom had brought over the night before and homemade cinnamon buns that Nell Gruber had dropped off first thing this morning. The casseroles would be coming later, I knew, and the disposable aluminum trays of lasagna. I wondered what atavistic ritual makes us want to overfeed the living right after there's been a death. I had to ask Chief Tyler to repeat what he'd just said.

"The car seat. We think there might have been a mal-function. There's a possibility, anyway. Something went wrong when the Jeep rolled over. So she was thrown— Well, the thing is this: it shouldn't have happened. We looked up the manufacturer on the Internet. Apparently, there've been complaints about another one of their products—something about faulty safety latches, I think."

"Oh," I said. "Oh my God."

"We thought you should know right away," the chief went on. "In case you wanted to contact a lawyer. I'm not a big expert on this or anything, but you might very well have a negligence or wrongful death suit here."

Wrongful death.

It was a phrase that would haunt me in the days ahead. Through the surreal hours of planning my daughter's funeral with Cal, his family, and my father, who came over later that morning without asking and insisted we pray together. But *the Lord is my shepherd* was shouted down in my brain by *wrongful death*. I kept thinking back on those final moments when I was talking to Tessa while buckling Betsy into the safety seat. Stopping midway to tell Tessa that Cal didn't know yet about Jude. Had I ever actually finished strapping her in? It was one of those things I do so often, one of those routines that becomes such a part of everyday life that the mind no longer really registers it. Like turning off the iron or locking the front door. Leaning into the back of the car and inserting the buckle into the clasp.

Of course I did. Surely I did. I kept rubbing the tips of my fingers together as if trying to bring back from somewhere deep inside the feeling of that *click*. That little shudder of metal kissing metal.

5

Cal

※

"I guess I just don't understand her reasoning," Edmund said. He, Kurt, Dad, and I were sitting around my parents' living room. It was nearly midnight. Empty beer bottles cluttered the coffee table. Jenny's father had conducted Betsy's funeral service that afternoon at the Lutheran church in town; then we buried my daughter in the Horigan family plot in the Roman Catholic cemetery out on River Road. Neither Jenny nor I am particularly observant, but we still managed to get into a fight about the right way to handle things with Betsy. Jenny came up with this crazy idea that we should cremate our baby and have her buried on our property.

"Up on the hill near where I want to put in the gazebo," she explained to me. "That way we can visit her whenever we want. And she won't have to be in some awful cemetery surrounded by headstones." I was having such a hard time reading Jenny's moods at this point. Neither one of us was sleeping very well, and I was running pretty much on fumes.

"People bury their pets in the backyard, Jen. My dad told me that there's a really nice sunny spot right behind my grandparents."

I thought we'd managed to talk it through and that Jenny was okay with the decision, but on the way back to my parents' house after the interment she'd said, "So now the Horigans get to have her for eternity."

I knew how much she was hurting. I understood the hell she was going through. So was I. Still, it seemed to me that if there was any solace to be had, it was the fact that Jenny and I were in it together. But I was beginning to think she didn't see it that way. She kept turning away from me just as I was turning toward her. After years of effortlessness, I couldn't seem to get into the right rhythm or set the appropriate tone with her. Case in point was our differing opinions on what to do about the car-seat manufacturer. I was ready to go in there and sue the pants off the sons of bitches.

"I can't think about that now," she told me the first time I brought it up to her; this was when we got back from my parents' house the night after Betsy died. They'd hosted a kind of open house for everyone who wanted to come by and share their grief; the place had been mobbed. Kurt and Denny Lockhardt had taken me aside during the evening and filled me in on what Denny had found out about Gannon Baby Products, Inc., including the two lawsuits the company had already settled out of court. I'd been surprised to learn that Chief Tyler had apparently already told Jenny about all this earlier in the day, because she hadn't said a thing about it to me. When I raised the subject again this morning, after Edmund had called to say he'd found a lawyer he wanted us to meet with, Jenny flew off the handle:

"What's the point? She's gone, Cal! And no amount of money in the world is going to bring her back. I think there's something wrong, something really kind of creepy about demanding payment for someone's death. People who do that sort of thing? They're like vultures as far as I'm concerned."

"It's not about the money," I replied, stung by her tone. "It's about making sure these guys don't get away with this kind of thing again. I mean, come on: Gannon was probably responsible for our daughter's death! Doesn't that make you furious? I can't believe you don't want to do something about this."

"Please, let's not talk about it right now, okay?" Jenny replied. We were up in our bedroom and she was standing in front of her open clothes closet, trying to decide what to wear to the funeral service. She looked like she'd lost about ten pounds in the last couple of days. Her shoulders were slumped, her arms locked across her chest. Along with everything else, I knew she was having a tough time dealing with her father, who had called her idea of having Betsy's favorite children's songs played at the beginning of the service "not in keeping with the sanctity of the occasion." I knew she was also dreading having to face her sister, Jude, who was supposed to be coming down from Boston in time for the funeral. The situation with Jude alone was enough to make anybody act crazy. I felt myself relenting. Unlike me, Jenny grew up without any real love or support. But somehow, through her own fierce will and determination, she managed to turn herself into this strong, brave, beautiful person. I went over and put my arms around her.

"Whatever you say," I'd told her, pulling her close. "I just want to do the right thing." Her breathing was quick and ragged, her body rigid.

"I've got to find a way to get through this," she'd said. She'd circled her arms around my chest and squeezed tight, then stepped away. Now, though, sitting there with my father and brothers, I was having a hard time recapturing the sympathy I'd felt for Jenny's position earlier in the day. Edmund had been on my case about a lawsuit for the last half hour or so. And a lot of what he said was making sense to me. But I wanted to at least try to present her point of view.

"Jenny feels that whatever we might get would be like blood money," I explained. "That it would be tainted. And, besides, she says she can't think about any of this right now. We're doing everything we can to just keep things together."

"Sure, I get that," Edmund replied. "But later? When the anger sets in? I think you're going to change your mind, and I just hope it's not too late. This product liability lawyer I'm talking to in Albany told me he heard that Gannon settled one of those suits for a million two."

Leave it to Edmund to know the exact amount of the settlement. Or to know somebody who would know. I have my problems with my oldest brother, but I concede that his grasp of the wider world of business and finance is far greater and more sophisticated than mine. He kept up with and then built upon all the contacts he made at Cornell, and at this point the friends in his network—at least those on his Facebook page—number in the hundreds. Yes, he can be a total asshole. He actually had the balls to tell Kurt and me that Horigan Lumber and Hardware financial reports were "proprietary information" these days. But if you need to find the go-to guy in any given situation, Edmund will start thumbing through his iPhone address book and have a name and number for you in a matter of seconds.

"I filled the lawyer in on what happened," Edmund continued. "He thinks you have a case. Why don't you at least meet with him? Hear what he has to say. You can catch Jenny up on what you learn when you feel the time is right."

Do I trust Edmund? Not really. He always seems to be operating with some kind of hidden agenda, angling for something I don't understand, looking over my shoulder to see if someone more important than me might be in the room. But his outrage over the way Betsy died feels genuine to me. There were tears in his eyes when he hugged me at the cemetery. Because Edmund can be so cool and contained, that display of unguarded emotion really touched me. And I do trust his information. If he says Gannon settled for one two, they did. If he says the lawyer thinks we might have a case, we probably do.

"Why don't you sleep on it, Cal?" Dad suggested, sighing as he rose from his La-Z-Boy. He scooped up a bunch of the empty beer bottles by their necks and headed toward the kitchen with them. Then he stopped, turned back to us, and said: "But, you know, Jenny may have a point. No amount of money is going to make up for losing Betsy; I can tell you that right now. And I've never really understood this business of assigning blame. It's just not all that productive in the long run."

"Okay, Dad," I said, rising as well. "Let me think about it." The Jeep had been totaled. Jenny had driven our second car, a Volvo wagon, back to the house hours ago. Kurt would be dropping me off on his way to his place, which is just a couple miles north of ours. The three of us helped the old man straighten up downstairs. My mother had long ago re-signed herself to our late-night revelries—"it's the cross I have to bear for having only sons"—but she's a stickler about coming down to a neat kitchen in the morning.

"Give me a call when you're ready," Edmund said as he double-clicked the key to his BMW. "But don't wait too long."

Kurt and I didn't say anything for a while after we headed up Route 32. Farmland still encroaches on the town from every direction, and within a mile or two the street lights of Covington were swallowed up by darkness. Winter salt and grime had eaten away at the white safety lines on the roadway, and Kurt was taking things slow. I could feel a certain tension between us, though it might have been just my imagination. I felt all wound up and utterly exhausted at the same time.

"You think Dad was trying to tell me something?" I asked him finally.

"How so?" Kurt said.

"About Jenny having a point. And that business about not assigning blame. He can be so fucking cryptic at times, especially since his open-heart."

"I know what you're saying," Kurt replied. "But, no, I don't think he was sending out any secret messages. Just don't rush into anything."

"Meaning the lawsuit? Meeting with this lawyer Edmund's lined up?"

"Yeah. You want my opinion? I don't think you're ready. Jenny *or* you. You know how Eddie gets—everything's got to be ASAP. Well, it doesn't. You and Jenny need to come down from this. You need to—what does Tessa call it?—*process* the whole thing. I'm not saying you shouldn't pursue it at some point down the pike maybe. I was there. And I've seen my share of accidents. I can vouch for it: something about the way that car seat came loose was fucked-up. But wait until the time's right, until you two have had a chance to talk it all through. And I would definitely *not* go doing anything behind Jenny's back."

"Right," I said. "You're right. But you don't think Dad was trying to say like—that maybe I'm the one to blame?"

"How the hell did you hear that? I sure didn't."

"Yeah, well. I had been drinking. You know, I keep thinking about that, keep wondering if—"

"No way, Cal. You blew like a .03 on the BAC at the hospital. That's just about dead sober in my book."

"I don't remember taking a breath alcohol test. When did that happen?"

Kurt glanced over at me through the darkness and then back to the road ahead.

"When we got to the hospital. In the ER. It's standard procedure. You were still pretty out of it. You had a concussion. People sometimes have whole hours at a time wiped right out."

"I remember enough that you wouldn't let Tyler Breathalyze me at the scene. And it was over an hour, nearly two, between my last beer and the ER. So you probably figured I'd be just about sobered up by then."

"What's going on with you?" Kurt asked, turning into our drive. He pulled up by the back entrance but kept the engine running. "You actually trying to say you think you're responsible for what happened? Because if you are—I'll tell you right now that that's total bullshit. God—or whoever the hell's in charge here—has a plan for each of us, even if at times it seems really cruel. It's not going to do you or Jenny any good if you start playing these kinds of stupid mind games. Understand me? What you need to think about now is how to help Jenny get through this, how you both can come out of this stronger and better people."

I want to believe what Kurt said. And most of the time I'm able to. It's usually only late at night, after Jenny's gone up to bed, that I begin to think about how Kurt has always protected me. He shielded me from bullies when I was boy, helped me toughen up for high school sports, pushed me to hang out with the kids my age he thought had their shit together. He also taught me by example how to play it straight, stay strong, be a guy other people can count on. And how to avoid getting taken in by liars and users, and even—without ever saying it out loud—how I should keep a wary eye on Edmund. But then, too, I know he loves me, perhaps in the way only siblings can. I'm a pretty genial guy, but if anyone ever hurt Kurt in any way, I'd probably want to kill the person. I think he feels the same way about me. So what's that say exactly about his ability to judge me—innocent or not?

I went back to work a couple of days after the funeral. An hour after I walked in the door, Ravitch called to say the project was still on. So at least Kurt and I have our hands full deciding on the crew, ordering materials, applying for the permits and insurance. But I feel like I'm just going through the motions. It's like a big part of my brain is out of commission, like I'm still suffering from that concussion. I have to keep consciously reminding myself to do the simplest things: turn the key, step on the gas, downshift, brake. I borrowed Dad's ancient Oldsmobile convertible until we can decide what to do about a new car, and each time I glance into the rearview mirror my heart stops.

I see Betsy everywhere. She's in the kiddie seat of a stranger's shopping cart at the Price Chopper, or riding on someone's shoulders into the Covington Public Library, or running crookedly in a gaggle of other kids across the baseball field where she spent the last hours of her life. I cry at every excuse and for no reason at all. I can't concentrate for more than a minute or two on the newspaper, or a book, or the evening news. My mind keeps wandering. At first, I didn't know where. I'd just find myself snapping back from some trancelike state. But I can remember fragments—like bits and pieces of a dream—and I'm beginning to suspect that I'm drifting back again to the moments right after the Jeep rolled over. When Betsy's fate was still undecided.

Kurt must have said something, because everyone's been going out of his or her way to make it clear that I shouldn't in any way blame myself for what happened. My mother. Tessa. Dad. Even Edmund's wife, Kristin, gave me a call at the end of my first week back at work.

"You know, I looked up the meaning of 'fox' in my compendium of symbols," she told me. Kristin leavens her lack of humor and perfectionism with an avid interest in the occult and new age spirituality. "The Chinese connect the animal to the afterlife. Apparently, a fox sighting is considered a signal or message from the world of spirits."

On one level I'm touched by these assurances; on another I wonder why they have to be made at all. Why the need to declare my innocence unless there's actually some question about my guilt? The only person who hasn't broached the subject of my blamelessness is the one I need to hear from most. In fact, she avoids all discussion of the accident itself. That whole hour or two from the time I left with Betsy in the Jeep to the moment I met Jenny at the hospital seems to be off-limits. It's as if Jenny is insisting on a kind of mutual amnesia—as if she's decided to appropriate the dreamlike oblivion of my own concussed state of mind.

We can talk about how much we both miss our baby. We can discuss Betsy's funny, rambunctious personality. Her stubbornness, her determination. We read aloud to each other from the letters and e-mails our friends and family have sent. Nightly, we'll sit together in front of the Mac computer in the great room and click through our collection of photos, laughing and crying. We can even go over the events of the funeral and burial. The way Jenny's dad, after his rigid dictums about sanctity and propriety, had the good grace to let his voice quaver and then break on the final benediction. How Jude, ten minutes late to the church, wept loudly straight through the service and internment, probably the only one in the entire congregation who had never actually met the person she was mourning with such typical Jude-like self-absorption and theatrics.

But Jenny doesn't want to hear about the accident itself. She'll cut me off when I mention how the last thing I saw before the fox running in front of us across the road was Betsy laughing—or how a part of me still feels trapped upside down in the Jeep on the side of the road.

"No, Cal, please!"

Jenny will shake her head. Stand up. Leave the room.

And there I am alone in front of the computer with a shot of Betsy taken last Christmas filling the screen. She'd pulled tinsel from the Christmas tree and draped it around her shoulders like a fancy shawl. I remember taking the photo: her head turned slightly away from me, toward the kitchen where her mother had just called out:

Cal! Get that stuff off of her right now! I told you it's a choking hazard!

I think what a cautious, anxious mother Jenny had been. She'd seen danger lurking around every corner. I'd been just the opposite: tossing Betsy up in the air, running with her on my shoulders, pushing her on the swings as high as she could go. Driving fast down a back road, windows open, breeze whipping at my daughter's curls. I tell myself that even if I'd done things differently—drunk less, gone slower—it would have turned out the same. I reassure myself with Kurt's comment about God's plan. Or what Kristin had said about the fox being a messenger from the spirit world. Fate in the form of a red blur with a whitish tail, racing across the road at just that juncture, at just that moment, and then escaping into the woods without a backward glance.

6

Jenny

❧

$\mathcal{C}$al first mentioned Daniel Brandt a week or so after Horigan Builders broke ground for the Ravitch place. It was early May. I was spending most of my time in the garden, digging up the old overgrown beds that Cal and I inherited with the house. He must have understood that gardening was therapeutic for me on some level because, unlike Tessa and Jude, who kept dropping by to check up on me, he left me alone to work outside as much as I wanted. It was still daylight at seven when Cal came home, popped open a beer, and stood on the back porch watching me spade around a woody spirea I was planning to transplant the next day.

"Need any help?" he asked me. "That looks like quite a job." We've become very solicitous and polite with each other, like two patients in a convalescent home.

"No, thanks, I'm fine," I said. "I'm about to quit for the day anyway." It really was pretty grueling work: the soil around the shrub was congested with rock rubble and in-grown roots. I had to jump up and down on the spade, trying to force it down through the unyielding layers. But it was this kind of intense effort and concentration that was keeping me sane. I was going to bed exhausted at night, my muscles screaming but my mind nearly blank.

"We met with the landscape architect today," Cal told me. "Daniel Brandt. Ravitch was thrilled that he agreed to do the job. He's supposed to be some kind of big deal. He's won all sorts of awards." I detected a definite "but" in Cal's voice.

"So?" I asked. "What's he like?"

"It was a little weird," Cal said, setting his beer can down on the porch railing. "I felt that I knew him from somewhere. That we had this kind of *connection*. I don't really know how else to explain it. I kept trying to figure out where we could have met before. I probably annoyed him with all my questions. But he's new to the area. So there's no real chance our paths would have ever crossed. I'm thinking now that he maybe just reminds me of someone I know."

"Too bad you can't use Frank," I said. Cal usually recommends my old employer Frank Pellani for landscaping work. "But I guess you're stuck with this new guy if Ravitch wants him to do the job."

"Yeah, well, I don't know," Cal replied. "It might be interesting to work with somebody new. He comes across as very buttoned-up—and sort of cool. Maybe I could learn a thing or two from him."

"Great," I said, though Cal's reaction surprised me a little. He generally makes a point of being loyal to people he works with, but he seemed so willing to bypass Frank this time. And "buttoned-up"? Since when has Cal considered that a good trait in another person? But I let the subject slide. We're doing that a lot lately. Avoiding sources of friction or unease. Steering clear of people and situations that might make either one of us uncomfortable. He's finally stopped trying to talk to me about the accident itself. And, thank God, the subject of suing Gannon Baby Products has been dropped. I'm the only one who knows it probably wasn't the manufacturer's fault. But I can't tell even Cal what I believe might really have happened. I can hardly admit it to myself. I'm able to think back to the final moments with the seat belt, the weight of the metal buckle in my palm, the coolness of its surface on a hot day. But I can never seem to get past that. And my thoughts cycle back so often to that last clear moment that I'm beginning to fear I could lose even that, rework it one too many times, and end up destroying the few fragile threads that still connect me to my former, blameless self.

Maybe that's why I'm discovering that Jude is one of the few people I can tolerate being around these days. She'd been gone for several years by the time I was pregnant with Betsy, and she wasn't here when my baby was born. She'd never known my daughter—or seen me as a mother. So she has no real sense of the gaping hole at the center of my life right now. With Jude I can revert to a former version of myself, one where I outwardly appear to be pretty much a whole person again.

It helps, too, that Jude's so self-involved. She's not constantly asking me in hushed tones how I'm doing like so many women I know do, or giving me those long, meaningful looks and heartfelt hugs. I can hardly stand to be in the same room with Tessa these days; her sympathy and concern are so overwhelming. It feels like just an added burden to what I already have to carry.

And there's something else about Jude that I know makes no logical sense, but she reminds me so much of Betsy: stubborn, brashly confident, and yet playful and mischievous in a way that I could never be.

"I decided to take it upon myself to clean out the Reverend's basement," she announced a few days after Cal first mentioned Daniel Brandt. Jude often referred to our father as "the Reverend" or "His Holiness" when we were growing up. I think she hoped that poking fun at his uncompromising authority would diminish it and somehow help to dispel his power over us. It was a warm, sunny afternoon, and she was stretched out on one of our lawn chairs, stripped down to her bra and jeans, a glass of iced tea resting on her exposed stomach. From the three photos we have of our mother, we know that Jude takes after her: redheaded, lean, with the long, attenuated limbs of a dancer. Though Jude's always been a tomboy: full of energy, but clumsy and accident-prone.

I'd taken up most of the old flagstone patio by then and was stacking the slabs in the wheelbarrow. My hands and knees were caked with dirt. I'd decided just that morning to lay in a pathway, utilizing these stones, up the old haying field that rises to the north of the house, at the top of which I planned to eventually install a gazebo. A beautiful teak model had caught my eye at Pellani's Garden Center early this spring. Betsy seemed to have liked it, too, grabbing onto the wooden railings as she circled the octagonal interior. I decided it would make a great playhouse for her when she got a little older. And I could see her at fifteen or so, sitting next to a boy in the gazebo, being kissed for the first time. Somewhere in the back of my mind I think I also pictured her getting married under its wooden cupola one day. I know Cal thought I was crazy when I suggested we bury Betsy there, but it felt so right to me. I'm not new agey or anything, like Kristin, but the top of that hill is one of three or four places where I feel my daughter's spirit hovering. I can so easily imagine her running full tilt down through the field of wildflowers—and into my arms.

"I was thinking that I could turn part of the basement into a workshop," Jude went on. My sister collects odd-lot pieces of chintz and printed fabric and sews them into quilts, pillows, and kitchen mitts, which she sells at craft fairs. "Plus I guess I was hoping to find a little corner of that house where I could make a mess. The place is like a fucking museum, Jen. Everything in its little anal place. Anyway, I received the blessing of His Holiness to move things around down there. Guess what I found?"

Jude was shielding her eyes from the sun, waiting for me with a knowing smile when I looked up and over at her. The two of us have been searching for clues to our mother's abrupt disappearance from our lives for almost as long as I can remember. Her name was Lillian. I think my father used to call her Lilly. All I know is that she ran off with a man—a church consultant—who'd been working with my father to try to build up his congregation. I'm not sure how I came to learn that; it's just embedded in my memory somehow.

I was eight when she left and, though Jude can't recall a thing about her, I remember her vaguely. But even the few memories I have of her—standing in cutoff jeans in front of the sink, smoking a cigarette (I'm certain without my father's knowledge, let alone approval) while reading me a bedtime story, waving to me from the back of a motorcycle—seem to me both out of focus and larger than life. They're like big blowups of photographs where the details have blurred, the eyes and mouths unreadable smudges. Especially now, since Betsy's death, I resent how insubstantial these images are, how little I have to hold on to.

"Gotcha!" Jude said, laughing. "Oh, Jen, you should see your face! No, it has nothing to do with Mom, except in a roundabout sort of way, I suppose. Are you ready for this? I found about a two years' stash of old *Playboy* magazines! They're in perfect condition and—this is almost too good to be true—they're arranged in chronological order! Can you believe it? The lecherous old hypocrite! I almost lugged them upstairs and called him on it. But then I was afraid he'd change his mind about letting me have the basement."

I didn't smile back. I was stung that she'd tricked me into thinking she'd discovered something about our mother. Angry that she seemed to think I was in any kind of emotional shape to respond lightheartedly to her kidding around. Jude has always had a way of making me feel older than my years—more responsible than I ever wanted to be. She remains so immature and needy. She surely must know that the bottom has fallen out of my world, but she behaves as though nothing much has changed with me. She still seems to see me in the role I've always played for her: the reliable, uncomplaining caregiver. Would my sister ever grow up—and finally see me as a person separate from herself? I needed *her* now, not the other way around.

"Which two years?" I asked her, turning back to my work.

"What?" She seemed surprised that I wasn't sharing in her amusement.

"You said there were two years' worth. Do you remember which years?"

"Sometime in the eighties, I think. There was a lot of big hair—along with plenty of other big body parts, let me tell you. The whole thing really creeped me out. You know what I'd love to do? I'd love to donate them to the church sale this summer. Courtesy of the Reverend Karl Honegger."

"I bet he got them after Mom left," I said. "Don't you think that's kind of sad?"

"No, I do not!" Jude said, sitting up. "And I hope you're not starting to go all soft on him now. God, he remains so fucking sanctimonious. Do you know what he said to—"

"Oh, Jude, sorry—," Cal interrupted. He'd come around to the back of the house by way of the side lawn, so we hadn't heard him approach. He and Jude have kept their distance since the funeral. Betsy's death so overshadowed my sister's return that my earlier worries about how Cal would react to the news came to nothing in the end. He'd simply nodded and said "okay" when I told him Jude planned to stay on for a while. But I sense he still isn't particularly comfortable when she's around. That's one reason I try to limit her visits to times when I know he'll be working. I wondered what had brought him home this early on a Thursday afternoon. Then I realized he wasn't alone.

The man who'd come up to stand beside Cal was about my husband's height, but slighter. His dark hair, longer than I'm used to, was going gray at the temples and starting to recede. He wore sunglasses, so I couldn't see his eyes, but I knew he was looking at me. Then his chin tilted toward Jude, who was slowly pulling a T-shirt on over her head. You could tell that she knew she was being watched and that she enjoyed the attention. I don't think she can help herself, but it doesn't make her behavior any more acceptable. Even now, in front of me and Cal, whose relationship she'd nearly ruined by her impulsive actions, my sister needed to put herself on display.

"I was hoping to make this a surprise," Cal said, looking fixedly over Jude's head at me. He was clearly put off by her being there. "But, okay. Here goes: I'd like to introduce Daniel Brandt. He's going to be your birthday present. It's a week or two early, I know. But Daniel was up at the site today, and I wanted you two to meet and have a chance to talk."

"What? No ribbon?" Jude said, standing up. She walked right over to Brandt and held out her hand. "Hi, I'm Jude. The prodigal sister."

"Hello," he said, taking her hand, but he didn't keep it long. He looked over at me. "And, hello, Mrs. Horigan. Your husband tells me you're trying to renovate these gardens on your own. It looks like quite an undertaking. He thought I could help you with some design suggestions, if you're interested."

I understood now why Cal called Daniel Brandt cool. Except for the longer hair, he didn't come across as particularly hip or edgy; if anything he seemed a little conservative and reserved. He was wearing a checkered oxford shirt, a sports jacket, and a pair of chinos that looked as though they'd been ironed. No, he was cool in the sense that he seemed so contained and self-confident, so at ease within himself. Only his voice was a little jarring: froggy and hoarse, breaking in places like a pubescent boy's.

I was wearing my usual gardening outfit: leggings tucked

into white socks, work boots, and an old shirt of Cal's knotted at my waist. I hadn't bothered to shower yet, and my hair was matted down under my wide-brimmed gardening hat. It didn't really bother me that they'd found me covered in mud and looking like a wreck. That wasn't what upset me so much. It was the fact that this interruption—Cal's decision to bring in this stranger, a professional landscape architect, no less—forced me to step back and take stock of what I had actually been doing.

The rubble of the old patio lay scattered around us. There were oddly shaped indentations where the flagstones used to be, outlined by a maze of grass strips that had grown up between the slabs. The day before, I'd divided and cut back the bearded irises that ran along the back porch, so that now the front of the border looked as though it had been attacked by a weed whacker. I'd dug up plants and shrubs and had them waiting in black plastic tubs to be resettled, leaving gaping holes throughout the garden and yard.

Though I had an overall sense of where everything should eventually end up, in truth my plans were really nothing more than vague yearnings. Distant and shapeless. All I really wanted was to feel my hands in the earth, to be digging, pulling, uprooting. I'd assumed that Cal understood this. And now I was taken aback by what I considered to be his obtuseness. It alarmed me that he might have been secretly questioning what I'd been doing these past weeks, that he might have actually been viewing all my activity in the garden the same way I imagined Brandt must be doing now: the work of a crazy person—or someone crazy from grief.

I brushed my dirty hands against my leggings. Tucked a strand of hair that had fallen across my cheek behind my ear.

I heard a buzzing—a bee or mosquito—close to my head. I needed to be on guard, I told myself. Watch how I reacted, what I said. I had to be careful not to let Cal see what a stupid thing he'd done or Daniel Brandt realize that the last thing I wanted was his professional advice. I had to try my best to protect whatever wild impulse had been helping me move forward.

"Nice to meet you," I said, holding out my hand. "Excuse the mud. And my appearance—the garden's, too. I'm afraid we're not looking our best right now." Though his fingers barely closed around mine before slipping free, I felt how rough and dry they were. An occupational hazard, I thought. Maybe because of this, I had the feeling that he didn't much enjoy shaking hands.

"It's a work in progress," he said. "Like every good garden. Why don't we walk around a little and you can tell me about what you're hoping to achieve. Your husband told me that you haven't been working them very long."

Hoping to achieve? I wanted to laugh out loud. I had to lead the way through what looked like a minefield: side-stepping holes and pots, maneuvering past piles of earth and stone. Jude sat back down in the chair and picked up her iced tea, but Cal trailed behind me and Brandt as I pointed out what I considered some of the garden's better features: the decades-old tree peonies and lilac bushes, the day lilies that would run riot behind the lichen-covered stone wall come July, the hostas and ferns that blanketed the shady bank leading down to our seasonal brook.

"Jenny put in this whole new area last summer," Cal said, as we stopped in front of the sunny border on the south-facing side of the house. It was based on a garden I'd fallen in love with when I was working for Pellani's Garden Center: massed groupings of allium, echinacea, monarda, phlox, and catmint. I was proud of the way it had turned out. Though it would take another month or two to produce its full effect, I knew a professional like Brandt would be able to visualize the bright primary colors splashing up against our white clapboard, the butterflies and hummingbirds drifting above the blooms.

"Very nice," Brandt said.

"The monarda hasn't begun to fill in yet," I said. "It'll be almost six feet by the end of July."

"Yes, I can see that," he said. "I'm curious why you went with the straight rectangular shape."

"It's a border. It runs alongside the house. It seemed appropriate to me. What would you have done?"

"Appropriate," he said, turning to look down at me. I could see myself reflected in his sunglasses: the wide brim of my hat obscuring my eyes but highlighting my lips and chin, the pale slope of my neck. "That's the perfect word for it. This bed—in fact the entire garden, really, is just that. Appropriate, expected, respectable."

"And you'd probably go for the inappropriate and unexpected," Cal said. Something about his tone—knowing but also ingratiating—irritated me a little. I remember Cal saying that he had felt an instant connection with Brandt. I recalled the admiring way he'd talked about the awards the landscape architect had won. How Cal felt he could learn a thing or two from him. It occurred to me that this visit wasn't just about introducing me to Brandt. On some level, it was a way of showing off—me, the house, the property—to this man. But he was going about it in such an obvious, almost juvenile way, it seemed to me. I felt embarrassed for him when Brandt didn't answer Cal right away. Instead, Brandt took off his sunglasses and met my gaze. I took a step back; he suddenly seemed to be standing too close to me.

"No, that's not really the case," he said, turning slightly to include Cal in his answer, but he was really talking to me. He was older than I'd first thought: in his mid-forties, at least. His eyes were slightly pouched, heavy lidded; crow's-feet were grooved into the skin. "I prefer gardens to flow against a landscape. In this case, you could follow the line of those fields in the distance. Or the up and down of that stand of hemlocks over there. I'm not a big fan of imposed shapes. Of strictures. Have you ever heard the expression 'pathways of desire'?"

"No," I said.

"It's an architectural term. It refers to the tracks and paths we create naturally in our day-to-day lives. How we really get from place to place—from car to house, say, or across a vacant lot—rather than following the prescribed routes. I think a good gardener should be attuned to that as well. Think about how you move around your yard here. Where you sit, which way you like to face. When was the last time, for instance, you actually came to this side of the house other than to work? And yet you put so much effort into this. All that time."

"This is one of my favorite spots," Cal said, not understanding what Daniel was saying, or not paying enough attention.

"You're just talking about shortcuts," I said. I wanted to put him in his place, to put him down. He was absolutely right about my sunny border; I never spent any real time out here—except to garden. "The fastest way between two points."

"Not really. I interpret the phrase a little more broadly than that. In fact, I think that sometimes it can actually be a much longer route. The scenic one, say. It's 'pathways of desire,' not 'expediency.' In my mind, it means paying attention to where—unconsciously, perhaps—the body leads, where the eye follows. Which way the heart wants to go."

7

Cal

☙

"So?" I asked Jenny as we watched Daniel, then Jude, pull out of the driveway. Jude had made a point of leaving at the same time Daniel did. She'd walked right beside him as they'd crossed the lawn to their cars, talking and looking up at him in that way she has.

"I guess I should say thank you," Jenny replied, turning back inside the house. I'd been expecting a much bigger response from her. The Daniel Brandts of this world don't come cheap—and they carry a professional cachet that I thought Jenny, being an amateur in the field, would really appreciate. But it seemed to me she'd been barely civil to him when I first introduced him and, toward the end, almost combative. But, as I've been doing so often these days, I told myself not to call her on it. Not to take any of this to heart.

"What did you make of him?" I asked, unable to let it rest completely. "That 'pathways of desire' business. I thought that idea alone was worth the price of admission, didn't you?"

"Yes," she said, walking in front of me to the kitchen. "I did." We haven't made love since Betsy's death. For the first couple of weeks, we held each other at night when we crawled into bed—and wept. But we aren't even doing that anymore. The last week or so, I've been making little attempts to get her attention. I used to rub her shoulders after dinner as a signal that I was interested in heading upstairs, but when I tried that the other night she just shrugged me off.

"Don't, Cal."

"What? I can't even touch you anymore?"

"That's not what that was," she replied. "I'm not ready, okay? I'm not anywhere near ready."

What exactly is the appropriate amount of time, I wonder, before a husband and wife can make love again after losing their only child? There seems to be no good answer to that—or to any of the other questions that keep coming up for me. For one thing, I don't know what to do with all my feelings about Betsy. I don't know where to put them. There's just no good resting place that I can see. So I carry the weight of her death—which seems to be getting heavier—around with me everywhere. But, as Edmund predicted, the grief is slowly starting to morph into anger. I've stopped talking to Jenny about the lawsuit because it only sets her off, but I haven't stopped thinking about it.

"Do you know where the car seat ended up?" Edmund asked me a few days after Daniel's visit. Edmund called me on my cell. I was up in Harringdale, meeting with one of the cement contractors who was bidding on the Ravitch job. "You're going to need it as evidence. The sooner we get it to the lawyer, the better."

"No, I don't know where—," I began, and then I caught

myself. "I'm still not all that sure about going ahead with this, Eddie. I mean, you remember what Dad said: what's the point of assigning blame?"

"But it isn't about blame," he replied. "It's about restitution. It's about someone destroying the most precious thing in your world—and you saying, 'Guess what: that's not okay.' Listen, to tell you the truth, Dad's just tired. You don't work with him every day the way I do. He's keeping up appearances most of the time. Getting by. He's not interested in rocking any boats right now. But I'm totally convinced that if this thing happened two, three years ago? He'd be banging on that lawyer's door louder than anybody."

"Kurt's against it, too," I said. "At least as long as Jenny is—and I don't see her changing her mind. I've stopped trying to even talk to her about it, honestly. It just seems to make an already bad situation worse."

"Jenny—I don't know what to say there. But Kurt? We both know the deal with him. I love the guy, but he's just not a fighter. Not like you and me."

"I hear what you're saying," I told him. I was tempted, but there are so many things about moving ahead with the lawsuit that make me uncomfortable. Maybe top on my list is the idea that I'd be doing it under Edmund's auspices. "I appreciate what you're trying to do for me. But, honestly, I have to ask: what's in this for you?"

"I'm really kind of hurt by that question, if you want to know the truth," he said. "You think I don't have any feelings? Betsy's death did a number on all of us, Cal. I guess it's because I'm more on the business side of things than the rest of you are, but as far as I'm concerned this lawsuit is just how the real world operates. Maybe not according to Kurt's insular small-town rules. But, believe me, ask around: I'll bet you most objective people would tell you that you're crazy not to pursue this."

I think that was probably in the back of my mind when I suggested to Daniel at the end of the week that we grab a drink together. He'd been up at the Ravitch site with his two-man crew most of the afternoon.

"Sure," he said. "But I'm buying. You're a client now."

We agreed to meet at Ernie's in Northridge. Daniel was renting an apartment not far from there. He was waiting at the bar when I arrived, talking to the bartender about the Yankees' chances.

"Yeah, well, if A-Rod could only keep it in his pants for a night or two, we might begin—"

"Jesus, man," I said, pulling up a stool. "You're taking your life in your hands even discussing those bastards in here. Plenty of Red Sox fans in this neck of the woods."

We went through the usual song and dance—weighing how many good games Mariano had left in him, whether Jeter was starting to fade, when Manny was going to hit that five hundredth—enough for me to appreciate the fact that Daniel is at least as knowledgeable as I am about the game. Then we moved on a little gingerly to the economy. What a mess the real estate market was in. How badly Wall Street had been trashing Main Street. I don't think either one of us was about to give out the details of our own business prospects, but I did say at one point:

"Thank God for Phil Ravitch."

"I'll second that," Daniel replied as he signaled the bartender for another round. "At least all this white-collar crime is keeping him in the clover."

"Yeah," I said, sipping the foam off my draft. The first beer had slaked my thirst; I hoped this one would start to ease the deep-seated pain between my shoulder blades that's been with me since Betsy's death. In the little lull that followed, I could sense Daniel starting to wonder what this was all about. What did I want from him? On paper, we have so little in common: he's ten or fifteen years older than me. A recent transplant from Manhattan, but still definitely citified: the sports jacket, the expensive haircut. He's way better educated than me, a big deal in a competitive field, championed by the likes of Philip Ravitch. And yet, as I'd told Jenny when I first met Daniel, I felt that we had a kind of immediate rapport. Maybe it's just that I'm having a harder and harder time communicating with Jenny these days, but for some reason I had this sense that Daniel was someone I could talk to.

"Things going okay with Jenny and the garden?" I asked him at last. "She said you came by yesterday for a while."

"Yes. I took some photos. And we talked a little," Daniel said. "I'm not sure—" He laughed to himself, shook his head, and went on: "This is going to sound a little egotistical, but I don't usually get this reaction from women. I'm not sure she likes me. She seems very—what?—defensive? Defended? In any case, I should probably tell you that I don't think she's all that thrilled with your birthday present."

"You don't know what happened to us, do you?"

"Happened?" he said, turning on his stool to look at me. "No, I'm afraid I don't."

"I guess I assume everybody knows. This area—it's really just a bunch of small towns. And it was all over the local news. We lost our baby daughter in a car accident about six weeks ago. I was driving. The Jeep rolled. I walked away without a scratch, but her car seat came loose and—"

"I'm sorry," Daniel said. "I had no idea. You both must be going through hell."

"Yeah," I said, suddenly overcome. It was only then that I realized I had brought Daniel there to unburden myself. That I'd been longing to tell him the story. The whole story. From my point of view. I was as brutally honest as I could be. I told him about the pickup game, how we'd all been drinking. That even now I couldn't swear how many beers I'd actually had. And I told him about my fight with Edmund. How that had really riled me up, distracted me. I was probably going too fast. It was a rough road, too, and it was beginning to get dark.

"This fox ran out of nowhere right in front of the Jeep. And I swerved to keep from hitting it and—"

"I'm sorry," Daniel said when I couldn't go on. He looked down into his half-filled glass and said again: "I'm really sorry." I'd been hearing variations on that theme from so many people over the weeks since the accident, all so heartfelt, often accompanied by tears. But there was something about the way Daniel said it that was different. It took me a moment to grasp what it was: he didn't really mean it. He didn't really care. He'd never known Betsy. He was new to the area. Covington, the Horigan family, our little domestic tragedy—it was all pretty much an abstraction for him. None of this touched him very deeply. He wasn't actually sorry; he was just being polite. But the funny thing? Rather than being embarrassed or hurt by this realization, I was relieved.

"You're actually one of the few people I know who's not

personally involved with what happened," I told him. I was aware that I could be trying his patience, but I felt I had to push on; this was too important to me. "My family and friends keep telling me that I shouldn't feel responsible in any way, that it wasn't my fault. What do you think?"

"Honestly?" Daniel asked, looking over at me again. Maybe he was trying to gauge what kind of impact his answer would have on me, or perhaps he was just pausing for dramatic affect. The overhead light gleamed on his high forehead and softened the wrinkles around his eyes and mouth. Suddenly I had no idea how old he was, or who he really was. He stared back down into his beer for a moment as if weighing his words. Then he said:

"As far as I'm concerned, the whole idea of guilt is probably the worst concept mankind has ever come up with. I don't buy into the idea that actions necessarily result in consequences. That way of thinking? I think it's just a very clever system for keeping people in line, holding them back. I believe life simply unfolds—as mysteriously and inevitably as a flower. And, if you have any sense at all, you'll do everything in your power to enjoy the process."

"Wow," I said. He looked more serious at that moment than I'd ever seen him. Then, suddenly, as if reading my thoughts, he laughed and said:

"Sorry, I can get a little carried away."

"No, that was great," I said. Maybe it was just the alcohol starting to hit me, but I felt looser. Lighter. He'd given me a whole new way of looking at things. It wasn't just that he'd provided me with a possible answer to something that had been gnawing away at me: he'd managed to reframe the whole question. It didn't matter whether what happened was

God's will—or my fault. Because, for Daniel, it wasn't about guilt and innocence. Right or wrong. It was liberating to think that these were just man-made concepts anyway, ideas people could choose to dismiss. Or ignore.

"I've got one last question for you," I said. I told him about the car seat and the possibility of suing Gannon Baby Products, but I think I already knew what he was going to say.

"Why not?" he asked, signaling the waiter for the check. "What do you have to lose?"

☙

The Ravitch job gives Kurt and me a reason to get up every morning and climb the stairs to the office, make calls, move pieces of paper around, drive over to the site to see how the foundation is coming, shoot the breeze with the small crew we've cobbled together. But we're not kidding anybody, especially each other. We're barely covering expenses, and we have months to go before we see another dime out of Ravitch. I feel so grateful now that my folks handed Jenny and me the farmhouse free and clear. We have our problems, but at least we don't have to worry about mortgage payments the way Kurt does. He got one of those interest-only loans at the top of the market, and at this point his house is deep underwater in terms of equity.

"I'm thinking of selling the Bayliner," Kurt said one afternoon toward the end of May. We were enjoying a run of beautiful weather: hot and clear, with the daylight hours stretching ever deeper into the evening. Last year at this time, we'd had five places under contract and were working twelve-hour days. Between us, we'd juggled crew and contracts, bids and building inspections—and had developed a highly synchronized, almost instinctual way of keeping all those balls in the air. Now, though, with so little to do, we kept finding ourselves making stupid mistakes: Kurt wiped out two weeks' worth of phone messages by pushing the wrong button, erasing a callback number for a possible job in Red River; I forgot to send in the check for our standing ad in the *North County Real Estate Guide*, and those ass-holes in the ad department—claiming they were getting stiffed right and left since the downturn—dropped our full page from the May book, usually one of the biggest of the year.

"The hell you are," I said, looking over at Kurt, who was busy flipping through his digital deck of solitaire cards. "You love that thing."

Kurt's twenty-eight-foot Ciera outboard cruiser has a Mercruiser V-8 engine that, five years old now, still purrs like a kitten. It was the only high-ticket item he bought for himself after the company took off, and over the years he's loaded it up with options: microwave, stove, fridge, Bose radio and CD player. Every spring, until this one anyway, we haul it up to Lake George or Lake Champlain and spend a long weekend cruising and fishing. Kurt's never been particu- larly possessive or acquisitive, but on one of those trips a few years back I managed to gauge an inch-long scratch in the Bayliner's fiberglass, and Kurt fussed over that thing like a mother hen with an ailing chick.

"I could probably get over fifteen thousand for it on eBay," Kurt replied, not looking up from his game.

"You really need the money that bad?"

"It's not just that. Tessa's on this kick about cutting back on our carbon footprint, doing our bit to stop global warming or whatever. We're decluttering."

"Oh, come on," I said. "The Bayliner isn't clutter. It's almost like a collectible at this point. I remember you saying you wanted to hand it down to Jamie someday. And weren't we going to start teaching him how to fish in a couple of years?"

"Well, that's another thing," Kurt said, sighing and turning away from the computer. He ran his hands through what was left of his hair. "Now Tessa doesn't want Jamie going out on the boat until he's like eighteen or something. Says it's too dangerous. She's suddenly gotten a little nuts about safety issues. So what's the fucking point, right?"

That did it for me. I'm not sure why, but suddenly I felt like I had to push back. Make a stand. Betsy's death hadn't just fouled up my own life; its ugliness was starting to seep into the lives of those around me. Jenny couldn't see it, I told myself, because she was still so wrapped up in her own suffering. I thought back to what Edmund had told me: that the lawsuit wasn't about blame. *It's about restitution. It's about someone destroying the most precious thing in your world— and you saying, "Guess what: that's not okay."* That's exactly how I was feeling now. It was time to get some answers. Stop the self-doubt and recriminations. How else were we going to be able to move on?

"I've been meaning to ask you," I said to Kurt. "Do you know what happened to Betsy's car seat?"

"Why?" Kurt replied.

"I just don't want it thrown away by mistake," I told him. "I mean, if you do happen to have it, I don't want it getting tossed out with all this decluttering you're planning, okay?"

"Why not just let it go? It's not really something you want to keep."

"Yes, it is, actually," I said. "It's hard to explain, but I'd like to hold on to it. It's the last thing that touched her."

Kurt seemed to buy my explanation. It had just the right tone of sentimentality for him, the correct note of sorrow. Old Kurt. I don't think he suspected what I was up to. He trusted me. He believed we saw eye to eye on just about everything. He thought he knew me so well.

"I stored it away in the garage," he told me. "Up in the eaves. I'll get it down for you on your way out."

into some kind of perspective. It didn't help that he looked so different from the man I'd been imagining these past few days. Perhaps it was just being indoors, but he seemed taller and a little heavier now. Also, I'd remembered him as fairly pale, with finely drawn features. But I realized that his skin was actually deeply tanned with the kind of swarthiness that often comes from teenage acne—and that you might associate with a pirate or Gypsy. It was hard to imagine what he might have looked like as a child. He seemed so adult and completely evolved. Not really a handsome man, I thought, though he was clearly someone who took a great deal of care with his appearance.

It occurred to me that he had very likely made himself over from some former, less acceptable persona. That the image he projected to the world was a calculated one, created to both dazzle and obscure. He'd successfully put that facade over on Cal, I decided, as he probably tried to do with all of his clients.

"Do you mind if I just roam around and take some pictures?" he asked as we walked out onto the back porch.

"No, go right ahead," I said. I sat down on the wicker settee and picked up a magazine. I wasn't about to show him around again. I knew I was being a little rude, but I didn't care. Since Betsy's death I've stopped worrying about the niceties. In fact, I've become abrupt and dangerously frank. I finally told Tessa a few days ago to please stop dropping by so often, that her outpouring of love and concern wasn't really helping me right now.

At the same time I've grown far more intuitive and alert to the world around me. Our house, the garden, my friends, our two families—everything has a kind of hyperreal quality.

More than that, I'm now acutely aware of possible dimensions beyond this one—especially the feeling that Betsy is often hovering nearby. Sometimes, when I'm working in the garden, I can so easily believe that she's playing just behind me the way she used to with her trowel or one of her dolls. I'll turn—as quickly as I can—hoping to catch her there, only to find an empty stretch of green summer lawn and the unbearable reality of her absence. My arms ache to pick her up, to hold her to me. I can almost breathe in the scent of her skin and hair. But not quite. And this physical longing—and deprivation—dominates my waking hours now. It permeates my dreams. As the days pass and she remains just beyond my grasp, I can feel the need building and intensifying.

Without being aware of it, I keep rubbing the tips of my fingers together. I know why, of course. Though I've managed to block out all thoughts of those final moments with the seat belt, I can't seem to stop this unconscious questioning. Weighing. Wondering. Thumb against index and middle fingers, over and over.

And here I was, doing it again! I flexed my hands, shook them out, and started to leaf through the magazine, pretending to read while I watched Daniel move around the property. Stopping at the stone wall to take a series of photos. Turning toward the sunny side border and lifting the camera again. Then turning back toward the house, camera blocking his face, but his fingers clearly moving. Tapping the lens button. Focusing in. Closer and closer. There was no way I could prove it, but I was suddenly certain he wasn't taking shots of the garden anymore. He was photographing me. I felt threatened in a way that I couldn't account for—and that was probably ridiculous. Still, it made me realize that there's something about Daniel's physical presence that alarms me—that the air around him feels charged and expectant—like the seconds between a lightning strike and the clap of thunder. I have to remind myself that Ravitch handpicked him, that Cal admires him, that he's an established and respected professional.

As he walked back toward the house, I could feel my whole body tensing.

"Is there anything in particular you're hoping for?" he asked as he climbed the porch stairs toward me. I had one of those flashes I've been experiencing lately—like a door opening a crack and closing just as quickly—of Betsy climbing up those same steps calling *My Yay Yay!*

"What?"

"About the garden?" he asked, leaning against the railing. "Any favorite plants or shrubs I should know about? Did you have any kind of plan in mind already?" He crossed his arms in front of him, cradling the camera in his hands. It seemed an oddly protective gesture, and I had the outrageous notion that he was aroused and concealing an erection. I could feel my neck and face flushing with embarrassment. Where in the world were these thoughts coming from? I've never thought about anybody but Cal in that way. I looked past Daniel to the garden. To the hill of wildflowers where I'd wanted to put in the pathway leading up to the gazebo.

"No," I said. But he must have seen something in my expression, because he said, "I think of it as my job to make this the garden of your dreams, Mrs. Horigan. How can I do that unless you tell me what they might be?"

It startled me that he called me by my married name. It seemed to me that we'd already moved beyond that somehow.

I'd been thinking of him as *Daniel* almost from the moment we first met. Had it all been one-sided? Could it be that I'd just been imagining all these crosscurrents between us?

"No. You're the expert," I told him. I dropped the magazine beside me on the settee. "I'm looking forward to seeing what you come up with. Would you like a drink of water or anything before you go?"

"I don't think so," he said, smiling, "but thanks for the offer." He had a little gap between his two front teeth, and his smile made him look younger and more harmless than I believed he actually was. He tilted his head, studying me in a knowing kind of way. It struck me then that he was actually fully aware of the interior argument I'd been conducting with him and that he was simply toying with me.

"My dreams have nothing to do with this," I added, standing up and leading him back down the porch steps. He could walk up by way of the side garden to the driveway and his car. I didn't want to take him through the house again. I suddenly didn't want him anywhere near me.

❧

"Hey, Daddy," I said, knocking on the door of my father's study. It worried me that he hadn't heard me come into the house, even though the screen door to the kitchen screeched as usual on its rusty hinges. And the old hickory floors creaked as I made my way down the side hall to the room where the Reverend Honegger spends most of his waking hours, surrounded by his books, papers, church bulletins, and—I like to imagine—regrets. The air was filled with dust motes, swirling upward through the late afternoon sunlight, no doubt set in motion by the draft I'd created coming into the house. Though my father's prostate cancer treatment two years ago was declared a success, it seems to me that he's been slowly failing in other ways: both his hearing and his eyesight have been getting worse. He turned at the sound of my voice.

"Jennifer?" he said, taking me in over his rimless glasses. "I wasn't expecting you." He looked so mild mannered and unassuming with his wispy white hair cross-combed over that freckled pate. Some ironic quirk of physiognomy makes it look as though he's always half smiling; his lips curl sharply up on either end and the skin around his mouth is soft and dimpled. Yet I've never known a harder, more unbending man.

He was in his early forties when he married my mother: a stunning but, from what I know, demanding and headstrong twenty-two-year-old who forced my father's hasty departure from the small Maryland community where he'd been ministering. Covington gave him a chance to start over and rebuild his reputation, which, with my mother's charismatic presence, he'd started to do. But within five years of settling here, my mother ran away again, leaving his church with a lot of unanswered questions, and obliging him to raise two unruly daughters on his own. His congregation soon began to abandon him, as well. More gradually, it's true, but no less decisively. And the rejection must have been that much more humiliating because so many of his former parishioners gravitated to the livelier and more tolerant Congregational church just down the street.

Despite these many setbacks, something makes me believe he was always headed this way, blinkered on his straight-and-narrow course. His convictions seem so bred-

in-the-bone and calcified. And he wears his many disappointments with a kind of martyrish pride. I sometimes think that
he considers his unpopularity proof positive of his own righ-
teousness.

"Yeah, well, I haven't seen you for a while," I said,
leaning against the doorframe. Did I need to remind him that
my daughter had recently died? *You're a minister,* I longed to
tell him. *Shouldn't you be dropping by to see how I'm doing?*
And yet, I remember when he had come to the house the day
after Betsy was killed and forced me to pray with him, I
couldn't wait for him to be gone again. I've always felt this
kind of ambivalence toward him: needing and wanting his
love, then bitterly rejecting whatever feeble gestures he tries
to make in that direction.

"Judith isn't here," he replied. "She's down in Hudson at
some crafts fair."

"Yes, I know." I'm not sure why my father has never
called Jude or me by our nicknames, but I suspect it's because it would force him to acknowledge that we've long
been our own independent selves. Both a far cry from the
sweet, submissive offspring he had probably hoped for. "I
spoke to her on the phone this morning. No, I came by to
talk to you."

"Oh?" he said, looking from me to the papers on the
desk. I'm sure he wished he could claim that he was too
busy. That he had a sermon to write, or letters to answer.
I've been aware for many years now that my father dislikes
dealing one-on-one with people. His ideal form of discourse
is speaking down to a congregation, preferably from an
altar. He's even uncomfortable having to mingle with the
crowd at the monthly church teas and potluck suppers. It

doesn't help that I'm his own daughter. It actually makes it much worse. The two of us have a long history of bruising confrontations in this very room. I could almost see him bracing for combat.

"Well, come in, then," he said, moving a pile of books off a chair and onto his desk. He pushed the chair several feet away from him and waved me into it. He crossed his legs and steepled his hands on his knee. "What can I do for you?"

"Ah—," I began, but then almost immediately realized that I didn't really know how to put my question into words. I'd fled the house a few minutes after Daniel had driven off, knowing only that I needed guidance. I couldn't turn to Cal for this—or Tessa, my usual confidante. Oddly, I sensed the only person who might remotely understand what I was experiencing would be my sister-in-law Kristin, with whom I have zero rapport.

"Daddy," I began again. "What happens when someone dies? Where do they go exactly?"

"Are you asking because of Betsy?"

"Yes. Of course."

"Well, I can promise you that she's in heaven. Our Betsy went right to heaven."

"Yes, but what does that mean? Where is that in relation to where we are on earth?"

"Now, you know there's no definitive answer to that. We no longer think of heaven as somewhere above us—like the stars, say. Because it's eternal, it's not something the human mind can really conceptualize."

"So it could be right here," I said. "Like in a parallel kind of universe we can't see but can sometimes sense."

"No, that's really not the right way to think about it,

Jennifer. Heaven isn't parallel to earth—it's infinite, far beyond any sort of relation to this small, finite globe."

"I see," I said, seeing only that we could go around in circles endlessly with the question. "I guess what I'm asking is—well, sometimes I feel like Betsy's right here still. I mean, in the next room, or just on the other side of that wall. Sometimes I feel that, if I only knew how to do it, I could push through whatever's separating us. And I could pick her up. I could—pick her up again."

Did he see my eyes fill with tears? Did he hear them in my voice? All I know is that he started to shake his head and look past me down the hall as he said:

"No. I'm sorry, but, no, you can't. And the sooner you realize that and accept it, the easier it will be for you to move on. To pretend otherwise is wrong and possibly even damaging. Because it will only worsen and extend your sorrow, and keep you from finding—*closure*."

Last summer, my father was forced to participate in a church-sponsored sensitivity seminar up in Albany. He returned sporting a new politically correct vocabulary. He now "reached out" to his congregation and tried to "connect" with those who needed his help. "Closure" was one of his favorite new words. Meaningless to anyone in real pain. An insult, really, to someone crying out for help, like "time heals all wounds." Perhaps I should have argued with him more. We could have gone at least a few more rounds before retreating to our separate corners. But I was quick to decide he'd failed me once again. Though I think a part of me realized I'd actually set him up to do just that.

ॐ

The house was filled with people when Daniel stopped by with the plans for the new garden. It was my birthday, and Cal had insisted on throwing me a big party. I wasn't in the right frame of mind to entertain, to say the least, but I also didn't think I could stand spending that particular night alone with Cal. In my mind, Betsy's absence was becoming an almost palpable presence between us—as suffocating and pervasive as smoke. But Cal pretended not to notice. He refused to take offense at my sulks or react to my angry outbursts. I could see how hard he was struggling to make believe everything was normal. That we were okay. Despite the fact that I'd moved out of our bedroom and had taken to sleeping on an Aerobed in Betsy's old room. Or that, even if we brushed together accidentally in the bathroom, I flinched.

"I'm really glad you guys decided to go ahead and do this—," Tessa was saying to me when I saw Cal open the front door. I knew just by Cal's greeting who it was:

"Hey, this is great! I thought you said— Well, sure, but come in for a minute anyway. You'll at least want to say hello to the birthday girl."

"Who's that?" I heard Tessa ask, as Cal led Daniel down the hallway toward us. He had his arm around Daniel's shoulder. Daniel had a bouquet of white roses and a mailing tube under his arm.

"What—?" I asked, turning back to Tessa and trying to pick up the thread of our conversation.

"The man with Cal. That's the landscape architect guy, isn't it? I see what Kurt means."

"What did Kurt say about him?"

"That he's"—Tessa lowered her voice and leaned in

toward me—"totally full of himself. I can see why, though. I guess he *is* kind of attractive."

"Jenny!" Cal was calling over people's heads as he attempted to steer Daniel through the crowd that had formed in the kitchen. "Look who's here!"

Cal eagerly introduced Daniel around to our friends and family. When he explained that Daniel's redesign for our gardens was actually my birthday gift, I saw Tessa look over at me sharply. I don't know why I hadn't told her about any of this. But I realized now that my reluctance to do so was connected somehow with my asking her not to come by so often.

Jude, on the other hand, greeted Daniel like an old friend. She went right up to him and asked him what he wanted to drink.

"Sorry, I can't stay."

"But that's crazy," Jude said. "You just got here."

"No, really," he said, stepping toward me with the flowers and tube. "I just wanted to drop these off."

"Thanks," I said, taking the gifts from him.

"Tell him he has to stay a while," Jude told me.

"You have to stay a while," I said, looking past him as I spoke. I knew my tone wasn't particularly welcoming.

"I'm sorry," he said. "But I really can't."

"Okay, then," Cal intervened, slapping him on the back. "Let's try to get you out of here. Come on, Jenny."

People were still arriving as we made our way back down the hall. Cal and I had to stop a couple of times to greet the new guests:

"Paul, Maddie, great to see you."

"Hey there, Lori. Food and drinks out back."

I noticed that Daniel quietly pushed ahead of us through

the crowd. He was waiting for us on the front porch. If anything, it was even warmer outside, the night air thick with humidity and the thrumming of insects. It was too overcast to see any stars, but I could feel them there above the cloud cover, the millions of invisible universes, pulsing with life.

"Thanks for coming," Cal said again. "And for the plans, too, of course."

"Don't thank me yet. Who knows? You may not like what I've done."

"Why do I doubt that?" Cal said, laughing.

"Well, it's actually *Mrs.* Horigan I'm worried about."

"Mrs. Horigan?" Cal asked, turning from Daniel to me. "Honestly! Aren't you two up to first names yet? Here, let me introduce you: Jenny, this is Daniel."

Oh, he was so pleased with himself. So happy. Standing there between Daniel and myself, not understanding anything.

"Hello," I said. "Daniel."

"Happy birthday, Jenny," he replied, leaning forward. I lifted my hand to try to ward him off, but instead I felt my fingers brushing against his shirt front. I had to steady myself, leaning against him for support, my fingers closing around his upper arm. All Cal saw was Daniel kissing me on the cheek. Though, in fact, Daniel's lips managed to graze mine—so quickly that at first I didn't quite realize what had happened. I just felt the shock. I looked at him. Yes, he'd done it on purpose. Though it had the feeling of an accident. A moment of thoughtlessness. Something that in retrospect seemed to unfold in slow motion. But, in fact, was actually so fast. In the blink of an eye, really—but that's all it takes. How easily your whole world can be overturned.

Part Two

9

Cal

❧

I told Jenny I was going to the baseball game. At that point, it didn't bother me that I was lying. We'd had a fight about Daniel's designs for the garden, and I was so pissed off that my decision to meet with Edmund and the lawyer he'd lined up suddenly seemed totally justified. I really think I'm doing everything I can to cater to Jenny's moods, but she's just becoming more and more impossible to live with. When we looked at Daniel's blueprints together that morning, she kept finding all these nitpicky little things to complain about. I'm starting to think that maybe there's nothing in the world I can do to please her.

"Okay, I get it," I finally told her. I was supposed to see Edmund at three o'clock, and I didn't have time for any more of her craziness. "Okay. We'll just shelve the whole business for now. I'll tell Daniel that we're not ready."

She seemed a little startled by my sudden capitulation, maybe even contrite. Well, let her suffer a little, I told myself as I slid the blueprints back into the storage tube. But, like so many of our arguments these days, I suspected this one wasn't over yet. Since Betsy's death, Jenny's usual self-control and equilibrium have gone totally to hell. And she's grown so combative and outspoken. Sometimes I feel like she's actually spoiling for a fight—that she'll grab onto any excuse to lash out at me.

I'd already stashed Betsy's car seat, wrapped in a big black plastic garbage bag, in the trunk of my dad's Oldsmobile. A couple of nights after Kurt had turned the seat over to me, and an hour or two after Jenny had gone up to bed, I took a series of photos of it from different angles with my digital camera. A part of me actually did want to hold on to the thing, just as I'd told Kurt. But that was before I really focused on the seat itself: the straps were mangled. I was a little drunk at the time I took the photos, and I had the weirdest feeling that I was being watched. At one point, I even pulled open the door from the garage to the kitchen— thinking I'd catch Jenny there. Obviously, I had been imagining things, or letting my conscience work me over again.

Because that's the thing: no matter what I tell myself, or how hard I try to listen to what other people say, I still feel guilty about how Betsy died. And I believe Jenny thinks I'm guilty, too. What else could it be, after all, the way she's been treating me? The sulks. The turning away from me when I make even the slightest attempt to touch her. That nasty, biting temper. I think she must look across the table at me and see the person who let her baby daughter die. The fox, the Jeep overturning, the car seat—Jenny still doesn't want to hear about any of it. And why is that? I'm alive. Betsy's not. I think Jenny's just making a simple equation.

"Hey there, little brother," Edmund said, coming across

the lawn to meet me as I pulled up in front of his house near Hudson. He and Kristin have gussied up an old Victorian, and its maroon and pink-trimmed facade dominates their suburban neighborhood. Edmund, lord of the manor, was wearing a blue blazer and pressed chinos.

"I didn't know I was supposed to dress up," I said. I had on my Horigan Builders baseball jersey and a pair of jeans.

"You look fine. Where's the seat?" he asked, peering into the back of the Olds. "Didn't I tell you they—"

"In the trunk, Eddie," I replied. "Where the hell else would it be? You actually think I'd leave it out where Jenny could see it? She doesn't know I'm doing this, remember? She'd throw a total fit if she knew."

"Calm down, Cal. Grab the seat and we're off. We'll take my Beamer."

Driving from Edmund's place to Albany takes about an hour. My older brother spent the time filling me in about all the work he'd been doing on my behalf. Except for quick cell phone calls on the subject, I haven't had much of an opportunity to talk to him about any of this, and I actually did have a lot of catching up to do. For one thing, it turned out the original lawyer he'd contacted—his old Cornell buddy—wasn't whom we were going to be meeting with that afternoon.

"But I thought you were so high on him," I said.

"Gerry? He's a good guy, but frankly, he doesn't have the expertise we need. Law firms tend to specialize. Some outfit wins a big suit, or scores a major settlement in a particular area, and it suddenly becomes the go-to firm for that thing."

"And Gerry doesn't do our 'thing'?" I asked, looking out over the fallow fields and broken-down farmhouses. Summer heat—or some kind of smog—blurred the horizon.

"No. He's more in the personal-injury area. He actually told me that dead kids aren't worth all that much. I mean in terms of payouts, of course."

"Jesus!" I said. "We're talking about Betsy here. You know, I don't think I can do this."

"Sorry," Edmund said, glancing over at me. "Look, I'm really sorry. But I've been having to sort through a lot of stuff—things I didn't want you to have to deal with. I've been looking around, talking to different firms. I don't think there's any sense in pursuing this if the right people don't have our backs. And, from everything I could learn, Stephens, Stokes, Kline—these guys—bring the experience we need to the table. They're supposed to be the best in the state in terms of product-liability litigation. They handled a case similar to ours a few years back and, well—" He paused and looked over at me again when he realized that I wasn't responding to any of this. Then he sighed and said, "In the future, I want you to tell me to just shut the fuck up when I touch on something you find painful. Okay?"

"Listen," I said, letting my head fall back against the headrest. I closed my eyes. I'm not sure why I feel the need to fight Edmund every step of the way—but then, we've always had such an adversarial relationship. And there's something about his eagerness to help me now that seems forced. Unnatural. But, to be fair, I wasn't really feeling all that great. I'd stayed up too late the night before and probably drank a little too much at the party. Then there was that scene with Jenny. Frankly, I was pretty wiped out.

"I just want to be clear," I told him. "I'm still not sure I want to go ahead with any of this."

"Understood," Edmund replied firmly. "And Stephens,

Stokes get that, too. This is all just very preliminary. A meet and greet."

❦

The law firm took up the top three floors of one of the old ornate granite buildings downtown. The interior design was sleek and contemporary, though, with tinted glass partitions and custom-built mahogany workstations. I think to keep me from any further misgivings, Edmund insisted on carrying the car seat. When he told the receptionist who we were, she nodded, got up from her desk, and walked us down a carpeted hallway to a corner conference room. The floor-to-ceiling windows faced west and north over downtown Albany and out to the distant green of the summer suburbs.

There were two men and a woman waiting for us at the end of a long table. As we entered, the older of the two men stood up and walked across the room to greet us. He'd obviously met Edmund before, because he came right up to me.

"Cal," he said, both hands closing over mine. "We're all so very, very sorry to learn about your loss. I'm Lester Stephens. And these are my associates"—he took my elbow as he led me back to the table—"Janet Graystone and Carl Zeyer. Please take a seat. There's coffee, tea, soda, bottled water—help yourselves to whatever you want."

Edmund and I sat across from the two younger lawyers, facing the view, while Lester sat at the head of the table. His colleagues—both fair haired and dark suited—looked almost typecast for their positions, but Lester, broad and beefy, could have passed for some sort of ringmaster with his orange suspenders, French cuffs, and a pocket square in his jacket. He had receding hair and a dark, carefully groomed handlebar mustache.

"Edmund has already given us the basic outline of what happened," he said. "I won't pretend to know what you've been going through. I've never experienced that kind of terrible tragedy myself. But I can tell you that I've helped many, many people in your position. And one thing I really do understand is that nothing—nothing ever—will truly compensate for Betsy's death. It's ridiculous to even talk about that, isn't it, Cal?"

"Yes, it is," I said, meeting his gaze. I was on the alert for fakery or false notes, but, despite his showy appearance, Lester struck me as straightforward and sincere.

I don't know what I'd been expecting, but I realized that a part of me had been readying myself for some sort of confrontation with this man. It hadn't really occurred to me that he'd be on my side.

"At the same time, Gannon Baby Products has a documented history of some very, very serious problems. They've faced a number of lawsuits and fines. They've been forced to issue recalls on a couple of separate occasions. We successfully litigated against them in a portable-crib death several years ago. I'm sorry to say that we know them—and their legal strategies—all too well. I thought then that we had helped teach Gannon a lesson they would never forget."

"You're saying you sued these guys before?" I asked. "And won?"

"Yes, that's what I'm saying," Lester replied, running his index finger over the bottom ridge of his mustache. "They settled out of court for two point three million dollars."

"Some other lawyer told Edmund that quote-unquote

dead kids aren't worth all that much," I blurted out. The line had been burning in my throat since I'd heard it.

"Well, it depends on the context," Lester said, glancing from me to Edmund. I sensed he was picking up on some of the tension between us. It occurred to me that he used his eccentric appearance as a kind of cover; you were too busy looking at Lester Stephens to realize just how much he was taking in about you.

"The sad truth is," he continued, turning back to me, "that if a child has been seriously injured in an accident—suffered brain injury, say—then the plaintiff's lawyers will draw up what we call a 'blackboard' of costs for a lifetime of medical and emotional needs. The list could easily run into the tens of millions. Obviously, that's not going to happen in your situation. But, believe me, I wouldn't be sitting here talking to you now if I didn't think you had a potentially very strong—and very important—case."

I sat forward.

"In what way important?" I asked.

"Too many parents—especially first-time parents—just don't realize the danger so many of these so-called safety seats pose. Allergic reactions to chemicals in the fabrics . . . straps that can strangle when twisted . . . insufficient headrest padding—and head trauma is the leading cause of car-seat fatalities. It's truly frightening. Young parents trust manufacturers like Gannon to know what they're doing, to be thinking first and foremost of their baby's protection. But these are companies, Cal; they're out to turn a profit, plain and simple. Do you know what an outfit like Gannon figures into their cost of doing business—right along with advertising budgets and plant costs? Insurance to pay off and hush up people like you when the worst happens . . ." Lester paused, staring down at the blank legal pad in front of him for a second, then looked up at me and said:

"If you give me the opportunity, I intend to make such an example of Gannon this time that no parent in this state would even consider buying another one of their products."

I slumped back in my chair. My heart was racing. *Yes!* I thought. It was as though Lester had been able to put shape and meaning to the anger and confusion that I'd been living with these past three months. He reinforced what I was just beginning to understand: that this wasn't really about me. It was bigger than what had happened to Betsy. I was so sick of beating up on myself. I was more than ready to turn all that rage on somebody else. Suddenly the answer to everything that had gone wrong recently seemed clear: I needed to go after Gannon Baby Products and bring them down. It wasn't their money that I wanted. Like Lester, I wanted to see the company totaled.

Edmund must have misread my silence and body language, because he interjected:

"That's all very well and good. But we don't want to lose sight of our case."

"Of course not," Lester replied. "I just felt your brother might want to understand some of the overarching issues that concern me."

"They concern me, too," I said.

"Good," Lester replied, smiling for the first time since we walked in. "Then, if you don't mind, I believe that Janet and Carl have a few questions for you."

Lester sat back while Janet Graystone, a severe-looking blonde, walked me slowly through the last hours of Betsy's life and Carl Zeyer took down what I said on his laptop.

Though Lester mostly just looked out the window during the proceedings, I sensed that he was actually as alert to Janet's questions as he was to my responses.

"I'm sorry," she said about ten minutes into the interview, "you say you had a few pops with the boys. Do you mean sodas?" She had the broad vowels of Boston.

"No, we sometimes call beer 'pops,'" I said. "We usually bring a cooler or keg with us to the games."

"So how many 'pops' do you think you had?" she asked.

"I don't remember," I said. I could feel my neck flushing. "It was a hot day. The game went on for over three hours. It's not something I would normally even mention except—"

"I talked with him after the game," Edmund said. "He was totally fine. And he was Breathalyzed at the hospital."

"Not at the scene?" she asked, frowning a little and turning to Lester.

"Cal has no record of DWI," Lester told her, "either at the time of the accident—or at any other time. We know from Edmund—and we know just listening to Cal's story— that he's the kind of loving, protective father who would never, ever drive drunk."

It was a not-so-subtle verbal slap on the wrist, and I thought I saw Janet actually flinch. Only later would I wonder if the whole thing hadn't been prearranged by Lester and his staff as a way of both feeling me out on a sensitive issue and reassuring me of their confidence in my integrity. I remembered, too, Edmund's crack the afternoon Betsy died about my "putting away the old brewskies," the comment that had almost escalated into a physical fight between us. I wasn't the only one who wanted to reweave the story of Betsy's final hours, reworking any dark and messy patches that might make me appear less than a totally exemplary father and human being.

Though Janet continued to question me for another twenty minutes or so, that was my only moment of discomfort—until the very end.

"How is your wife holding up?" she asked.

"Not so well," I replied. "Not well at all."

"That's to be expected, Cal," Lester interjected. "We often find that one spouse is able to handle a tragedy like this better than the other. You never know how these things are going to affect people."

I think it was Lester's fatherly, almost affectionate, tone that did it to me. I found myself telling him:

"Jenny doesn't like the idea of a lawsuit. In fact she's dead set against it. She says that people who do this kind of thing are like vultures."

"Well, that's a little rough," Lester said, laughing. "But those of us in the legal profession have been called a good deal worse in our time. However, if we're going to move ahead together on this we'll eventually need her cooperation. Ideally, we'd want her to be an integral part of the process. At the very least, we'll need to depose her—that is, have some fairly detailed discussions with her. Do you think you'll be able to talk her around?"

"Of course he will," Edmund said. "She's just grieving."

"There's no 'just' about grief," Lester replied. "It can be a very lengthy and debilitating process. We want to be very careful not to interfere with that. And, believe me, there's a hell of a lot of work to do and still plenty of time before we need to talk to your wife. What do you think, Cal? Will she be there for you when the time comes?"

I was pleased that Lester had put Edmund in his place. I was impressed by the lawyer's depth of expertise and humanity. He seemed able to see all sides of our situation—and respond with compassion and even humor. Lester Stephens was someone I felt I could work with. It occurred to me that I'd already pushed past my initial objections and was ready to move ahead with the lawsuit and with Stephens, Stokes, Kline. I actually couldn't wait to get the ball rolling. For the first time in many months I was feeling good about myself again. And I was beginning to realize how irrational Jenny was being. About Daniel and about the lawsuit. I'd reached the point with her where I could no longer take her objections seriously.

"Yes, she will be there for me," I told Lester. The fact of the matter was, I didn't intend to give her a choice.

As we were leaving, Lester asked us for the car seat. The firm planned to have a series of forensic tests run on it, hoping to pinpoint exactly what had gone wrong. It was weird, but I felt my heart constrict when Edmund turned the thing over to Janet. She took it from Edmund with both hands and cradled the black plastic bundle in her arms as though holding a baby. She must have seen the look of pain that flashed across my face because she said:

"Don't worry. We'll take good care of it."

☞

"So?" Edmund asked halfway across the lobby. "You kind of liked them, right?"

"Yeah, I liked *him*," I said. "But what's the story there? Do they wheel the top guy out to make the sale—and then pawn you off to the underlings once you've signed on the dotted line?"

"You don't get it, do you?" Edmund said, laughing. "This case is potentially a very big fucking deal. A lot of money could be involved. I kind of admire your restraint in not asking him outright for a number—or at least a range. Because I did when I met with them two weeks ago."

We were approaching the car. I waited until we were inside, buckling up.

"And?" I asked.

"One to five," Edmund said, gunning the BMW as he turned the motor on. "Million, that is."

We drove back down the Taconic through the soft summer twilight, the jagged silhouette of the Catskills backlit by the setting sun. I watched the orange ball expand for a moment, then collapse into strokes of lavender and pink.

I suppose it was because I was feeling at peace for the first time in so long that my thoughts turned to Jenny. Not the difficult and demanding person she's become. But the fun-loving girl I used to know. The first person, honestly, besides Kurt, whom I loved for herself alone—because of who she was, not for what she could give me. You don't get the chance to feel that way about too many people in your life. My heart began softening toward her, all my earlier anger melting into sadness. I didn't want to hurt her. I vowed to do everything I could to keep this lawsuit from upsetting her. But, at the same time, I felt a real need to pursue this new course. I owed it to Betsy, didn't I? And, though she couldn't see it yet, I owed it to Jenny, too. In time, she would come to understand that. Someday, I told myself, she would thank me for it.

10

Jenny

&

*T*he farmhouse that Cal's folks gave us as a wedding gift was originally built in the 1820s by the first Horigan to settle in the area, Jeremiah Livingston Horigan, who immigrated west from Boston, seeking his fortune in lumber. He established the first sawmill in the newly incorporated settlement of Covington, then an area of sparsely populated rocky farmland, heavily wooded hills, and rushing streams from which local industries looked to harness power.

The original homestead, according to plans Kurt located at a "house histories" Web site a few years back, was just four downstairs rooms: parlor, kitchen, bedroom, scullery. Over the years, succeeding generations of Horigans added floors and porches, a barn and outbuildings. Each era left its own stamp and personality, so that today the house is a hodgepodge of styles. There's a fanlight transom over the front door, gingerbread molding on the side porch, a circa 1950s picture window in the breakfast nook. When we first moved in, I seemed to be discovering some remnant of the past—yellowed-newspaper-lined canning shelves in the basement, a cider press in the barn—almost every day. I loved the sense of history and tradition permeating these things; my own family's roots in Covington are so relatively recent and shallow.

The grounds, too, offered a testament to long-forgotten enthusiasms: the circle of blackberry bushes half-hidden in underbrush, the cracked-cement remains of a goldfish pond. With Betsy in tow, I spent hours exploring the property, gradually charting our new domain in the notebook I carried with me in my gardening bag. I began planning how to turn these notes and drawings into a grand renovation project, one that would incorporate some of the property's idiosyncratic elements into an enlarged and more contemporary design of my own.

Since Betsy's death, though, I often lose track of what exactly I'm supposed to be doing—indoors or outside. It's hard for me to concentrate, to think ahead as I once did. At the end of an afternoon, say, I'll find myself staring out over the distant hills, uncertain of where my thoughts have drifted. The only clue is that kick to the heart—that *wham!*—as I remember all over again, as I'm forced to do every morning when I wake up, what it is that I've lost.

The morning after my birthday party, Cal unrolled Daniel's computer-generated blueprints on our kitchen counter while I stood beside him, holding my coffee mug. I hadn't slept well, which isn't unusual for me, but it wasn't Betsy who had kept me awake. Instead, I kept replaying the memory of Daniel leaning toward me, the way I felt when he kissed me.

My training at Pellani's Garden Center enabled me to

look at Daniel's designs and see right away that he planned to rip out all the old gardens and start with a landscape tabula rasa. The peonies that Cal's grandmother had planted—one for each of her five children—were to go, as were the day-lilies, hostas, and hollyhocks. In place of these two-hundred-year-old plantings, Daniel had proposed a series of large, undulating beds set on raised banks of fieldstone. His plans favored shrubs over flowers—buddleia, continus, heather, dogwood—interspersed with tall stands of grasses. The color palate was muted and cool: silver, blue, plum, white. It was all very professional. He'd solved the problem of the uneven sloping grade of our property. Still, I didn't sense he'd put much time and thought into the project. The designs looked generic to me—just another showy, expensive garden like the ones that surround so many of the new second homes in our area. Daniel, I thought, had simply cobbled together a few signature ideas.

"Wow," Cal said. He leaned intently over the printouts, though I suspected he didn't really know what he was looking at. "These are pretty impressive, don't you think?"

"All that stone is going to cost a fortune," I said.

"Well—I already told you that's not an issue."

"And those specimen shrubs? Do you know what a Harry Lauder's Walking Stick is going for these days? And look—he's asking for three of them here."

"Jen? Enough, okay? The question is—what do you think of it—the big picture, I mean?"

I hesitated a moment, knowing how much my resistance to the project upset Cal. Then I remembered the warmth of Daniel's breath in my ear the night before—and shivered.

"I don't know. There's just something about him that—"

"Oh, for chrissakes!" Cal said. "I'm not asking what you think about him as a *person*. And, anyway, you've made your feelings pretty clear on that point. You were really almost rude last night."

"What are you talking about?"

"It was like you couldn't get him out the door fast enough. I was kind of shocked by the way you acted. Especially because I think I made it clear I *like* the guy, okay? I *invited* him to the party. Every once in a while you might want to think about how *I* feel. What I want."

"Oh. Sorry. You know, for some stupid reason I thought this was supposed to be a birthday present for me. But since it's really all about you—then I say: great! These plans are just totally fantastic!"

"What the hell's the matter with you?" Cal asked. He looked utterly bewildered.

"I don't know," I said, deflating suddenly. "I'm just—I'm sorry. I think maybe it's that I don't want to touch anything. To change anything, you know? I'm afraid that if we do, it'll be like saying we're ready to—move on." Like so many of our exchanges these days, this is half-true, or only partially a lie. Usually, we let these minor deceptions slide. But, for whatever reason, Cal decided to call me on this one.

"You were tearing up the patio when I first brought Daniel over."

"You're right," I said, looking at the floor. "But that felt different somehow. I was in control of it, I guess. I could do it in my own way. It was more—"

"Okay, I get it," Cal said. "Okay. We'll just shelve the whole business for now. I'll tell Daniel that we're not ready. All right? That we really like what he's done—but we're going to have to wait to actually put the gardens in. I'm sure this kind of thing has happened to him before. Especially now, with the downturn."

"But—" I hesitated. I could tell by Cal's tone what this was costing him. It was going to be an embarrassment for him. He'd probably been hoping that the project would solidify his friendship with Daniel, and this wasn't going to help on that front. For the first time, I actually did make an effort to see the situation from his point of view. Aside from what he'd wanted for himself by commissioning Daniel, I knew that Cal had only been trying to please me. To help me. He wasn't the one to blame for the outcome.

And what was I actually afraid of? So Daniel had come on to me a little bit. Was that really such a big deal? I knew perfectly well that some men did that kind of thing as a matter of course. That this felt different to me—somehow deeper and more complicated—was probably just a result of my hypersensitive state of mind. If Cal halted the project now, wouldn't it look as though I was running away from Daniel? Wouldn't I seem like a woman who was simply too insecure or inexperienced to know how to gracefully deflect a man's attention?

"What will you do about reimbursing him?"

"I'll pay him for the plans, of course. And—I don't know—I'll have to check the contract, but I think I should at least give him some kind of a kill fee for the rest."

"Oh, Cal. I feel badly about this."

"Yeah," he said. "Well, so do I."

❦

Cal had a baseball game over in Red River that afternoon. Betsy and I used to always go with him—and then often out with a group of the guys and their families for drinks and dinner afterward. But I've been begging off a lot this summer. It isn't, as I think Tessa believes, because the games are such a painful reminder of Betsy's last day. It's more the agony of seeing everyone carrying on with their lives, of knowing that the weeks, and now months, are passing.

I can understand why the Victorians used to stop their clocks at the moment of death. It feels as though a big part of me has stopped, actually. Or more that I'm willing it to stop—forcing time to stand still. If I don't, then I know that, slowly but inevitably, Betsy will start to disappear. For now, though, because I work so hard at holding her memory close, she's still alive for me. I can hear her voice—though less and less clearly these days. And it's already the third week of June. It's still daylight at eight o'clock in the evening.

I'm not sure how long I'd been sitting on the back steps, looking out over our view of fields and distant hills. But whatever startled me—shaking me out of my reverie—made me realize that the evening shadows had begun to lengthen across the sloping lawn. Mist lay over the wildflower field. Fireflies drifted through the updrafts with their sad little searchlights. Something stirred below me in the field. I sat up, alert. The whirring of cicadas filled the air.

I got up slowly, so as not to frighten whatever was there. I kicked off my sandals and made my way barefoot across the dew-dampened grass. What was it? I asked myself. But I knew. I knew! And then, suddenly, I couldn't help it. I started to run toward her down the hill. The darkening world tilted toward me, and I felt almost weightless with joy. *Mama! Mama!* Did I actually hear those words, or was it only a great flapping of wings as one of the red-tailed hawks that hunts on our property rose, shrieking, from the far side of the field?

It wasn't the first time I imagined I saw Betsy. Though it's more sensing her presence than actually seeing her. These visitations never feel scary or crazy to me. For the brief seconds that I know she's there—reaching out for me—everything actually feels right again. Normal. It's the rest of my life that seems so out of kilter. It's as though I exist in a constant state of vertigo. I've convinced myself that if I could just break through whatever it is that separates me from Betsy, my world could be righted again. Sometimes it feels so simple, as though all I need to do is find the right moment, push open that secret door.

Tonight, though, as I walked back up to the house, it came to me just how inadequate all my yearnings for my daughter are actually turning out to be. What am I doing, really, besides chasing phantoms? Wasting time? While every day the smell of her hair, or the exact feel of her skin, becomes a little bit harder to recall. How can I stop her from slipping ever further away? I knew that I had to do something radical—something real—soon.

☞

There's nothing more treacherous than longing. By the time Cal returned later that night and I told him that I'd changed my mind, that we should go ahead with Daniel's plans after all, I'd actually managed to convince myself that I was doing the right thing.

☞

I hadn't been expecting a backhoe. It arrived on a flatbed truck about an hour after Cal left for work. At first, I thought it must have had something to do with the Ravitch project, that maybe one of Cal's subcontractors had confused addresses and had come to our place rather than the construction site. I walked outside to set the driver straight. It was then that I noticed Daniel's Lexus pulling up behind the flatbed. I stopped where I was on the front lawn while Daniel walked over to talk to the truck driver. A few minutes later, a pickup pulled in beside Daniel's car. Two young men hopped out, wearing work boots, jeans, and gray T-shirts with "Brandt Landscape Design" emblazoned in blue across the front. They huddled around Daniel.

I watched while he gave the men instructions, pointing to the side lawn, laughing at something one of the younger workers said. It seems incredible to me that I've actually seen Daniel in person only three other times now. I know so little about him, really. And yet I've allowed him to seize such a large part of my imagination. I know it's because so much of me feels damaged these days. Lost and alone. I've simply let Daniel—or whoever I fantasize Daniel might be—fill that vacuum. That's all it is, I tell myself. There's nothing real between us.

As the men started to unload the backhoe, Daniel walked across the lawn toward me. He was wearing jeans and a blue-and-white-striped shirt with the cuffs rolled back. Something about him had changed again. Was his hair a little shorter? Then I realized that he'd left a stubble of beard on his chin—like some male model or movie star. With anyone else, I might have assumed he just hadn't gotten around to shaving that morning. But I was sure Daniel was too self-aware for that. And the salt-and-pepper stubble did make him look younger. Both rugged and a little reckless.

"You sure you want to be here for this?" he asked with a smile. I noticed that little gap between his front teeth again. Almost two weeks have passed since my birthday party, yet I can remember the brief pressure of his lips against mine as though he'd just kissed me. I was wearing cutoffs and an old T-shirt of Cal's. As usual when I'm alone in the house, I wasn't wearing a bra. The morning sun was in my eyes, but I could sense—rather than see—Daniel looking me over. I folded my arms across my chest.

"How bad is it going to be?" I asked.

"Well, we're basically planning to level the whole back area. It'll be noisy as hell, too."

"Are you suggesting I leave?"

"In a way," he said, tilting his head as if to take me in a little better. "I'm suggesting we both get out of here—and have lunch together. I'll need an hour or two with the crew before we go, but we'll just be in the way once the heavy lifting starts."

My first impulse was to say no, of course, and I guess he saw that in my expression, because he went on before I had a chance to respond.

"No strings attached—I promise," he said, raising both hands as if to show me he had nothing to hide. "I think—no, I know—we've gotten off to a kind of rocky start, you and I. But I'm really not the big, bad wolf you seem to think I am."

He looked so harmless, so very *un*wolflike at that moment, that I almost laughed. A strand of hair had fallen across his forehead. Once again I wondered: just how old is he? And how does he manage to keep changing—size, shape, persona—almost before my eyes?

"Ah, an excellent sign: she's smiling," he said. "I'll

interpret that as a yes. Let's say one o'clock. How about Deer Creek?"

"Sure," I said, relaxing. You couldn't ask for more of a fishbowl than Deer Creek Bistro at lunchtime. Besides all the Covington regulars, the restaurant was always busy in the summer with the second-home crowd and tourists.

❧

The place was jammed, just as I'd thought it would be. Larry Bisel, the owner, looked distraught when he saw me. Larry and I have known and liked each other—in a passing sort of way—for years. He always makes a big deal of seating me at one of the better tables.

"I'm afraid I'm going to have to ask you guys to wait in the bar for a while, Jenny," he said, running his eye down the reservation list. "I have two whole busloads of ladies on their way up to Williamstown for the matinee. We're a total madhouse today."

"How about outside?" Daniel asked, pointing to the circle of small café tables on the terrace, an area usually reserved for evening cocktails. The umbrellas were furled and the chairs tilted against the tabletops. No one else was out there.

"Sure, if you don't mind," Larry said. "I can have them set things up in no time."

It was either that or the dark intimacy of the bar, so I followed Daniel outside again, and we were soon sitting across from each other at a round metal table so small that, if I didn't shift my legs to one side, our knees would have touched. I felt uncomfortable being in such close proximity to him, but I soon realized there was no need to worry. He seemed determined to set a friendly, breezy tone, and in a number of self-deprecating anecdotes that cast him in the role of clueless city slicker, he filled me in on how relocating to our area had affected him:

"I couldn't get over the noise at first. Especially earlier in the summer. Those damn birds! All that squawking and calling and peep, peep, peep! Manhattan is an oasis of silence in comparison."

"That's probably because you keep your windows closed and the air conditioner going all the time," I said, trying to get into the spirit of the thing. We'd finished our salads and quiches, and Daniel was nursing the last of his white wine. When the waiter came by to clear our plates, Daniel ordered an espresso.

"You sure you won't have some dessert?" he asked me. "I've had the chocolate soufflé cake here. It's addicting."

"As I know all too well," I said. "I had to join a twelve-step program to wean my way off of it."

He laughed. Then he stopped laughing.

"What?" I asked as the waiter moved off.

"You have a beautiful smile, Jenny."

"Please—"

"Okay. How about this: it's really wonderful to see you smile. You should do it more often. Is that better? I told you I'd behave. Haven't I been behaving?"

"Yes," I said, my gaze shifting past the terrace, over the stores and homes along Route 32, to the fields beyond, blurring in the midday haze into the distant swell of hills. What was I doing here—flirting with this man? Or allowing him to flirt with me? There's hardly any difference, really, and both are so unlike me. Jude's the one who enjoys exciting men's interest. She needs to be constantly looked at, looked over, desired. I think maybe my mother was the same way. One of my few clear memories of her is watching her put on lipstick using her compact mirror. We were waiting in some line together—for the movies, maybe, or at the fairgrounds—and I saw her wink into the compact at the man standing behind us. My own mother! I remember feeling so ashamed of her. Later, after she abandoned us, I wondered if maybe she'd been able to sense how I'd felt about her. Did my childish awareness of her shortcomings factor into her decision to move on? Sometimes, oddly, I find myself confusing my memories of Betsy—or more my sense of loss and longing—with those that I have of my mother. As if all tears trickle down into a single pool eventually—and all great sadnesses become one.

"Why don't you tell me about it?" Daniel said after the waiter had come by with the espresso and the check.

"I'm sorry," I said. "I'm afraid I'm not much fun."

"You don't have to apologize," he said. "I know what happened."

"You do?" I asked, looking over at him. I was shocked. He'd never given any indication that he was aware of our tragedy. The very fact that he'd kissed me, that he seemed to be coming on to me, made me assume he didn't know. But I realized—all in one clarifying moment—that I've actually been wanting him to ask me about it. Almost from the moment I met him, I've been longing to tell him. In fact, it's clear to me now that every unspoken thing between us has been building up to this.

It didn't take me long. Five minutes, maybe. By the time

the waiter came back to pick up the bill folder and Daniel's credit card, I'd told him the whole story. Or almost all of it.

"I'm sorry," he said. "I know it's a cliché, but life really isn't fair, Jenny. I imagine that must be the hardest part of this for you in a way. Wondering why these things happen—why you and Cal?"

❦

When we'd arrived at the restaurant, the parking lot had been full, and Daniel had been forced to park far in the back under a stand of hemlocks. By the time we left, the parking lot was almost empty again. We walked across the macadam in silence. Daniel unlocked the car and we both climbed in. It was then that I turned to him and said what I'd really been waiting to tell him all along:

"Actually, I know why it happened."

"What?"

"I keep replaying those last moments I was with her over and over again in my head. I haven't told anybody this."

"You can tell me."

"I haven't even told Cal."

"You can tell me."

And I knew I could. Not because he was more sympathetic than Cal or Jude or Tessa. If anything, he was less so. He'd never met Betsy. He didn't really understand what I'd lost. Or care about the unforgivable thing I might have done. He wouldn't hold what I told him against me. I think he was just interested in what I'd been hiding from everyone. I believe my sense of guilt intrigued him—and that he found the depth of my anguish seductive in some way.

"I think—there's a good chance—I didn't finish strapping Betsy into the car seat. There are these two buckles that you need to secure—and I know I fixed the bottom one. But then I stood up and said something to my sister-in-law—and I can't remember if I actually finished buckling the top one that straps her in at chest level. It's the kind of thing that becomes such a routine, you know? I keep trying to remember clearly. I keep trying to separate out that last time, that one particular moment, from all the other times I did the same thing. But I can't. I can't remember. I rub my fingers together, trying—"

I didn't realize what I was doing until Daniel grabbed hold of my fingertips—stopping me. Startled, I looked over at him. He took both my hands in his, held them tight for a moment, then, bending his head, turned my hands over and kissed my palms.

"I haven't even told Cal," I said again, knowing that this, more than letting Daniel kiss me now, was the true betrayal. This secret was the darkest thing I ever had to share with anyone—and I'd given it to this stranger.

11

Cal

"So what's up with you and Eddie?" Kurt asked me, seemingly out of the blue. The two of us were driving back from a meeting outside Northridge with a prospective client, a couple Ravitch had generously referred us to, Sherry and Alan Faggiano. We met them at their mountaintop property to go over our numbers. The heavily wooded land went almost straight uphill and was embedded with a number of large limestone outcroppings. It was going to be a bitch to build on. But when Kurt started to point out some of the difficulties, Sherry Faggiano said that Lovell Construction hadn't raised any such concerns. Fucking Danny Lovell had lowballed us out of at least two other projects in the past year. The Faggianos merely looked annoyed when Kurt mentioned Danny was being taken to court—something almost everybody in town already knew about—for shoddy workmanship.

It was so unlike Kurt to stoop to that kind of thing, but this was the first big project we'd been asked to bid on all summer. We didn't talk about it on our way home. As usual, we carefully sidestepped any serious discussion about how badly things were going business-wise, but I think Kurt understood as well as I did that we could probably kiss the Faggianos good-bye.

"How do you mean?" I replied. Eddie and I had agreed to keep a tight lid on the lawsuit until Stephens, Stokes actually filed a claim, which could end up being months from now, apparently. It's already been three weeks since our initial meeting and we've yet to hear back from them on the forensic tests. I'm still feeling good about things, but I'm also starting to get a little antsy.

"You guys just seem to be talking to each other a lot more," Kurt said.

"Yeah, well. What can I say? Things changed for me after Betsy died. I'm trying to get rid of a lot of old baggage. Reset my priorities." I wasn't going to lie straight-out to Kurt. But I know how he feels about going after Gannon, and I'm not eager to face off with him on the subject until I absolutely have to.

"That's good to hear," Kurt said, nodding at the road ahead. "That's great. Sometimes I think all Edmund really needs is a pat on the back from time to time. I don't think it's any picnic working with Dad these days. I walked in on them at the store on Tuesday and Dad was reaming him out about something. They didn't want to talk about it then, but Eddie told me later Dad's getting really short-tempered."

"Like that's something new?"

"I got the feeling it's getting worse. You noticing that at all?"

"Not really," I answered. But I think we both know what

the problem is: the old man just doesn't seem to be getting any better. And it's been almost a year now since his open-heart. When he complained recently about being so tired all the time, his doctor switched his medications around, but that only led to dizziness and nausea, and a quick change back to the original lineup. One of which is a blood thinner that makes him have to piss every other minute. I was driving him home a week or so ago when he had to ask me to pull over to the side of the road so that he could take a leak.

"Don't get old," he told me angrily as he climbed back in and slammed the door so hard the whole car shook. He's always been so much larger than life. I think it infuriates him to feel helpless, to feel anyone's pity—maybe especially his sons'.

"Want to come take a look at the eighth wonder of the world?" I asked Kurt when we pulled into our driveway. "Daniel's crew put on the finishing touches yesterday."

"Sure," Kurt said. "Tessa was asking me about it."

"She should come down and see it for herself," I said, leading him around to the back by way of the side lawn. "I don't think I've seen Tessa since Jen's party. Everything okay?"

"I could ask you the same thing. Did you know Jenny told Tessa to start *calling* before she comes by now? After how many years of the two of them being like sisters? I think it really hurt Tessa's feelings."

"Yeah, well, tell her I know how *that* feels," I said. I stopped when we reached the first terraced level. The new gardens cascaded down our hillside like some kind of floral waterfall. The raised beds, supported by the newly constructed stone walls, flowed one after the other down the lush green incline. I still can't get over how thoroughly Daniel has transformed our backyard. Every time I walk outside now, I feel a little like Dorothy stepping into that dazzling Oz Technicolor for the first time.

"Wow," Kurt said. "You weren't kidding—this really is pretty amazing. It must have cost a fortune. I sure hope you got that bastard to cut you a deal."

I've known for a while now that Kurt doesn't much like Daniel. When we started working with him on the Ravitch project, Kurt complained that Daniel's "air was a little too rarefied" for him to breathe. It was one of the first times in my life that I thought my brother was totally off base about someone. Every once in a while I do see what Edmund means about Kurt's "insular small-town rules." Kurt just prefers staying in his own particular comfort zone, I think, while I'm beginning to understand the value of embracing new experiences, new people—like Daniel with his nonjudgmental way of looking at the world.

"Yeah, well, he was great to work with," I said. I was feeling too good about how the new gardens turned out to let Kurt dampen my spirits. But in fact, the whole thing had come to over a thousand dollars more than I'd anticipated. Cost overruns, as Daniel explained, all well within the budgeted allowances. Well, I had plenty of money put aside. It had piled up during our boom-boom years, and I thought of it as our rainy-day reserve. After Betsy was born, I started earmarking it in my mind for her college fund. I guess that's one reason I don't particularly care that this project will take such a big bite out of the thing.

I also think that a part of me is already anticipating the Gannon money. Edmund told me that, depending on whether we go to trial or work out a settlement, Stephens, Stokes's cut could be as much as thirty-three to forty percent of the payout. But even with that, worst-case scenario means more money than I ever dreamed possible could be coming my way. I try not to dwell on it—consciously, anyway. But it does have a way of breaking into my thoughts from time to time like a ray of sunshine. No, more like a pot of gold, glittering in the back of my mind. Still, it's really not so much about the money. I think it's more the awareness that I've finally decided to take up this fight—to make a stand—that's changed my attitude lately. I feel like things are finally turning around for me again. That I'm back in the game.

"Was that Kurt?" Jenny asked when I came back up to the house through the kitchen. She was sitting at the counter, Betsy's collection of stuffed animals arrayed in front of her.

"You know it was," I said, reaching into the refrigerator for a beer. "You should have come down and said hello. What're you doing?"

"Trying to make some decisions," she said. "The church rummage sale is Saturday. My father said he thought it was a good opportunity for me to go through Betsy's clothes and toys and donate a lot of stuff. What do you think?"

"That it's a really great idea," I said, leaning against the counter as I took a swig of beer. I was surprised, honestly, that Jenny had even gotten this far. Surprised and pleased. "Let's keep one or two of those guys, though. Let's keep her favorites, okay?"

"They were all her favorites."

"Yes, I know," I said. "So keep the ones you like, then. I've got to get going. I'm supposed to meet Daniel at six."

Jenny had actually apologized to me a few days ago for

being "such a nutcase" about Daniel and the garden. It wasn't like her to be overly enthusiastic about anything right now, but I think she has to be pleased with the way the job turned out.

"What for?"

"I asked him out for a drink—to thank him for his work and to give him the final payment."

"You asked him?"

"Sure," I said. "Is something wrong with that?"

She turned around and looked at me. At the bottle in my hand. The way I was standing. Then she just shook her head.

"No, I want you to tell me," I said. "You think there's something wrong with that?"

"Just that maybe *he* should be asking *you*," she said, turning back around to the stuffed animals. She picked up a panda with big black glassy eyes and asked it in a babyish singsong, "Don't you think so, Pandy Bear? Otherwise, don't you think it kind of looks as though great big Daddy here has a little tiny crush on this guy?"

"He insisted on buying the last time," I said evenly, though I was really pissed off. I thought we were getting somewhere, but obviously I was wrong. Where the hell was all this weird nastiness coming from? "It's my turn."

❧

We met at Ernie's again. I think it's become something of a hangout for Daniel. When I walked in, two waitresses were leaning in talking to him at the bar as they waited for their drink orders to be filled. As I approached them, I thought I heard one of them say:

". . . for all the action you're going to see in *this* town."

They started to go back to work as I pulled a stool up next to Daniel, though the prettier of the two gave me a once-over and a smile as she walked away. It's not that I still don't get checked out from time to time, but I had the feeling that I was just reaping the benefits of being in Daniel's electromagnetic field.

"Hey, man," I said, ordering a draft. I slid the envelope with my check in it down the counter toward him. "Great job. The gardens look fantastic."

"I'm glad you're pleased," Daniel said, slipping the envelope into his sports jacket. As usual, he was dressed a little too well for Northridge. I think that he must enjoy standing out, being noticed. He definitely gives off a certain aura of—what exactly? Celebrity? Glamour? It's hard to define, but I could feel people glancing over at us from time to time. Kurt complained about the air around Daniel being too rarefied. But, honestly? I enjoy breathing it in.

"Jenny seems pleased, too," I told him.

"Good," Daniel said. "Because that's what this was all about, right? Trying to make her happy."

"Yeah," I said, looking down into my half-empty glass.

"Did she tell you I took her out for lunch the day the gardens went in? That we had a long talk?"

"I don't think so—," I said, trying to remember. I'm so focused on the future now—on the Gannon thing, honestly—that for a moment or two I really couldn't recall exactly which day that had been. Then I remembered Jenny complaining about how the trucks had torn up the side lawn. How we'd have to reseed that whole area. And we'd argued about her being so negative all the time. I mean, for chrissakes! There was this beautiful new wonderland right in front of her eyes—and all she could see was a couple of tire tracks? If she'd said anything about lunch with Daniel, it had been forgotten in the heat of another fight.

"Well, I enjoyed it, anyway," Daniel said, looking over at me. I'd finished the draft and was fingering the coaster, still trying to cast my mind back. In fact, since Betsy's death, my memory's been a little clouded. Maybe it's the result of the concussion—or just the stress of trying to deal with everything. Maybe it's all these days and weeks without real work beginning to blend together into one long, aimless stream of wasted time.

"Looks like you could use a refill," Daniel said, nodding to the bartender. He was nursing a scotch straight up and put his hand over the glass when the bartender made a move to top it off.

"You're right," I said. "Long, bad day. We're in the running for a big job right now, but one of the guys we're up against wouldn't think twice about undercutting his own mother. And the bottom line is all anybody seems to care about these days."

"Yes, I know," Daniel said. "The first six months I was up here it didn't seem to matter what I charged—people kept throwing commissions at me. Now? I've clients who are getting cross-bids from local nurseries. I can't beat that kind of wholesale pricing. That's not what I'm about."

"So what are you going to do?" I asked. I was pleased that he was talking to me in this way. Confiding things.

"Put my feet up—for a while, anyway. I've been at it pretty much nonstop since I relocated. But I can't complain. It's been a good run."

"That's how I feel, too," I said, which was still mostly

true. The business would start turning around again, I told myself. These things always tend to go in cycles. And there's that Gannon jackpot waiting for me somewhere in the future. Just the idea of it, the possibility, makes me feel lucky now, expansive. I made Edmund promise not to talk about Gannon with anyone, but then I remembered that I'd already told Daniel about it—and that he'd encouraged me to pursue the lawsuit.

"You ever hear of a law firm called Stephens, Stokes, Kline?" I asked him.

"I don't think so. Should I know them?"

"They're probably the top product-liability law firm in the state," I said. "It looks as though they're going to take our case."

"Really?"

"Yeah. We had a meeting with them a few weeks ago, and Lester Stephens—he's one of the partners, okay?—was really encouraging. They're running some forensic tests on the car seat for us."

"When you say 'we,' you mean you and Jenny?"

"No," I answered. "My brother Edmund is riding shotgun with me on this. Jenny doesn't know we're doing it. And there's really no point in trying to talk to her about it: she's against the whole thing. She's being totally irrational. I figured I'll put her in the picture when I'm told that it's a definite go. I know she'll get behind it when she understands how important it really is. That it's not just about Betsy or us. It's about stopping a corporation like Gannon from getting away with murder—again."

"I see," Daniel said. "That does sound pretty serious. But—"

When he didn't go on after a second or two, I glanced over at him and realized that he'd been studying me in the mirror that hung over the bar.

"What?" I asked his reflection. "Tell me."

"This isn't any of my business."

"That's not true—I made it your business by telling you something in confidence. And if you have any reservations, I'd really appreciate you letting me know."

"No, listen," he said, turning on his bar stool to face me, "no matter what you say, I really don't think it *is* my business. Go with your gut. We've talked about this before. I'm a big believer in following your instincts. Just, at some point before it goes too far, I assume you'll have to let Jenny know. You'll need her cooperation, right? I imagine this law firm has already told you that."

"Sure," I told him. "And I'm not worried about it in the long run. But the thing is—Jenny and I are at really different stages with Betsy's death. Jenny's still pretty bogged down in what happened. She's afraid to let go. I think she sees it as a way of holding on to Betsy." Somehow, I'd finished off my second draft. I looked into the bottom of the glass and thought about the truth of what I'd just said. Of course, a part of me already knew Jenny felt that way, but for some reason explaining the situation to Daniel helped me see things more clearly. I found myself telling him something I hadn't even yet fully admitted to myself.

"But the thing is: I *am* ready to let go," I said. "To move on. After we nail those Gannon bastards to the wall, that's it for me. I don't want to spend the rest of my life on this—do you know what I mean? Does that sound heartless?"

"Of course not," Daniel said. "Things go by so fast."

I had another beer. The pretty waitress came back and began to flirt with Daniel—and with me, too, I think. Her smile seemed to include both of us, anyway. She was dark haired, big breasted, with long, shapely legs. Jenny doesn't have much use for makeup, but this woman's face was slick with the stuff: heavily defined eyebrows, thickly coated lashes, lips so shiny you could almost see your reflection in them. She was good-looking enough that I had to ask myself why she thought she needed to slather herself up like that. What would it be like, I wondered, to kiss someone with all that gloss on her lips? I must have been trying to get a better look at her when my elbow slipped off the counter.

"Whoa there, baby," she said, putting out an arm to steady me. Then she turned to Daniel and whispered something to him before she started to move off with a loaded tray again.

"Why not?" I heard him say. "Just give me a call when you're ready. You've got my cell."

"I gotta get going, too," I said. I felt a little foolish losing my balance like that. I slid off my stool and fumbled in my pocket for cash. "Here," I said, slapping a couple of twenties on the counter. "That oughta take care of things."

"You okay to drive?" Daniel asked.

"Oh, sure," I told him. "I'm nowhere near my limit."

❦

It was nearly nine o'clock by the dashboard clock. So I'd had a total of four beers across almost five hours. Not such a big deal, I told myself, considering I'd been metabolizing the alcohol right along. I don't know when exactly I began to think about my drinking in these terms. When it was that I started consciously pacing myself. Since Betsy's death, I know I've become much more circumspect about how much I put away, at least in public, more aware of how others might view me. In private, I've taken to regularly monitoring myself. As I started the drive home, I decided I was really feeling pretty steady. Maybe I had a little bit of a buzz on, but I was definitely in control. Still, that *whoa there, baby* from the waitress bothered me. It rankled, honestly, because I didn't think I deserved it. My elbow had slipped.

The house was dark when I pulled into the driveway. It's not unusual for Jenny to go up to bed this early. I know she has trouble sleeping and feels exhausted a lot of the time. But it bothered me she hadn't thought to leave even one light on for me. I try to keep reminding myself that she's hurting, but sometimes all this nonsense just seems like pure selfishness to me. I have feelings, too. I have needs. I'm the one who keeps this roof over our heads. I'm the one who's given her the freedom to sit home every day and feel sorry for herself.

I went through to the kitchen. She hadn't left anything out for me for dinner. I could feel my anger building. I thought about that waitress at Ernie's. How Daniel would no doubt be screwing her later on tonight. *Why not?* That was all he needed to say. It's been almost five months for me and Jenny. Maybe that's our problem. No, I decided as I turned out the kitchen light and headed upstairs, that's *definitely* our problem.

Jenny's taken to sleeping in Betsy's old room on a blow-up mattress. She told me it's because she's so restless at night. Up and down. Lights on and off. She claims that she doesn't want to disturb me. As I walked down the hallway to Betsy's room, I realized that I'd reached the point where—for both our sakes—I just had to say "bullshit" to all these excuses.

The door was half-closed. I pushed it open. Moonlight washed over the familiar room: the crib with the musical mobile hanging above it . . . the old wooden chest Jenny had painted pink and stenciled with little brown teddy bears . . . the miniature quilt depicting a barn and farm animals that my mother had hand-sewn and that Jenny had hung on the wall. The blow-up mattress was wedged between the crib and the closet. Jenny was curled up on her side, her legs drawn to her chest, hair fanned out over the pillow. She was wearing an old T-shirt of mine. She'd kicked the sheets off. My anger began to ebb—and something else took over.

I unbuttoned my shirt. I stepped out of my chinos. I lowered myself onto the mattress, but the damned thing started to bounce like a trampoline.

"Cal—?"

"Shhhh—," I said, crawling toward her. She slid toward me as the mattress buckled under my weight.

"What are you doing?"

"I just—" I worked to keep my balance as Jenny rolled into me. But my right arm slipped out from under me, and my elbow landed in her hair—jerking her head back.

"Damn—that hurts! What the hell are you doing?"

"I just wanted to see you," I said, trying to sit up. I felt a little sick to my stomach as the mattress rolled beneath me. Each time I moved, the whole room seemed to shift precariously. My hand closed around something soft and giving. For a brief moment, I thought it was my wife's breast. Then I realized that I'd grabbed onto one of Betsy's stuffed animals.

"Are you drunk?" she asked. "You stink of beer."

"No—," I began. But what was the point? Whatever I tried to say, I knew I would be in the wrong as far as Jenny was concerned. Which is right where she wanted me to be. Which is where she's made sure I've stayed for the last five months. I sat up and started to ease my way off the air mattress. I kept bumping into furry little creatures, and I realized that Jenny had brought all of Betsy's stuffed animals up to bed with her. She'd surrounded herself with them, but my weight had scattered them across the mattress, and a few had slipped onto the floor. When I stood up, I stepped on something that squeaked. I kicked it across the room.

"Close the door behind you," she told me.

But I did her one better. I slammed it.

12

Jenny

❧

"Well, what do you think?" Jude asked, throwing her arms up over her head as she cocked her left hip. She was wearing a strapless yellow-flowered sundress with a flared skirt that came halfway up her thighs. She recently had her red hair—which has darkened as she's gotten older—styled into one of those newfangled shags. Her body can still pass for that of a teenager. But the many disappointments of the past few years have etched little grooves around her mouth and cast shadows under her eyes.

"You look just fine," I told her. "But I'm facing into the sun. Move to your left a little. Yeah, that's better."

We were out on the new terrace. It was an almost balmy late October afternoon. Indian summer. Sugar maples sent bright red flares up the hillside. Below us, Daniel's plantings patterned our sloping yard with the jewel-like hues of an oriental carpet: the reddish purple of the sedums, the hydrangeas' dusky rose, the straw and greeny gold of the many different grasses. I'm still not accustomed to the reality of

Daniel's almost too-perfect composition: the way the different shapes and groupings lead the eye, the subtle balance of color and texture. How could I have ever thought Daniel's plans were generic? They're like photographs I've seen of the gardens at Versailles, or paintings of paradise. The kind of place you might dream about, but where you could never imagine actually living.

In that sense, it's not really my garden anymore. It's Daniel's. It's almost as if he's left a part of himself behind. When I walk along the pathways that wind through the beds, or down the new stone steps that are carved into the hillside, I feel once again the sense of relief—and release—that began to wash over me in the days following my lunch with him. The guilt that gripped me when I first told him about Betsy's car seat has slowly eased, replaced by a real if fragile tranquility. It no longer feels wrong that I told him my secret. I know it's safe with him. It's been almost three months now. Three months since I've seen him, but the tactile memory of his lips on my palms still lingers. It went no further than that. Still, it was enough to make me feel absolved in some way. It seemed to me that his brief touch was both gentle and forgiving—like a kind of benediction.

"I'll want a full-body shot," Jude was telling me. "And a couple of close-ups, too. Can you do retouching on your computer? I'd love to have these damned frown lines removed." She made a face at me, pulling at the sides of her mouth with her thumbs, scowling like a gargoyle, and sticking out her tongue.

"Do you think you could hold still for a second or two?" I asked her, just barely able to control my irritation. Without Besty—or the garden now—to care for, I have more time than ever on my hands. Yet the simplest tasks seem burdensome to me. And Jude's request that I take some new head shots for her feels like an enormous imposition. Having spent the summer selling her work at craft fairs and growing increasingly bored and restless, my sister has now decided she needs to get her long-dormant acting ambitions back on track. She simply wouldn't hear my attempt to say no, showing up earlier that afternoon with a couple of changes of clothes and a bag of makeup. It stuns me sometimes how narcissistic she can be. She still seems utterly oblivious to my pain and loneliness.

"They're mounting *A Christmas Carol* in Stockbridge over the holidays," she said. "Maybe I could audition for that old hag who tries to sell Scrooge's bedclothes." She began to pluck invisible fabrics out of the air and hold them out to me for inspection.

"I wager this'll fetch us a pretty haypenny, dearie," she said in an approximation of a cockney accent, then cackled as she bit down on an imaginary coin.

"Please, Jude," I said, frowning as I lifted the camera. "The light's starting to go."

She froze midpose, like a mime. Then she quickly repositioned herself and, shaking back her hair, smiled seductively into the camera. And there—between blinks of the shutter—I saw Betsy again. Betsy, rather than Jude, smiling impishly back at me. It's not so much that Jude and Betsy look alike, though they share the same high forehead, curving brow, and slightly crooked, definitely wicked grin. It's more that they have like spirits—fun loving, headstrong, unpredictably wild. Betsy, who would fling her arms around my neck for no reason and whisper, "Love, Mama!" Jude, who'd call me collect from strange towns and tell me drunkenly, "You're the only person in the whole world I believe in." Betsy, who would throw a temper tantrum without warning, her screams echoing across a crowded Walmart. Jude, who tried to seduce my husband.

So when Jude said, "You're beginning to feel better, aren't you?"—it seemed to me as though somehow Betsy, too, was asking.

"Yes," I said, lowering the camera. I felt my anger ebbing. So she *was* aware of the hell I'd been going through. "Maybe I finally am. Finally."

"That's great. And things are okay with you and Cal?"

It's unlike Jude to pry. In general, I think she's usually too self-involved to really focus that much attention on those around her. And, since that business with her and Cal, she's got to be aware that I've stopped confiding in her. She's my sister and of course I love her. But I'm not sure I'll ever really be able to trust her again. And I think she knows that. Knows, and has been careful not to push her luck, especially when it has anything to do with my husband. So I had to wonder where these questions were coming from. Then it occurred to me:

"Why? Is His Holiness worried?"

"Can't I be, too?"

"Sure you can," I said, raising the camera again. But I felt I had my answer; my father had obviously asked Jude to quiz me. How silly of me to think she'd bother asking on her own. I know my father's upset with me that I still refuse—despite the kind of tragedy that often brings a person back to organized religion—to attend his services. Does he truly want to help? I wonder. Or does he just worry that his congregation might find it unsettling that their minister and his grieving daughter are so obviously estranged? Whatever his motivation, the fact remains that his rote answers to my life-and-death questions are useless to me. Just as I know how ineffectual any advice he might want to offer me about my marriage would be. Cal's and my problems won't be fixed with any of the usual bromides. I can't begin to imagine how we'll ever find our way back to the couple we used to be before Betsy was killed. It's like we're in Hansel and Gretel's dark forest, and the birds have eaten the trail of breadcrumbs that was supposed to mark our way home.

I spent a few seconds adjusting the camera before I finally told Jude:

"You can tell him that there's really no need to worry. Everything's fine. We're good."

By the time the light faded altogether I felt I had a decent range of shots to select from. I'd used Cal's digital camera, rather than my old Nikon analog, so that I could work in iPhoto to crop and enhance the best ones. I decided just to get the whole damned thing over with. After she left, I went right into the great room, where we have our computer set up, and started to import the afternoon's work. It's a process that usually takes a few minutes, so I wandered into the kitchen to make myself a cup of tea.

The postage stamp–sized images filled the screen when I sat back down. I started from the last photo I snapped and worked my way backward, enlarging each one, deleting those with obvious problems. I had a chance to really study Jude's face as I did so, thinking back to that flash of Betsy I'd seen earlier in the afternoon. It was harder to detect any real similarity in the still photos. The likeness is far more obvious in the actual laughter, the brightness of the eyes, the turn of the head. Looking at Jude's prominent cheekbones and her wide, eager smile, I was reminded again of the couple of grainy photographs we have of our mother. And though my memories of my mom are as blurry as the photos, I've long felt that she and Jude shared more than just good looks. In the same way Jude reminds me of Betsy, I've often sensed my mother's temperment playing out in my younger sister's behavior.

"I hate this!" Jude told me one summer evening when she was eight or so. "I'm running away." There was still a little light on the horizon at nine o'clock, which my father had designated the hour of her bedtime. She'd just thrown her nightgown on the floor, refusing to change into it. For weeks now she'd been objecting to the fact that I was allowed to stay up until ten o'clock in the summertime. When it came to my father's rules, Jude saw only injustice, never mind that a lot of kids her age were put to bed even earlier.

"But that's crazy," I told her, though already alarmed. Even then, Jude didn't make idle threats. "Where will you go?"

"I don't care!" she said, kicking her nightgown across the room. "Why do you get to stay up? This isn't fair! I can't live here anymore!"

Did she know how frightened I was of being abandoned again? Just the thought of it made me go numb: the one person I loved more than any other leaving me behind as our mother had done. Of course, a part of me realized that she'd have a very difficult time making good on any of this, but fear had gotten the better of me. Before I thought twice about what I was doing, I was pulling back the covers on my own bed and crawling in.

"Okay, so now we're equal," I told her. "Now it's fair."

I went to bed when she did for the rest of the summer. And, of course, Jude didn't talk about leaving again. At least not then. But in many ways, it was only the beginning of her complaints and ultimatums. The more I tried to placate her, the more restless and demanding she became. Until, of course, she crossed the line from bad behavior to betrayal. Until she took a step too far—one that forced me to agree that, after all those years of threatening to do so, the best thing she could do finally was walk out the door.

How sad, I was thinking as I stared at her frozen coquettish expression on my computer screen, that things couldn't be easier between us. How sad that even now, when I was feeling so uprooted and unstable, our old, entrenched patterns of behavior remained the same. Why couldn't she be there for me—when I needed her most?

Angrily, I clicked on the backward arrow for the next shot.

And my heart stopped.

A part of me knew instantly what I was looking at, even while my mind refused to focus. But the bucket seat was so familiar. And it looked perfectly normal, except for the fact that the left shoulder strap had been wrenched loose from the frame and dangled from a few frayed strands. A part of me knew what I was looking at, but the shock of seeing Betsy's car seat again—the evidence of my own, unspeakable negligence—kept me from taking in the reality of the thing all at once.

In fact, I don't know how long I sat there, staring at the screen, before I clicked on the backward arrow again. And there was another shot of the car seat, this time from a more head-on angle. I clicked again. And again. There were thirteen shots of the seat altogether, each taken from a slightly different position. For the first time, I allowed myself to imagine how my daughter's life had ended. I don't know why I'd never really thought it through before. Perhaps it was because I'd seen her body at the hospital. I'd held her in my arms. But then Kurt had carefully arranged her for us in the chapel, wrapped her in that sheet, maybe even hastily borrowed somebody's makeup to cover the bruises. Staring at the photos, I began to see how it must have really been. What she would have looked like when Kurt first found her. When the EMS crew tried everything, as Kurt assured me they had, to bring her back to life. The car seat had made it through with just a mangled strap, but she'd been thrown from the car like a rag doll, her body bloodied and broken.

I could hardly breathe. It felt as though my rib cage was being crushed. What were these photos doing on Cal's camera? Where was the actual car seat now? I hadn't thought to ask after the accident. No, I hadn't wanted to know. Now I felt panicky, trying to understand what had happened. Why Cal had taken these shots. Why he'd never told me. Had he somehow figured out what I'd done? Had he taken the photos to confirm his suspicions? What else could I think?

☽

His car lights swept through the downstairs as he pulled into the driveway. I remained seated in front of the computer with one of the photographs of the battered car seat enlarged to fill the screen. I heard him open the front door. Walk down the hall. Stop in the kitchen to get a beer.

"Jenny?"

"I'm over here," I said. I heard him cross the room and come up to stand behind me. I could feel him staring at the screen.

"Oh Jesus," he said.

"I don't understand. Why did you take these?"

"I was going to tell you," he said, putting his hand on my shoulder.

"Don't touch me!" I swung around in the chair to face him.

"Listen, Jenny," he sighed, closing his eyes. "I know how you feel—"

"No, you don't," I said. "You can't. You can't possibly know."

"She was my daughter, too! I have every right to do this. More than a right. It's an obligation. To Betsy. To other innocent kids."

"What?"

"It's not about the money," he said. "I mean that; I really do. But someone has to stop Gannon. Someone has to step up to the plate."

"You're going ahead with the lawsuit."

"I want *us* to go ahead with it. We need to do this together."

I just stared at him, my heart racing. He didn't know. But now was the moment to tell him. How it had happened. Why. That exchange with Tessa. The worry about Jude. I thought about how to begin. How to explain. But my thoughts kept circling. My mind wasn't working right. I felt as though I was falling back into the dark hole of those first days after Betsy's death. The walls were closing in. Cal was talking, but I wasn't really tracking what he was saying.

". . . a firm Edmund contacted in Albany . . . Already

sued Gannon and won . . . a huge settlement . . . forensic tests should show . . ."

"You gave this law firm Betsy's car seat?"

"Yes, they're conducting some tests to pinpoint exactly what went wrong."

"You went behind my back. You lied to me."

But what were Cal's lies compared to mine? He did have every right to try to find out why his daughter had been killed—and to hold the guilty party responsible. Would these tests be able to show that Betsy hadn't been correctly buckled into her safety seat? If so, the law firm would certainly want to drop the suit, wouldn't they? Then Cal would come home and ask me why I'd been deceiving him all these months. And what would I say? That I'd begged him not to go after Gannon. That he hadn't listened. He hadn't even tried to understand. But the truth was, I didn't tell him because I was so ashamed. And now I was afraid. How would he react when he found out what I'd done? But if he didn't pursue the lawsuit, he'd never have to learn what had really happened. I knew I had to find a way to stop all this. I was so rattled, I could hardly stand up.

"I'm doing this for Betsy. For all the—"

"No," I said as I walked away. "I can't hear this. I can't take any more of this. I've got to get out of here."

∾

I drove south. I didn't know why at first. I drove south into Covington and then east along Route 206, which winds up through the mountains. A moon rose above the trees. It was the harvest moon, nearly full, the orangey red of a bonfire. When I was a teenager and first got my driver's license, I used

to steal out of the house at night and take my dad's secondhand Camry on joyrides through these same mountains.
Sometimes Cal would come with me, and we'd park along
the side of one of the back roads and make out right up to
the point of no return. But never beyond it. What a pure
pleasure it was kissing him then! How special and powerful
I would feel when he'd reluctantly pull away and tell me:

"That's it. Or we'll be sorry." Though, honestly, I think
Cal cared a lot more than I did about saving the ultimate
step for our wedding night. If he'd pushed me at all, I know
I would have given in. But he had such a definite sense of
right and wrong. A vision for our future life together. Does
he still? I wonder. Betsy's death has managed to blur so many
once-clear moral lines. I'm not the only one hiding things.
For instance, I know Cal's drinking more than he lets on.
He's taken to stashing six-packs in the extra refrigerator in
the garage and drinking out there at night after I go up to
bed. He crushes the empties and puts them right into the re-
cycle bin, thinking I won't notice.

I'm partially responsible for that, too, I guess. I know he
feels frustrated. Well, probably far more than that by now.
But having sex with him at this point would feel so utterly
dishonest. I'd only be faking it—the way I'm faking so much
else. Every social interaction these days feels like such a
burden. I can hardly face going down to the Covington
Public Market and making small talk with the cashier. How
could I possibly expose myself to the most intimate of acts?
And with Cal—from whom I'm already trying to conceal so
much? I flinch when he touches me. If he knew the truth—
would he ever really want me again?

It wasn't until I was on the outskirts of Northridge that

I fully realized why I was heading in that direction. Whom it was I wanted to see. I don't know where Daniel lives, but Cal told me that he hangs out at Ernie's. It was early evening still; it wouldn't look too odd for me to drop by. I could pretend I was in town and thought Cal said he might be there. I parked in the public lot and put on some lipstick. The weak little light on the back of the visor hollowed out my cheeks; my eyes and mouth looked roughed in like in a child's drawing.

I've been avoiding crowds for months. So when I walked into Ernie's, the noise unsettled me—all those voices, the laughter, the heavy electrified bass line thumping out over the sound system. I scanned the bar, but it was hard to see more than a long row of backs from where I was standing. I made my way across the crowded lounge area, looking for that distinctive profile.

"What'll it be?" the bartender asked me when I reached an empty space near the service station.

"Nothing, thanks," I said, hesitating. "I was just looking for Daniel Brandt?"

"Haven't seen him yet. But Gail will know. Hold on, she'll be picking up her order in a sec."

Several minutes passed before a tall brunette waitress approached, and the bartender asked her if she'd seen Daniel, and then nodded at me:

"This lady's looking for him."

She sized me up, hand on hip.

"He's in the city for a couple of days on business. Whom shall I say was asking?"

"Nobody," I told her. She continued to stare at me, a half smile playing on her lips. "It's nothing. I just thought that if he was here, I'd tell him . . ."

Her smile widened as my words trailed off.

"I'd be happy to tell him for you," she said as she picked up a tray and hoisted it to her shoulder. "What's the message?"

"Just that Jenny came by to—to say thanks."

‽

I drove around aimlessly for another few hours, north, then west. I ended up looping back and picking up Route 206 again at some point. Retracing my steps home. I'd resolved nothing. I didn't have a plan.

The downstairs was lit up when I pulled into the driveway. I felt so alone. I sat in the car for a few minutes after I turned off the engine, thinking about Daniel. I tried to imagine what he would have said if I'd been able to talk to him. *You can tell me,* he'd reassured me that day we'd had lunch. In many ways that was all I really needed to hear. Needed to have. Someone who would listen. Who wouldn't judge. I could still feel the touch of his lips against my skin.

"There you are," Cal said, rising from the sofa when I came into the great room. "I was getting worried. I thought maybe something had happened."

"Something *has* happened, Cal," I answered. I heard the righteous anger in my voice. Lying was becoming second nature to me now. But I knew I just had to do whatever I could to keep Cal from proceeding with the Gannon suit. I felt that my whole life—our future, really—depended on it. "You've stopped listening to me. You're not hearing a single word that comes out of my mouth. So I'm begging you, please—pay attention! Don't do this to me. Don't do this to us! It's only going to bring more heartache. It's just going to drive us further apart."

13

Cal

❦

When I lifted the grill hood, smoke hit me in the face, making my eyes water. Half-blind, I poked at the turkey breast with my grill fork, and I checked the temperature gauge. Another fifteen minutes or so, I figured. I knew I should head back inside and make nice with Jenny, Jude, and my father-in-law, but I couldn't stand the atmosphere in the house. In the past I've gladly suffered through these Thanksgiving meals with Reverend Honegger, knowing that, having done Thanksgiving with him, we'd be freed up to enjoy Christmas with my side of the family. But this year, the first without Betsy, and with things such a mess between me and Jenny, it's been torture. Cooking the turkey—my annual holiday contribution—provides me with a built-in excuse to slip outside, check on the bird, and nurse along my coffee mug of Jack on the rocks.

The reverend doesn't approve of drinking, so Thanksgiving ends up being a dry meal in just about every sense of the word. And all day long I've been feeling Betsy's absence—

like a sharp pain riding under my rib cage. This time last year she helped me rake the leaves in the front yard with a little toy rake we'd gotten her. She loved jumping in the big pile we built, the leaves flying into the air above her. I can see her eyes, wide with joy and excitement.

I've already called Edmund twice this week about where things stand with Gannon. I feel so frustrated. What the fuck can be taking so long?

I heard the door slide open behind me, followed by the reverend's tentative, shuffling gait. My dad still tries to stride along like a man in his prime, but Jenny's father seems eager to play up his frailty and advancing age. He's got a quaver in his voice now—making what he says often sound testy and uncertain.

"Well, here you are!" he announced, as if he'd been searching the globe. We've never much liked each other. I've heard too much about the dictatorial way he raised Jenny and Jude to feel much sympathy for him. We've got nothing in common but his daughter and, I suspect, the conviction we both hold of each other—that she deserves a whole lot better. I've also been pretty shocked by his fumbling response to our tragedy.

"Yeah, here I am," I said, not really caring if he picked up on the irritation in my voice.

"I wanted to come out and see these new gardens I've been hearing so much about," he said, grunting under his breath as he made his way down the steps to the terrace, where I'd set up the grill.

"Not much to see now. Except the stonework." But even in late November, with all the leaves gone, I liked looking out over what I've come to think of as Daniel's landscape:

the way the stone steps lead from one level to the next, the neat ledges of shrubs and trees, how the pathways snake through the beds in an almost mazelike way. Whenever I start off on one of the artfully designed paths, I'm never quite sure where I'm going to end up.

"My goodness," Jenny's father said, stopping beside me and taking in the scene below. He crossed his arms. "Pretty fancy."

"What's that supposed to mean?" I asked, not liking his tone. It was typical of him to sound both judgmental and aw-shucks.

"Oh, well now, you know Jenny's the gardener in the family. I'm really not equipped to weigh in on the pros and cons of something this—this elaborate. My tastes are pretty uncomplicated."

"You don't like it."

"I think I preferred the old garden," he said, taking off his rimless glasses and polishing them on his scarf. It's something he tends to do right before he starts to pontificate. I braced myself.

"But, now, you know me," he went on, slowly putting his glasses back on. "I'm of the old school. Keep it simple. Stick to the straight and narrow and you won't end up where you don't belong."

"Is there something you're trying to tell me?" I asked him.

"I heard Jennifer and Judith discussing this lawsuit you're planning. I think it's ill-advised. It's not going to bring Betsy back."

"I'm already aware of that," I said. His know-it-all, holier-than-thou tone really pissed me off.

"You think you're justified, I'm sure," he went on, not

picking up on my anger. "But I'm aware how much this is upsetting Jennifer. Your first obligation is to her, Cal. And to your marriage. Both of you need to heal—and then start to move ahead together with your lives. It looks to me like this suit is starting to come between you. And that's not right. You might lose a great deal more than you're going to gain."

"It's not the money. I don't give a damn about the money," I said. I usually try not to swear in front of Jenny's dad, but I was beyond thinking about his feelings. He'd been of zero help to us after Betsy's death. What prompted him to want to throw in his two cents now? I wondered if Jenny had enlisted his support in her efforts to stop the suit. I had a hard time believing that she would turn to her father for this—or for anything else—but, then, I'm beginning to feel I understand my wife a little bit less every day.

"I believe you mean that," he said. "I imagine you're pursuing this with the idea that you're going to right a grievous wrong. You're hoping to punish the manufacturer. But lawsuits of this kind can take years to settle. It could take over your life, Cal. In the meantime, you'll be neglecting your own salvation and your precious marriage—the most important work you've been given to do on this earth."

"I don't think I need a lecture from you on marriage," I snapped. Even as I said the words, I realized that I'd stepped over the line—but, then, I felt he'd done the same with me. We've never discussed the matter—we've never gone into depth about much of anything, frankly—but I've often wondered how he squared counseling his congregants on matrimonial issues when his own marriage ended in such a public fiasco. Karl Honegger didn't flinch. If anything he grew more still. Stolid. We stood there together in silence. Then he said:

"Do as I say, not as I do. In the end, that's really all any parent can advise a child. Think about it, Cal. That's all I'm asking."

I waited until the meal was over. I had the requisite second slice of pumpkin pie. I even helped clear the dishes. Then I said, "I'm heading over to see the game. Anyone want to come with me?"

For Dad's seventieth, we all pitched in and bought him a fifty-four-inch, wall-mounted flat-screen Panasonic for his "den" in the refinished basement, a pine-paneled expanse where he keeps his guns and fishing gear and a lifetime accumulation of medals, ribbons, and framed citations. It's where our family and friends congregate to watch "the game," baseball or football, depending on the season. Thanksgiving is wall-to-wall college ball, which, because no one really gives a damn about the outcome, means most of us only glance at the set. We're there to party. Last year, someone brought out a hula hoop and everyone took turns. Jenny lasted the longest, her hips barely moving as the hoop circled around and around. I remembered her heart-stopping crooked smile and how sexy she looked.

"No, thanks," Jenny said, not even looking up as she loaded the dishwasher.

"You know, I think I'll tag along," Jude replied, surprising the hell out of me. We've been avoiding each other since her return. But I should have known. We weren't even out of the driveway before she turned to me in the front seat and said, "I'm really worried, Cal. I've never seen Jenny like this. You know I wouldn't be talking to you about it unless I thought it was really, really important. But someone has to tell you: I think you're making a huge mistake with this Gannon thing."

"Someone already *has* told me. Your dad. So all you Honeggers are lining up against me, huh? Honestly, Jude, I don't understand your reasoning. My daughter died because of these people's carelessness. And other kids are liable to end up the same way—unless we stop them. That's what this is about. Where's the problem?"

"My sister. Your wife. *There's* the problem," Jude said. "She's always been the rock of my existence. There for me when everybody else walked away. There for me when I didn't deserve it, when she should never have spoken to me again. All I'm saying is: I can't believe you don't feel the same way. That you don't want to protect her. I think just the idea of this lawsuit is tearing her apart."

"You never knew Betsy," I said. "You don't have any idea what I'm fighting for. What we lost."

"Well, I do know what you *could* lose," Jude replied. "And she's very much alive and hurting."

There were cars lining both sides of my parents' drive when we pulled in. Jude and I walked into the house side by side, not speaking. She disappeared into the crowd upstairs, mostly women and younger kids, headquartered in the kitchen. I assume that someone gave her a ride home at some point, because I didn't see her again that night. And I didn't want to. What she'd said had ticked me off. I hated the idea of Jenny confiding our personal problems to someone as un-predictable as Jude. Or as preachy and unbending as Reverend Honegger. Edmund and I had agreed to hold off telling our family about Gannon until Stephens, Stokes actually filed the complaint, but here was Jenny—already out there, sounding the alarm. And I wasn't exactly in a position to tell her not to talk about it.

"Hey there, Cal," Tessa said, coming over to me. Jamie was following his mom in a red plastic truck—one of the toys my dad keeps around for the grandkids—beeping the little toy horn with glee. He'll have been too young when Betsy was alive to remember her when he gets older. He's probably already forgotten her now. "Is Jenny upstairs?"

"No, she didn't come. I think she was feeling kind of wiped out. We had her dad and Jude over for the big meal."

"Oh, lucky you," Tessa said. She knows how Jenny feels about her dad and is fully aware of the fireworks surrounding Jude. They used to be close, Tessa and Jenny. Tessa used to be in and out of our house just about every day. It makes me sad to see them drifting apart. Tessa's so smart and tough-minded; a good person to have in your corner. Is Jenny closing her out because of Jamie? I wonder. Watching him talking and walking now—and knowing that Betsy will forever remain only two years old?

"We're off again!" she said as Jamie pedaled away. "New worlds to conquer."

We had a big crowd that year. It looked like Dad had invited the entire office staff. I know Edmund wouldn't have been so generous; he tries to make the case that Dad shouldn't fraternize with his employees so much.

"It's hard to discipline people you party with," Edmund has pointed out.

"It's harder to motivate people who don't feel appreciated" is Dad's position. But, the truth is, the old man just loves his business and takes a real interest in everyone who works for him. In another couple of weeks, this whole group—along with suppliers and clients—will be invited to reassemble in the showroom for the annual Horigan Lumber and Hardware Christmas bash.

I got talking to a couple of the salesmen, Nicky Odhner and Joel Price, both old friends from high school. Kurt joined us, along with Lori Swinson, who handles phone orders at the store. I couldn't remember if she was in high school with us, or if she settled here from out of the area. She's pretty in a kind of moon-faced way, with bottle-blond, shoulder-length hair. She's one of these types who seems to take her personal style cues from the Marilyn Monroe school of fashion: fuzzy pink sweater, low-riding jeans that accentuate heavy thighs, lots of lipstick.

"Well, I think it'll do just great," Lori interjected at one point when Kurt and Joel were debating the prospects of a new movie complex that was opening that month in Harringdale. The centerpiece of an urban renewal project that had been in the works for years, the theater was months overdue and nearly a million over budget. "I hate having to go to the mall at night."

"Yeah, but at least you don't take your life in your hands there," Joel pointed out. "Harringdale is like the crime capital of the county."

"What do you think, Cal?" Lori asked, nudging me with her elbow. "Don't you want to try it?" I'd only been half listening to what the others were saying. What had I been thinking? Once again, I felt myself emerging from a mental fog.

"I guess time will tell," I said. "In the meantime I think we could all use another round."

Kurt moved away after a while. My dad came by and wrapped his arms around Nicky and Joel.

"Glad you two could make it," he said, giving them both a squeeze. "The beating heart of the best sales team in the whole damned county."

"Yeah, if only we could round up a couple of customers to sell to," Nicky said in that sheepish tone so many of us are using these days.

"Oh, they'll come back," Dad said. "They'll be back."

At some point, Nicky and Joel drifted away, too. People were starting to leave now. I was stuck listening to Lori go on about her mother, who lives in a retirement community out in Arizona, and how she's just barely scraping along, importing her prescription drugs from Canada. It was all *blah, blah, blah*, as far as I was concerned. I nodded and smiled just to be nice, but I was thinking back on what Jenny's dad and Jude had said. How determined Jenny seemed to be to fight me. But why? There's only one conclusion I can draw, the same one I keep coming back to again and again: she blames me for Betsy's death. Blames me and is going to do everything in her power to keep me from getting the satisfaction I need from Gannon. In fact, she seems intent on making *me* pay for everything.

"You're sure you don't mind?" I suddenly heard Lori asking. "I'm afraid I'm really kind of out of your way. But my ride here had to leave early. You're sure you don't mind?"

"No, it's fine," I told her. The party was breaking up, but I was in no hurry to get home to a dark house and Jenny asleep upstairs in Betsy's room. We stayed and helped clean up first. Lori seemed delighted to be collecting bottles and carrying trash bags upstairs.

"I just dote on your dad," she said as we walked out to the Olds at the end of the drive. We were the last to leave. The temperature had dropped. Tiny snowflakes drifted in the headlights. She wasn't kidding that she was out of the way. She lived in a double-wide near Amesville in something called, according to the beat-up sign at the entrance to the place, Meadowbrook Village. Her trailer was dark, snow already icing the front steps.

"I better see you in," I said.

I followed her across the frozen little yard. A bucket filled with plastic flowers and snow sat at the bottom of the steps. She fiddled around with her keys, got the door open, flipped on a light.

"Thank you, Cal," she said, stepping inside but holding the door open. "You're the best. And I just want you to know that I think you're being so brave. I know how sad you must be. How hard losing your little girl has to be for you, especially this time of the year."

"Thanks," I said, looking down so that she wouldn't see my expression. Her little-girly voice had always irritated me. But it didn't now. She'd blindsided me with the very words I longed to hear from Jenny. If I'd been looking at her it might not have happened. I might have seen what was coming and done something to avoid it. Instead, the next thing I knew her arms were around my neck, and that pillowy body was pushed up against mine. Before I could catch my breath, her tongue was halfway down my throat. She smelled spicy and sweet. But her mouth tasted salty and a little sour. It's been such a long time for me. But that's not why I started to kiss her back. Why I began to fondle those heavy breasts. I wanted what her body could give me, of course, but it was more that I needed what her kiss said, what her touch implied. That I *am* brave. I'm still carrying a burden that is almost too heavy to bear. And I've been going it alone for too damned many months now.

While we were kissing, she somehow managed to pull me inside and close the door. I held her against me the whole time, surprised by how substantial she actually is. She probably weighs as much as I do, but it's all so soft and pliable. I pulled her sweater up and started to kiss her breasts. They were wedged together by a large black lacy bra. I fumbled around in the back for whatever it was that held the thing together. Jenny goes in for these little sports jobs that just lift up over her head. I couldn't remember the last time I had to deal with wired cups and tiny little hooks.

"Hold on," she said finally, with a high, breathy laugh. "Let me do it."

It gave me a second or two to think. To come to my senses. Lori's breasts, freed from their constraints, swung between us: milky white, enormous, a teenage boy's fantasy come to life. But I've loved one woman for so many years now, my idea of what is beautiful and desirable has been utterly reshaped to fit her exact dimensions. The little hollow at the base of her throat. Those long, slim, slightly bowed legs. Her upturned breasts. Lori's face was flushed, her lipstick smeared. She looked so pleased, expectant. I felt like a total asshole.

"I'm sorry," I told her, pulling her against me. "I'm really, really sorry. You're very pretty. And very sweet. And I'm just feeling . . . so down. But I can't do this, Lori—I've got to get home."

14

Jenny

✣

"It's so great to see you," Kristin said as she hugged me. Then she held me at arm's length and looked me over. "How are you doing?"

"Okay," I said. It seems that every other woman I've run into at the Horigan office Christmas party has felt the need to embrace me—and ask how I'm holding up. Without my baby daughter. A week before Christmas. It's every mother's nightmare. Terrible to even consider. They all know me and my family. I'm sure Betsy's death sent a tremor through the lives of these women. I can see it in their eyes: *thank God it didn't happen to me!*

"How are you really, Jenny?" Kristin asked me again. Blonde and superthin, my sister-in-law always seems so burdened down and humorless to me. Though Edmund makes a lot of money, she still insists on raising the twins without the help of a nanny, tutoring underprivileged kids in Hudson, and taking on every school and community project that comes down the pike. And all in a martyrish, self-righteous kind of way. She once told Tessa and me when we asked her why she couldn't cut herself a little more slack: *I just think it's so important to give back.*

But there's another side to Kristin—one that seems at odds with her uptight public persona—that I've found myself increasingly drawn to since Betsy's death. She studies the occult, believes in the presence of spirits in our lives, and has actually called me a couple of times since the tragedy to say that she wants me to know that Betsy is okay. A friend of hers named Harriet Elder is a new age medium, channeler, or something, and Kristin has been in her presence when she's supposedly communicated with my daughter.

"And what did Betsy say to her?" I'd asked. I was more than a little skeptical. For one thing, Betsy was still basically speaking baby talk when she died.

"Oh, it was really more that Harriet felt her aura—and heard her laugh. You could come with me next time I see Harriet. I'm sure she'd be happy to try and contact Betsy for you again."

But I have no intention of going through Harriet Elder to reach Betsy. It's not simply that I'm afraid Harriet might be a fraud, and Kristin her well-meaning dupe. Because a part of me does believe in the possibility of what someone like Harriet claims. It's more that I resent the idea that strangers feel they have the right to contact my daughter. Betsy was always a little wary of people she didn't know. She'd never let anyone but Cal or me pick her up without a struggle. I'm sure Harriet and Kristin believe they're helping, but I also know that Betsy will come only to me.

And throughout these first few weeks of December, I've actually felt closer to my daughter than I have in months.

The season is so full of nostalgia and easy sentiment. You can't turn on the radio or walk into a store right now without being bombarded by Christmas carols. *Through the years we all will be together, if the fates allow.* Just last week, I saw Betsy in the child's seat of a shopping cart at Rite Aid: the mop of curls, the chubby little legs kicking. My heart raced as I walked toward her. I was five or six feet away when the child's mother returned with an eight-pack of paper towels and wheeled my baby off. Though initially upset that I'd been mistaken, I've since allowed myself to imagine that Betsy is simply playing with me—that this is a kind of hide-and-seek—and she's just pretending to be the child in the shopping cart, or the baby in that stroller, or the little girl waiting in line for Santa at Pellani's Garden Center Christmas Fair.

"Honestly?" I said to Kristin. She was obviously expecting something more from me. "It doesn't ever stop hurting. But you do start to get used to the pain." This was a response I'd heard from someone else who'd lost a child; was it Elizabeth Edwards? I'd admired the sound of it: tough-minded, frank, even though I knew it couldn't possibly apply to me. Because the only way I will ever be able to get used to Betsy's death is if I first somehow manage to forgive myself for it.

"Well, listen, I think it's so great you came to this," Kristin told me, finally letting me go. "We're all pulling for you."

"Thanks," I said, though I felt exhausted by everyone's well-intentioned concern. Tessa had hugged me so tight and for such a long time when I first ran into her that afternoon, I thought I was going to faint. And, if anything, I feel worse now than I did before I came. Being surrounded by so many family members and friends for the first time since Betsy's funeral only reminds me how little right I have to their pity and love. What mother here would look at me the same way if she knew what I had done?

Ever since I discovered the photos of the car seat and learned what Cal was up to, we've hardly been speaking to each other. I know Jude and my father both tried to talk him out of the lawsuit—but that just seems to have hardened his resolve. He was fuming on the telephone last week with Edmund, demanding to know what's taking the lawyers so long. I live under the shadow of that return phone call—the one I know is coming any minute now—from the law firm.

In fact, I would never have had the courage to show up this afternoon if I hadn't managed to overhear Cal on a different phone call a few days ago. There was something about his voice—a little self-conscious and ingratiating—that made me suspect he was talking to Daniel.

"I don't know if you're into this sort of thing. It's really nothing fancy. But I thought it might be a good place for you to make some contacts. We're tight with just about every major contractor and supplier in the area. Sure—it's one of these open-house-type deals—feel free to drop by at any time if you're around."

I could tell by Cal's tone that he was hoping Daniel would show. But I'm desperate to see him again. The sense of relief I felt when I first told him my secret has been wearing off—replaced by a growing anxiety. It doesn't help that I have so little to do around the house and yard. The gardens are dormant now. Though we've yet to have any real snow, the ground is rock hard, the trees bare, the perennials skeletons of their former selves. I can no longer take comfort wandering through Daniel's garden. The pathways and steps are buried in leaves. His presence—which I once felt so strongly—seems to have been swept away with the wind.

I scanned the crowd as Kristin moved away, but Daniel had obviously decided to skip the party. It was nearly six o'clock and the two long buffet tables had already been cleared of their warming trays. The caterers were bringing out platters of cookies and coffee things. As they do every year, the Horigan staff had temporarily moved shelving and showcases so that the main floor of the store was open in the front, easily accommodating the fifty or so people who had gathered there. Holiday lights and evergreen swags hung along the countertops. My father-in-law, his gauntness accentuated by a loose-fitting green Horigan Lumber baseball cap, mounted the little platform next to the Christmas tree decorations display and stepped up to the microphone.

"Hello, everyone," he began. "And welcome. It's great to see you all here. Old friends and new friends. Family and employees—although in our case, I know it's sometimes a little hard to tell the difference . . ."

Jay tends to deliver the same speech every year, though it seemed to me his tone was a little different today. Slower. More subdued. He'd made his usual rounds through the crowd all afternoon, shaking hands and slapping shoulders, but I noticed him sitting down at one point, gazing out across the room at nothing.

"It hasn't been an easy year for most of you, I know. A lot of things hit hard all at one time, didn't they? In my own family, we—we had our—" I saw Edmund and Cal exchange a look when their father's voice broke, but then he managed to regain his composure and go on. "We had our problems, too. But life has a way of throwing curves, no matter how careful you try to be, right? I think the trick is to . . ."

Daniel must have arrived sometime during my father-in-law's speech. Though I'd been keeping my eye on the door most of the afternoon, I hadn't seen him come in. But there he was suddenly by the drinks table, applauding with the others as Jay stepped down from the dais. A good-looking forty-something redhead in a fur parka stood next to him, sipping wine, not even pretending to pay attention to the proceedings. I watched my husband hurry over and shake hands with them. Cal was smiling and nodding at whatever Daniel was saying, obviously delighted that his friend had finally shown up. It looked to me as if they had dropped in on their way to or from some other party. Daniel was wearing a sports jacket and turtleneck. It had been more than five months since I'd seen him. He looked different again. Was he starting to dye his hair? It seemed darker for some reason, accentuating the gray streaks at his temples. I saw him looking around the crowded showroom. I glanced away when his gaze fell on me. But I'm sure he caught me staring at him.

I busied myself talking with a group of wives I know from the baseball league, but I was secretly tracking Daniel the whole time. Cal had walked him and the redhead over to meet Edmund and Jay. My father-in-law launched into some anecdote that seemed to go on and on. The party was beginning to thin out. When I looked over again, Daniel and the redhead were gone. Cal and Edmund stood alone, heads together, talking. My father-in-law had made his way over to the front door and was saying good-bye to folks as they left.

"Hello, stranger," Daniel said from right behind me. A shiver went down my spine.

"Oh, hi," I said, turning around.

"I hoped you'd be here," he said. "How are you doing?"

"Not so great," I said, though, in fact, just being near him again lifted my spirits. "I've been going through a rough patch."

"I heard you came by Ernie's—and were asking for me."

"I was—" I still didn't know how to explain my urge to talk to him that night. Or why seeing him now made me feel so much better. "I just stopped in on a whim I was in the area."

"Really?" he said. "Well, I've missed our interesting talks."

"So have I," I said, meeting his gaze. I knew he wasn't thinking of Betsy when he looked at me. He probably hadn't given my confession another thought during these long, dark months when I've thought of little else. He didn't care what I had done. His indifference to Betsy's death and my role in it acted on me as a kind of balm, relieving me of my guilt and shame.

"Let's have lunch, then," he said, smiling. "I've been in the city a lot on business, but I'll be around for the next few weeks. I would have asked you sooner, but I wasn't sure you wanted to see me again. But now I think you do."

I was about to ask how he could tell, but I saw Cal break off his conversation with Edmund and start across the room toward us.

"You're right," I said. "When?"

"I'll be at the Clear Lake Inn in Lansbury next Wednesday at one o'clock. Do you know it?"

"Yes," I said as my husband approached. He looked so pleased to see me and Daniel together, engaged in what appeared to be a friendly conversation. It seems like years ago now that he first told me about Daniel—how he felt that he already knew this stranger from somewhere. That they seemed to share a bond he couldn't explain. Perhaps the Harriet Elders of this world are right, and we live alongside spirits and other dimensions every day. And we're influenced and moved by forces we can neither see nor understand. I still feel that way about Betsy. That powerful belief that she's right there—right *here*—just out of sight. That's what I was feeling now—that sense of mysterious possibility. *Connection*. I only had to reach out. A second before Cal joined us, I added, under my breath:

"I'll be there."

❧

Two days later, the day before Christmas Eve, Cal came home from work around five o'clock. I was wrapping presents. I'd decided to give everyone photos of Betsy. I'd put together a little collage of her—newborn with that downy halo of hair, grinning and gap-toothed in front of her first birthday cake, seated in a high chair next to Jamie last Christmas at the Horigan family party—and had five-by-seven prints made, which I was in the process of framing. The table in the great room was strewn with packaging from the frames I'd bought, wrapping paper, ribbons, scissors, tape. It's the only evidence in the entire house that Christmas is the day after tomorrow. Cal and I didn't get a tree this year. We didn't bring the lights and decorations down from the attic. We didn't even talk about it. Forgoing all the usual holiday trappings is one of the few things we seem to agree on right now.

"Hey there," Cal called from the kitchen. I heard him

popping a beer. He walked over to the table where I was working and stood there, looking over my shoulder at what I was doing. I hadn't told him about the collage. We were living like estranged roommates at this point. Eating at different times. Sleeping separately. Leaving notes for each other rather than talking.

"Hi," I said, not looking up. He didn't usually bother to greet me these days when he got back from work.

"Eddie finally heard from Stephens, Stokes this afternoon."

I put down the photo of Betsy I'd been trimming. She beamed up at me, the first of her baby teeth pushing through her gums, her eyes brimming with excitement. Though I'd been dreading this moment for months, now that it had finally come I felt an almost surreal calm. I've already endured the worst thing a mother can bear. I'd lost my baby. I'd lost her—and I had only myself to blame. Could Cal's fury really be any more terrible than my own?

"They're ready to file."

"To file?" I asked, turning to face him.

"They're ready to officially file the complaint against Gannon," he replied, then went on in a rush: "They've run a lot of tests. Not just on the car seat itself, but they actually did a series of these things they call 'sled tests,' where they recreate the accident somehow. Same conditions, Jeep, rollover, everything—the whole exact scenario. And each time, it turns out that the car seat should *not* have malfunctioned the way ours did. The seat should have kept Betsy safe. It was designed to protect her—and totally failed. Something was wrong with it—"

"What?" I asked. "What was wrong?"

"They're not absolutely sure. There are a couple of possibilities. But they think it was the probably something in the fastener mechanism. The way Betsy came out of the seat, it looks like that top part came loose or broke apart somehow and—"

"I guess I don't understand how this works. Don't they need to present one definite explanation?" I asked. "Won't the jury want to know exactly what went wrong?"

"The way Stephens, Stokes is talking, I don't think there's going to be any jury. They're saying Gannon will want to settle this thing out of court as quickly as they can."

"No," I said. "No, they won't." What I saw—and what Cal couldn't see—was that if Stephens, Stokes hoped to mount any kind of a case, of course they had to blame the manufacturer. They'd already spent how much time and money running tests on the car seat, re-creating this accident? Did they really think that my single thoughtless moment could be overwritten and eventually erased by their "sled tests" and theories, by their endless billable hours? Maybe Stephens, Stokes thought they could get away with it, but I was damned sure Gannon wouldn't. Gannon would point out the one thing that I bet Cal's lawyers must have already considered—the obvious explanation: my baby was killed because she hadn't been strapped into the seat correctly. It wasn't the car seat that failed. It was the mother.

"Well, it's not up to you to say no, Jenny," Cal said. "We *are* doing this. The law firm is filing the complaint the day after Christmas. They're going to hold a press conference— and they want us both to be there. This thing is going to make headlines. It's *that* important."

I couldn't imagine a worse nightmare.

"You're not listening to me, Cal!" I said, panic rising in my throat. "I don't want to go ahead with this. I don't think it's right. I don't think—"

"You know what?" Cal said. "I believe I know *exactly* what you think. I know what's going on with you. Why you really don't want anything to do with this."

"You do?"

"Of course I do," Cal said, draining the last of his beer. He crumpled the can up and threw it across the room. It hit one of the French doors and then rolled crookedly across the floor. "You blame *me*. You blame *me* for drinking. For driving too fast. For letting the Jeep roll over."

"No, that's not—," I said. I got up from the table. I started toward him, but he was backing away. He held his arms up as if to ward me off.

"Yes, you do. You think I let Betsy die. You blame *me*."

"No, really, listen, Cal—"

But I don't think he even heard me. He started down the hallway, but then turned back and yelled at me:

"And you want me to feel guilty about it for the rest of my life. Well, fuck that."

I heard him open the front door and then slam it shut behind him. After a moment, I got up to follow him. I had no idea what I was going to do or say—but I hated letting him believe that I blamed him. I heard the Olds start down the driveway at the same time something caught my eye outside. It was snowing. I could see sloppy, mothlike flakes fluttering down through the light from the great room. I opened the door and stepped out onto the terrace. Obviously, it had been snowing for some time and I just hadn't noticed. An inch or two coated the flagstones and blanketed the deck railing. Beyond, I could just make out the contours of the garden, the plants and walkways transformed by the snowfall into soft, amorphous shapes. So that what was actually a rock or a shrub could so easily be—my heart turned over at the thought—a child kneeling down, packing snow into a ball, her back turned to me forever.

15

Cal

❧

*E*dmund stood beside me. He was wearing his best suit, a rep tie, and a dark overcoat I hadn't seen before and suspected he'd purchased for the occasion. I had on my winter parka and jeans, and I was secretly sporting a hangover so bad I thought my head was going to explode. I wasn't expected to do or say anything, thank God. We were just part of the Stephens, Stokes dog-and-pony show. The bereaved father and caring older brother. We were standing to the right of Lester Stephens on the steps in front of the courthouse. A group of reporters and photographers had gathered below us. Two different camera crews were angling for position in the crowd.

"What you see here," Lester was saying as he nodded toward me and Eddie, "is a family torn apart by a senseless tragedy. Betsy Horigan—a beautiful, fun-loving two-year-old—was killed nine months ago in a car accident from which her father, protected by his seat belt alone, walked away unscathed. Why did this little girl die? Because her so-called safety seat, manufactured by Gannon Baby Products, simply fell apart when the Jeep turned over. Why did this little girl die? Because Gannon Baby Products once again put financial gain above product safety.

"My law firm, Stephens, Stokes, Kline, has taken on Gannon before. We've taken them on—and we were able to prove that one of their top-selling portable cribs was nothing but a cute-looking death trap. This time, I've promised my client, Cal Horigan, and his family that—once and for all—I'm going to stop Gannon and their total disregard for the lives of our precious, innocent children. I intend to make Betsy Horigan a name no parent in this state will ever forget. I promise here and now that Betsy Horigan will be Gannon Baby Products' very last victim."

It was bitterly cold. The wind was whipping across the courthouse plaza, ruffling Lester Stephens's hair. But he stood there calmly, taking questions from reporters for another ten minutes or so. I tried to follow along, but between the biting wind and my hangover, my head was throbbing so badly I had a hard time concentrating. These last twenty-four hours have been a real roller-coaster ride.

Edmund told everyone yesterday at our family Christmas dinner that Stephens, Stokes was going to be handling the lawsuit. It was the usual noisy, chaotic affair; three hours to open all the gifts, another two for the sit-down meal. Jenny hadn't come. We've barely spoken since our last fight, and she left a note that morning saying she'd be at her father's house. When I told my family, I made it sound as though Jude had bodily forced her to spend the day there. I said that Jude was fed up having to deal with the reverend on her own. I probably overdid the excuses; I saw Tessa exchange a look with Kurt when I was in the middle of explaining the situation. At the start of dinner, Edmund rose from his chair, tapped his glass, and launched into the big announcement.

I appreciated the fact that he managed to make it seem as though the whole thing was really Stephens, Stokes's idea—that they'd come to us and laid out such a convincing argument against Gannon that we really had no choice but to let them take the case.

"I thought Jenny had some reservations," my dad said.

"She still does," I replied. "But I've come around to thinking that we'd be wrong *not* to go ahead. This law firm we're dealing with sued Gannon before—and won. They had all sorts of really scary information about how dangerous a lot of their products are. Gannon needs to be stopped."

"But I worry, honey, if it's really up to you to stop them," my mom said. "Gannon is such a big name. Shouldn't the government be stepping in on something like this?" My mother's always been superprotective of me, her youngest. I think she still sees me as her baby.

"If enough people file suits the way we are," Edmund replied, "if enough people take up the fight the way we have—then, eventually, the government will have to do something. That's how the law works in this country, Mom. That's how justice gets done." I noticed that Edmund was taking on some of Lester Stephens's speech patterns and mannerisms. I used to think my older brother was kind of pompous and full of himself. But I've come to really appreciate his self-confidence—that take-no-prisoners approach to getting things done. It's true I was a little slow to sign on to all this; Edmund had to convince me we were doing the right thing. But now I don't think I could move ahead with any of it without his direction and support. He seems to *get* the whole process in a way I know the rest of my family probably doesn't.

I glanced across the table at Kurt. He was turned away from me, helping Jamie, who was in a booster seat beside him. Tessa and Kristin were busy moving back and forth from the dining room to the kitchen, bringing in plates of food. It surprised me that Kurt continued to keep quiet as the meal progressed and other members of the family weighed in. I'd been bracing myself, knowing how negative he'd been about going after Gannon. But both he and Tessa stayed out of the conversation.

"So everyone has to watch the local news tomorrow night," Kristin said at one point. "Cal and Edmund are going to be part of a press conference. And we think it's going to be televised."

"Daddy's going to be on TV?" Ava, Edmund's daughter, asked.

"Well, we'll see," Edmund said. "That's what the law firm's saying, anyway." He looked a little embarrassed that Kristin was making such a big deal of this. Maybe it was just me, but I felt pockets of unease around the table. My mom began to grill Edmund about who "these people"—meaning Stephens, Stokes—were. She grew up in Covington, daughter of a prominent lawyer, and tends to view anyone outside a ten-mile radius of our town as somewhat suspect. While Edmund gave her a rundown of the law firm's bona fides, my dad looked down the table at me and said:

"You'll want Jenny by your side on this."

"Yeah, I know," I answered. "Maybe not tomorrow, but she'll be there eventually."

Later, as the others were gathering their gifts and divvying up the leftovers, I managed to get Kurt alone. He was in the front hall, collecting Jamie's things. I pulled him outside. The frigid night air was like a slap to the face.

"You haven't said anything all night."

"You don't want to hear what I have to say."

"That's not true. Your opinion means a lot to me."

"Bullshit! You don't get to have it both ways. You already know what I think. I've been telling you for months and months not to do this without Jenny. But you're going ahead anyway. And the trouble is? I don't think you really even know what you're doing. What you're risking. How close you are to losing every fucking thing that matters."

"That's not—"

"And I'll tell you what else: I've been asking myself all night why you thought you had to lie to me about the car seat. Why not just tell me that day when you asked for it what you were doing? What you and Eddie were plotting? The truth is, you've been lying to me right along. I know you too well, Cal. I know how you work. You haven't just been lying to me. You're lying to yourself. This whole thing is bullshit. It's not taking on Gannon. Rounding up the bad guys. It's not about justice."

"What's it about, then?"

"Sorry, brother," he said, turning around to go inside. "I think you need to figure that one out for yourself."

So I'd gone back to my darkened house. To my wife locked away in my dead little girl's bedroom. I'd pulled down the bottle of Jack Daniels from the cupboard above the refrigerator. The next thing I knew, I was waking up on the couch in the great room in the blinding daylight, as sick as a dog.

Now, as I stood next to Edmund on the courthouse steps, I wondered again what Kurt had meant about my real motives. Hadn't he been the first one to assure me that Betsy's death wasn't my fault? *You actually trying to say you think you're responsible for what happened?* he'd asked me the night of Betsy's funeral. So what was he trying to tell me now? Did he really think so little of me at this point that he figured I was just in this for the payday? I'd been ready for Kurt to be a little pissed off. But it takes a lot to get him mad, and he's always gone so easy on me. So I wasn't really expecting much more than a lecture. Some complaints and caveats. In fact, I'd never seen him as angry as he was last night—at anyone. And it scared the hell out of me.

"What are you contemplating in terms of damages?" I heard a reporter ask Lester, who finally seemed to be feeling the cold. He'd pulled his coat collar up against the wind.

"It's way too early in the process for that discussion," he said, clapping his gloved hands together. "Okay, I think that will do it for today. Thank you all for coming out—and for interrupting your holiday week like this. I look forward to seeing you all in the new year."

As the crowd began to scatter, Lester turned to us and asked, "Would you gentlemen care to join me for lunch? There's a passable little Italian restaurant not far from here that I can recommend."

I was still feeling so rocky that I was about to beg off, but Edmund grabbed my elbow before I could say anything and told Lester, "Yes, sir, thank you, we'd really appreciate that."

Luigi's was a great deal more than passable. It took up all three floors of a restored townhouse down the block from the courthouses. The interior gleamed with mahogany wain-scoting, elegantly carved staircases, and cut-glass chande-liers. Lester seemed to have a regular table. With a nod, the maître d' picked up three menus and led us through the room to a quiet corner in the rear. Lester stopped to chat at a couple of tables while Edmund and I were seated.

"Pull yourself together," Edmund said, picking up his napkin and shaking it out.

"What do you mean?"

"You've been like a zombie all morning. I didn't say any-thing about it in the car coming up here because I figured you were nervous, but I could smell the booze on you. Don't drink anything at lunch."

"Are you my keeper?"

"Don't blow this, Cal," Edmund said. I could tell he wanted to say more, but Lester came up to the table. As he took his seat, he picked up the menu and put it to the side of his place setting, saying, "Don't even bother looking at that. Luigi will come by with the specials and you'll want to pick one of those." Lester ordered a martini, but both Edmund and I said we were fine with the iced water.

"But we have something to celebrate," Lester said. "Don't you think it went well?"

"Yes," I said, before Edmund could jump in. I was deter-mined to take charge of the situation. "You were great. It's just that—all this—it's still pretty hard. It's been a pretty rough Christmas, honestly, for me and my family."

"Of course," Lester said. "I'm sorry. That was thoughtless of me. Sometimes I get a little caught up in the dynamics of the legal process. It may seem dry to you. A couple of pieces of paper change hands inside a courtroom. So what? But, believe me, Cal, the equivalent of a bomb was dropped in there this morning. And I could hear the glass shattering all the way down at Gannon corporate headquarters in Raleigh."

Both Edmund and I followed Lester's lead and ordered something that turned out to be squash soup followed by stuffed pasta shells. I wasn't sure I was going to be able to eat anything, but it turned out to be really good. By the time we'd moved on to espresso and a plate of biscotti, I was almost feeling myself again. Lester led the conversation, but he was skillful at bringing me and Edmund into it, soliciting our opinions and advice. With the offhanded tone of a real insider, he talked about the never-ending political mess in Albany. He seemed to be on a first-name basis with prominent judges and the DA. He'd been at the governor's mansion for some party earlier that week. Over coffee, he swung back to our case:

"You feeling comfortable with Janet and Carl? I think pretty highly of them both, or I wouldn't have brought them into the initial discussions. But it matters more to me that *you're* happy with them. I want you to feel that you're part of a team. Think you can work with them all right?"

"Yes," I said, remembering how Lester had put Janet in her place about my drinking. I think we all knew perfectly well that it was Lester who called all the shots. The rest of them were his minions. "They both seemed fine. So—what happens next?"

"Gannon will come back at us, guns blazing. So be prepared. They'll refute everything we claim. Denounce us as money-grubbing charlatans. But that's all just part of pre-settlement foreplay, so don't let it worry you. And the press will probably start calling you. Wanting comments, et cetera. Now, this is very important: you have nothing to say. Okay? All such questions you refer to Janet. Please let everyone in your family know this, too. Tell them not to talk to anyone about the case—except us. How's Jenny doing, Cal?"

The question seemed to come at me from left field. I hesitated for a moment. How long could I keep telling everyone that Jenny was going to eventually come around? I'd stopped believing it myself.

"She's still in pretty bad shape. But I think maybe the holidays are especially hard on her."

"Of course they are," Lester said, signaling for the check. "Better let her know that Gannon might play rough, okay? I'd prepare her a little for that, Cal. If you like, I'd be happy to sit down and talk to her about all this. What to expect. How to cope with some of the media scrutiny. Please make sure she realizes that we're here for her—as we are for you. Any time of the day or night."

❧

"Sorry about what I said before," Edmund said on the drive back to Covington. "I was out of line. You did great with Lester at lunch."

"Thanks, but you were right to call me on it," I told him. "The drinking, I mean. Jenny and I are having our problems, as you've probably already guessed."

"Bad?"

"Bad enough," I said. I was feeling sick again. The fancy lunch was beginning to churn in my stomach. What the hell was I thinking, knocking back all that coffee? What I needed was a cold beer. Hair of the dog. And I was still reeling inside from the way Kurt had reamed me out. His anger, like Jenny's coldness, makes me feel off-balance. Concussive, all over again. That they're both against me feels wrong, unfair. It feels weird to me that Edmund—and Daniel, so new to my life—are the only ones close to me who seem to really understand. It's as though Betsy's death has fundamentally changed Jenny somehow. And now Kurt, too. Or maybe it's changed me.

"Want to come and watch the news in my office?" Edmund asked as we pulled into the Horigan employee lot behind the store. I'd parked the Olds there that morning and driven up to Albany with Edmund.

"Thanks, but I'd better head home."

"Did you see the Channel Six crew there today?" Edmund asked as we walked together across the parking lot. "Lester sure knows how to draw a crowd."

"Yeah. He's pretty impressive."

"We did good," Edmund told me when we'd reached my car. He patted me on the shoulder. "*You* did good. Don't worry about Jenny. Once she sees how big this thing is, she'll come around."

I stopped at the Cove, the local bar and grill, on the way out of town. It's basically Horigan Lumber's company cafeteria. Big old-fashioned jukebox in the corner. Pool table in the back. Wall-mounted television tuned to sports above the bar. I'm a regular. Darryl was pulling a draft before I even sat down.

"Tough day?" he asked.

"How'd you guess?" I said, tipping back the frosted mug.

"Joel was in for lunch. I think some of the guys are coming back to check out the news coverage. Way to go, Cal. I mean that."

I had another draft before Joel and Nicky and a few of the others showed up. I'd somehow known Lori would be with them. She gave me a smile and a little wave as she took a stool at the end of the bar. The video segment on Gannon lasted about a minute, if that: Lester making his announcement and then a couple of the follow-up questions. At one point the camera panned over to me and Edmund—then zoomed in on me. My eyes were tearing from the wind. I looked grim and heartsick.

A cheer went up in the bar when the news anchor cut to a commercial, and Nicky clapped me on the back.

"Great job, Cal," he said. "We're counting on you to stick it to those fucking bastards!"

I had another beer. I saw Lori get up and go to the ladies' room, then come back and pick up her coat and bag. She glanced my way as she paid up. When I signaled to Darryl for my tab, he shook his head.

"On the house tonight."

I followed Lori outside and down the steps.

"You maybe need another ride home?" I asked her.

"What? No, I have my—," she began, turning to me. She saw the way I was looking at her. "Actually, yes. Of course! I could use a ride."

I wasn't gentle. I wasn't affectionate. I don't think I said a single word when I got her back to her trailer and pulled off her clothes. She was so soft. But hard to hold on to. Her breasts kept slipping out of my hands; her belly wobbled under my weight. It wasn't until she hooked her legs around my back that I fell into a steady rhythm. Then it didn't take long. I was thinking only about me. I locked Jenny out of my mind.

"Yes, Cal, yes," Lori said at one point.

"Shhh," I said, kissing her on the mouth to shut her up. I didn't want to hear her voice. I didn't want to have to think about her. The shabby trailer. The underwear I'd seen drying in the shower stall. The fake miniature Christmas tree blinking on and off from the kitchenette. The scent of lemons that permeated the place, just barely concealing cooking smells—and something earthier that I didn't want to think about. I didn't want to think about anything. Except the blind and furious journey I was on. This narrowing path I'd found. Cutting through my anger and heartache. Obliterating all doubt.

16

Jenny

❦

"Is this Mrs. Horigan?" a male voice asked on the other end of the line. I'd answered only because I thought it might be Daniel. I was supposed to be meeting him for lunch in another two hours, and he was very much on my mind.

"Yes?" I said.

"I'm sorry to bother you at home, but I was wondering about your reaction to the story in the *Times-Union* this morning. Some of those comments from Gannon were pretty harsh. I imagine it must be hard for you and your husband to have to hear that kind of thing."

"I don't know what— Who are you?"

"I'm with the *Courier*. I thought you might want to tell someone—someone local and nonjudgmental—your side of the story. I know this whole thing must be a terrible ordeal for you, but—"

I hung up the phone. My hands were shaking. Cal had warned me the day after his television appearance that this might happen. He'd wanted me to sit down with his big-deal lawyer and be coached on how to handle the press.

"You don't have to worry about me," I'd told my husband. "I'm not the one talking about all this. I'm not the one standing up in front of the television cameras, trying to cash in on my daughter's death."

"Oh, please, Jenny, come on—," he began, but I said, "You know what? As far as I'm concerned, this whole thing just isn't happening. So don't worry about me. I don't have anything to say to anybody."

But, like everyone else in Covington, I'd watched the press conference. Alone, still in my pajamas at noontime, the winter sun slanting through my childless kitchen. I'd taken one look at that slick showman of a lawyer and known I'd guessed right: he'd seen our tragedy as an opportunity— and was running with it. Of course, it helped that he'd faced off against Gannon before. That business about "stopping Gannon once and for all" sure sounded convincing. I could see why Cal was drawn to this big, flamboyant, successful man—and his crusade for so-called justice. Of course Cal admires Lester Stephens. He's allowing my husband to feel like a hero.

I, on the other hand, appear to have taken on the role of martyr. Everyone in the family seems to know now that I'm opposed to the lawsuit. They've been calling—my father-in-law, Kurt, Tessa, Kristin—worried about me. I've been letting the answering machine pick up for the most part, and then playing back their messages. I know they think they understand: all this attention and media coverage must be intrusive and unsettling for me. They imagine that I want to be left alone with my grief. It's been useful to be able to see my situation through their eyes. Their concern has helped me piece together a kind of explanation for my behavior, an alternative reality to the lie that I'm living. And I've discovered that if you just keep lying long enough, it all starts morphing into a kind of quasi truth. Sometimes I can almost let myself believe that the pain that flows through my days is pure—untainted by guilt or deception.

In fact, I have been avoiding reading about the lawsuit and watching the news. Though I've been fully aware that it was only a matter of time before Gannon returned fire. Cal had warned me they'd be denying all charges, which of course came as no surprise to me. I've been trying to prepare myself for the next salvo, wondering how close it would come to hitting on the truth. I think the prospect of seeing Daniel again gave me the courage. On my way to Lansbury, I stopped at a GasMart and picked up a copy of the *Times-Union*. The story was below the fold on the front page.

GANNON BABY PRODUCTS
STANDS BY POPULAR CAR SEAT;
DENOUNCES LAWSUIT

I scanned the article, searching for the "harsh" comments the reporter had asked me about.

"We have sold tens of thousands of this top-rated child's safety seat across the country with no reports of any serious problems. Customers who would like confirmation of this should check the Consumer Product Safety Commission Web site, where they will see that our record for this model is, indeed, pristine. We are, of course, deeply saddened by the death of the claimant's daughter. There is nothing more terrible than losing a child. Our sincere regrets go out to the parents and family of Betsy Horigan. But the cause of this tragic accident lies elsewhere and, if forced to, we will indeed prove it. The reputation of our brand of excellent baby products is on the line, and we do not intend to see it blemished by unscrupulous and predatory legal posturing."

The printed words started to blur. I forced myself to take a deep breath. *The cause of this tragic accident lies elsewhere . . . and we will indeed prove it . . .*

I tossed the paper onto the seat beside me, started the engine, and turned around to back the car out. The backseat was empty, of course. It's been more than nine months since Betsy sat there—directly in my line of vision—buckled into her safety seat. So the ghostly image I saw of my daughter was, I knew, a trick of the eye—or of the memory. It was just some kind of mental imprint from the hundreds of times that I'd turned around in the past to find her there. The same thing happens when I glance at the end of the kitchen counter where her hook-on booster seat used to be. Or in the great room where her chest of toys still sits. Besides the children I sometimes mistake for Betsy, these vague, fleeting glimpses are all I get to have of her these days—just a feeling, a sense. Her voice is almost altogether lost to me now. And yet—for all that—she still seems so real to me. It feels impossible she's not *there*. Because, in so many ways, she's more substantial to me than I am. *I'm* the one who's fading, really. I'm the shadow whose laughter has disappeared.

🙠

The Clear Lake Inn is a rambling white-clapboarded early-nineteenth-century edifice that lays claim to being the longest continuously run hotel in the county. Its beamed public rooms have wide oak floors scattered with large braided rag carpets. The walls are crowded with quaint bric-a-brac: needle-point samplers, silvering tintypes, crossed oars from long-forgotten regattas on the wide, still lake that beckons from the inn's gingerbread porches. Its spacious restaurant is usually bustling, filled with tourists most months of the year. Midweek in mid-January, however, the dining room was nearly empty at lunchtime. Daniel was waiting for me at a quiet table by a window with a view of the frozen-over lake.

"I was beginning to wonder," he said, standing as I came up to the table. He kissed me on the cheek and pulled out my chair for me. At a quick glance, what did our relationship look like? I wondered. A little too close in age to be father and daughter. Uncle and niece? No, but then—not exactly friends either. More teacher and student. Promising student, but one who has perhaps not quite lived up to expectations. Because I got the feeling Daniel was disappointed in some-thing about me: was it my simple gray slacks and navy blue turtleneck? He was wearing one of his designer-looking sports jackets and a striped shirt open at the neck; his hair fell loose to his collar.

"Sorry. I guess I didn't give myself enough time," I said, picking up the menu.

"You look exhausted, Jenny," he said, scrutinizing me across the table. "Put that thing down. Talk to me."

"I *am* tired," I said, allowing myself to feel the full weight of not sleeping more than a few hours each night. For months and months now.

"What's going on?"

"What's going on?" I asked, staring at him. "Don't you know?"

"No. Sorry. I've been in the city," he said. He tilted his head, appraising me in that intense, half-amused way that he has. I sensed he was sizing me up, trying to plumb the depths of whatever new trauma had taken hold in my life. Not for the first time, I got the feeling that he found my anguish attractive in some way. Intriguing.

"Cal's lawyers officially filed the claim. It's been all over the television and radio up here. There was a big piece in the *Times-Union* today, quoting the car-seat manufacturer—Gannon—who said the claim was unscrupulous and predatory."

"Of course that's what they were going to say," he replied. "They're running a business. Which I imagine they'll fight tooth and nail to protect." He signaled across the room to a waiter. "I think you could use a drink."

I didn't stop him when he ordered a bottle of wine. Though I almost never drink at lunch, today I was beyond caring. I wanted to feel numbed. Lulled. Daniel's presence was already helping a little, but it only made me long for a more sustained kind of relief. Being with him again made me realize how much I'd been holding back, how long I'd been keeping everything bottled up inside me. Once again, I wondered why he was the only one I seemed to be able to trust with the truth.

"Gannon says that they're going to prove the car seat wasn't the cause of Betsy's death," I told him after the waiter had uncorked the wine and left us alone. "Do you think they really can? Prove it was my fault, I mean?"

"Take a drink, Jenny. Relax for a moment. Look out at that beautiful landscape. The way the sunlight plays across the surface of the lake."

I stared out the window.

"Nothing looks beautiful to me anymore," I said. "The world—this winter—everything just looks dead."

"You've been spending too much time alone. Too much time in your own head. Going over this one thing again and again."

"You're right. How did you know?" I asked, looking back at him. He was smiling, that little gap showing between his front teeth. Though I'd taken only a couple of sips of the wine, I was already feeling drowsy. For a moment, I had the craziest notion that Daniel was hypnotizing me. But I knew it was only because I was so exhausted. Exhausted—and so utterly relieved to be with him again. To be able to talk to him like this: freely and openly. I felt that I could tell him anything and that he wouldn't judge me for it.

"I'm hardly psychic," he replied, "but I do like to think I'm a little empathetic. Especially when it comes to desirable women."

"God, it feels like years since I've even thought of myself as a woman. Let alone desirable."

"You see? I knew that, too," he said with a laugh. "And I think we have to do something to remedy the situation."

I heard him, but I didn't respond. I heard him, but I didn't let myself really register what it meant. What he might be after. I was feeling too good—for the first time in how many months? Since the last time I'd seen him, I realized. This was all I needed, I thought. Just the chance to be with Daniel. If I had that, if I had him to talk to from time to time, maybe I could somehow find a way to make it through the lawsuit, the media, my own terrible doubts. We ordered lunch. The sunlight had shifted and was now streaming in the window, full on my face. I remembered what it was like to have the world feel safe and warm.

"You didn't answer my question before," I told him. "About Gannon being able to prove what I did—or didn't do. Do you think they can?"

"You're just assuming they know," he said, breaking off a piece of the bread the waiter had put between us. He buttered it before he continued. "Even *you're* not absolutely sure what really happened. I think you've convinced yourself that you're to blame—but, honestly, I doubt that anyone can prove anything definitively at this point. I don't think it's nearly as black-and-white as you seem to imagine it is. Life never is. Each side will argue its case, and whichever one is the most persuasive wins. In the end, I don't think the facts—let alone the truth—will factor all that much into the ultimate decision."

"Do you really believe that?" I asked. "It sounds so cynical."

"Cynical? No, I think I'm being realistic," he said, reaching over and taking my hand. "I'm just playing the devil's advocate, Jenny." I remembered the feeling of his lips on my palms, the roughness of his beard against my skin—and shivered. I pulled my hand away when the waiter approached with our plates.

The meal went by in a blur. I ate, or tried to; my attention was so focused on Daniel. He talked to me at length about a major project he'd been invited to bid on, landscaping the new corporate headquarters for a multinational bottling company in Westchester. I only half listened as I let myself bask in the pure pleasure of his voice—hoarse, breaking occasionally like an adolescent boy's—compelling in its intimacy.

Toward the end of the meal, I excused myself and got up to use the ladies' room. It was almost three o'clock and the restaurant and restrooms were empty. I looked in the mirror and saw that my cheeks were flushed, my eyes shining. I could still hear the cadenced rhythms of Daniel's voice in my head: *I think we have to do something to remedy the situation.* I knew what I had come for that day: the impartial hearing—and absolution—only Daniel seems able to give me. But, for the first time, I really forced myself to face why Daniel was there. What he was assuming about me—us—the rest of the afternoon. I should never have agreed to meet him in such an out-of-the-way place, I realized, an inn, no less. What was I thinking? I understood then that I had to leave immediately. Go back and thank him for lunch—and get the hell away from there.

"Are you okay?" he asked when I returned to the table.

"Yes, but I think I should probably—"

"Hold on a minute. I haven't finished telling you about the project," he said. "The best part."

"Okay," I said, standing beside my chair. "What is it?"

"They called me this morning: I got the gig."

"Oh, that's great—"

"So I'll be moving back to the city for a while."

I found myself sitting down again.

"You're leaving?" I asked. Abruptly, as if a cloud had cut off the sun, the afternoon fell back into shadow. "For how long?"

"Six months. A year. It's always hard to say for sure. I'm planning to sublet a place. These days I should be able to find something pretty spectacular."

He sounded so pleased with himself. Lighthearted. I just stared at him. I couldn't believe he'd known about this through the entire lunch and had just thought to tell me now. Had he no idea what it meant to me? How desperate I'd been for his company—and what solace he'd been able to bring to me just by listening? By simply being there. The very thought of losing him now panicked me. I tried my best to appear calm when I said:

"But—you'll be coming back to visit."

"Well, we'll see. Luckily, my place in Northridge is on a month-to-month lease."

"But—" My lips felt rubbery, and I found myself unable to form the words I wanted. I couldn't help it. Without him, I knew I would be utterly lost. I felt abandoned. How could I find the strength to keep going?

"What's the matter?"

"I don't want you to leave," I blurted out. It almost felt as though he'd kept this news from me on purpose—and then sprung it on me when I was at my most vulnerable. "I don't want you to go."

"I was hoping you'd feel that way," he said, standing up and coming around the table to me. "That's exactly what I wanted to hear. I don't want *you* to go either, Jenny. I could reserve a room for us. Come—"

"No—Daniel—that's not what I mean—I can't—"

He took both of my hands in his. He pulled me to my feet and kissed my palms. I felt a shock of recognition—the moment moving backward and forward in time, all in a split second. I'd been with him before. I would be with him again. I could feel tears burning along my eyelids. I had to find a way to keep him. He couldn't go. I couldn't let him go.

❦

I've never cheated on Cal. I've never even considered doing so. Perhaps this is the way it is with all adulterers—at least the first time—but what I did with Daniel didn't feel like that to me at first. Like a betrayal, I mean. Or a sin. A mortal sin, as my father would have it. The kind that could put my soul in jeopardy. Because my soul seemed to have so little to do with it. This was all about my body—almost as if it had become an entity wholly separate from the rest of me.

Daniel gave me no time to think about what was happening. He pulled me into his arms the moment he closed the door behind us—and didn't let me go. I caught a glimpse of the prettily decorated room with its four-poster bed and swagged curtains—the winter afternoon outside the paned windows already tinged with sunset. Then I closed my eyes. He seemed to be everywhere at once—lips at my neck, hands in my hair, along my shoulders, cupping my breasts. He knew what he was doing. I had just enough presence of mind to register that; he was an experienced lover. But also intuitive and generous. He knew what he was doing—and he enjoyed giving and taking pleasure. I think I'd sensed this about him from the very beginning: making love was what Daniel *did*. His real calling. He was in his true element now.

"Give me your tongue," he said. He had backed me up against the door, the length of his body pressed against mine. He put his hands under my backside and started lifting me up. Without thinking, I wrapped my legs around him. I gave him my tongue. I did what he told me. And he gave me a lot of instructions: faster . . . harder . . . slower. I literally put myself in his hands. I'm not sure why I was so utterly submissive. I wasn't thinking about what I was doing—just what Daniel told me I *should* do. I wasn't thinking about guilt then either. Or whether letting Daniel be in charge somehow made me less responsible. I just knew that I had to give myself over to him—to let him do to me whatever he wanted.

Only later would I wonder if what *I* really wanted was to be punished. Toward the end, especially, Daniel got a little rough. We were on the bed, and he had pinned my arms above my head before he straddled me again. I was sore by then, and it hurt. I cried out at one point, but he didn't stop. And slowly the pain eased, the pain changed. I heard myself whimpering from a long way off. Then I forgot everything. I was moving blindly. Toward some sort of light. I had a flash of pushing against a door that was half ajar—of the door falling open—and then of hurtling into oblivion.

Part Three

17

Cal

❧

The holidays were over, and Kurt and I were back at work. Or at least back in our office above the outbuilding at Kurt's where we store our heavy equipment. It's been totally dead business-wise. It's always slow in the winter months, but this year it feels like construction's never going to bounce back. You can't turn on the television or pick up the newspaper without hearing how the economy's still cratering. The stock market's down. And the country's just hemorrhaging jobs and money and confidence. How the hell did things get this bad? I know the problems started months before Betsy was killed, but I can't help but feel that these disasters are somehow interconnected. That the larger world and my own life are spiraling out of control together.

I'm lying to Jenny all the time now. Lying about where I am half the night. Who I'm with. I don't even need to put much effort into it. Jenny and I are communicating so little these days, it's easy to get away with things. It still bothers the hell out me, but at least I'm not lying to *myself* about

Jenny as Kurt accused me of doing with Gannon. I know full well I'm cheating on her. And it feels all wrong. I'm the first to admit that. For one thing, I don't much like the person I become when I'm with Lori. She keeps telling me I have every reason to be moody. But I know I'm just being selfish. Sometimes, I'm even downright mean. I probably drink too much when I'm with her, too. And I'm afraid I make it pretty clear that I'm not putting a whole lot of work into the "relationship," as she referred to it a few days ago.

"You must have guessed by now that I always had a thing for you?" she said, turning to me in that crappy fold-out bed of hers. I could feel the metal crossbars digging into my spine. "And I just want you to know that, no matter where our relationship is going? I'm happy. I just feel so happy and grateful every time I see you that I want to cry."

It's sad, really. I don't love her and, on some level, I think she has to know that. But she gives me things that I really need right now. Sex is part of it, sure. But she also seems to be doing everything she can to make me feel good about myself—and what I'm trying to do. She's been following the Gannon media coverage like a hawk, clipping out news items, surfing the Internet, watching the local television reports. I'll swing by her trailer after a few beers at the Cove and she'll have this little pile of Gannon stories waiting for me on her kitchen table. I think she must have somehow learned about Jenny's stand on the lawsuit, though we have yet to mention my wife's name. It feels kind of weird to be sharing all the details of my daughter's death with Lori. But I need to talk to someone who's behind me on this, and she's always so eager to hear how things are going. I think she believes that it's what brought us together—and what might keep us there.

At this point, though, I'm just thinking day to day. Edmund and I have been back up to Albany twice now to help Stephens, Stokes draw up a list of witnesses and prepare for our depositions. Each time I go over the details of my daughter's last day alive—the unseasonably warm weather, the baseball game, my home run—I find that I'm remembering things a little differently.

"Who brought the keg to the game?" Janet asked me last week. We were in a smaller conference room than the one where we'd first met. It was an interior space, windowless, nicely decorated with posters and leather chairs, but still a little claustrophobic.

"Keg? I don't think we had a keg. Just a cooler."

"And how many beers did you have? I think you said—was it a couple?—when we talked about this before. Do you remember?"

I'm no fool. I knew she was prepping me to go on the record, and then Gannon would have access to everything I said. I couldn't outright lie, but on the other hand, who but me would know the full truth? Edmund and I had given Stephens, Stokes names and numbers of people who were at the game: Burt Mayer, Mike Lerner, Denny Lockhardt, and, of course, Kurt. Who among them would be able say for sure how many beers they'd had that afternoon—almost ten months ago now—let alone how many I'd put away?

"Let me think," I said, closing my eyes as if trying to dredge up a clearer memory. "Yeah—I guess—that sounds about right. A couple."

Though I've been able to successfully skirt around certain issues with Stephens, Stokes, I've been having a much harder time trying to figure out how to finesse things with

Kurt. Everything's changed between us since Edmund and I went public with the lawsuit at Christmas. It's like some curtain's come down, or a wall's gone up. Kurt's there physically, but he's just kind of turned himself off when it comes to me. We never joke around anymore. I used to be able to just about read his thoughts. Now, half the time, I have no idea what's on his mind. He spends almost every minute he's in the office playing online solitaire, his broad back to me, hunched over his keyboard. So I was surprised—and momentarily elated—when, in mid-January, he banged up the steps, slammed open the door, and, before he even took off his coat, said, "We need to talk."

I was at my computer already, trolling for news about Gannon Baby Products. I've got them and Stephens, Stokes on Google Alerts, though most of the items are just a bunch of corporate PR gobbledygook.

"Sure," I said, pushing back my chair. "But shut the damn door. Stay a while."

He closed the door, and then leaned against it.

"That's just it," he said, digging his hands into his coat pockets. "I can't anymore. Stay, I mean, Cal. We both know this whole thing is pretty fucked up."

I decided to pretend he meant Horigan Builders.

"Yeah, well. Us and the rest of the construction business. Us and the rest of the whole fucking economy, right? What can you do about it?"

"I've been talking to Tessa," he said, looking at the floor. It hit me then that he was actually uncomfortable. Nervous. I've never known Kurt to avoid eye contact. He's the most laid-back guy imaginable. But now his unease filled the room like a bad smell.

"I've been talking it over with Tessa," he said again, "and we think it would be better for us—both you and me—if I stepped back from Horigan Builders for a while."

"What's that supposed to mean?" I asked, sitting up. My palms were sweaty even though the room was cold. "Step back?"

"I'm not happy sitting around doing nothing."

"Oh, come on, Kurt—it's January, for chrissakes—"

"No. We've been dead in the water over a year now. I've got a fucking mortgage eating me alive, okay? And . . . well . . . I just can't do this anymore."

It was anger and fear that made me say, "Well, good luck, there, brother, finding something else to do." I thought I had him. I suppose I thought that I was going to shame him somehow. Since when did I want to see Kurt humiliated?

But he didn't flinch. He just took a deep breath and said, "South County Regional needs an assistant coach. Tessa got me an interview, and they offered me the job yesterday. The money's pretty much chickenshit. But the head coach is set to retire next year, and they think I might be able to step up."

"Step up. Step back," I said. "Jesus, Kurt, which way are you heading? I don't think you know what the hell you're doing."

For years now, Horigan Builders has been such an ego boost. It had felt so good to take that initial risk—get out from under Dad's wing, borrow the money—and have it all pan out in such a public and spectacular way. In the beginning, Kurt and I could hardly believe our luck. The first year we cleared enough to buy our own truck—a Ford diesel Super Duty—and we had "Horigan Builders" painted on the sides. I'll never forget the look on my dad's face. He loved the fact that we'd made good on our own. And that was even before the business took off.

When the ball really got rolling, when we got more jobs than we could handle on our own and started adding crews and equipment, it still seemed so easy. We developed a reputation for being reliable, trustworthy, and cost conscious. But we'd been raised that way—anybody could tell you that. We were Jay Horigan's boys. I never felt we had to work hard at anything—despite the ten-hour days—it all just naturally came our way. It seemed like the phone didn't stop ringing for months at a time. You'd see our pickups and flatbeds emblazoned with the Horigan Builders logo throughout the county.

But, in many ways, the best part of the whole deal has been working side by side with Kurt. It's not just that I've spent most of my life looking up to him; it's that we've always had this amazing, almost psychic understanding—like that supertight harmony siblings' voices can produce. I loved the way we played off each other when we were pitching jobs, Kurt the laid-back, courteous good ole boy and me the more in-your-face sales guy. It's like we were in the zone: that state of grace so many athletes talk about. Kurt's been such a constant in my life. Always a few years and more than a few steps ahead of me. He's the one I've followed. Until lately anyway.

"So we have one bad year," I went on when Kurt just stood there. "One bad year in how many really great ones? We're going to pull out of this. Just like everybody else. I've never known you to be a quitter before, Kurt."

"Sorry," he said. "This is for the best."

"Bullshit. Don't you dare try to hand me that."

"You really want to get into it again?" Kurt asked, crossing his arms on his chest. He was the most out of shape I think I've ever seen him. In the last six months or so, he's put on twenty pounds easy, and it's gone mostly to his middle. I can hear him wheeze under his breath these days when we're going up the outside steps. We've both known for years now that I'd be able to take him in a fight. Today was the first time in my life I ever actually wanted to.

"Maybe we should," I told him. "Maybe you should tell me what's really on your mind."

"Don't push me."

"Well, I am—I want to hear."

"Okay," he said, rocking forward, then back on his heels. "I got a call from your law firm. Apparently, you gave them my name as a witness. They want to talk to me."

"Yeah, they're going to depose you—it just means they're going to ask you some questions about what happened that day."

"I know what a deposition is. The first thing you do is put your hand on the Bible and swear you're telling the truth."

"You make it sound like you're going to be on *Law & Order* or something. It's really not that big a deal."

"Maybe not to you, Cal. But then, you're not the one who's going to be asked these particular questions, are you? Under oath. About how much you'd had to drink. About what kind of shape you were in when we found you."

"What the fuck are you saying?" I said. My voice was shaking. I was that mad—or afraid.

"Do I really need to tell you after all this?" Kurt asked, shaking his head. "After all the times I tried to warn you off this goddamned lawsuit? Do I really have to explain it to you? How I made a decision that afternoon—at what was probably the worst moment of my life—how I made the decision to try and protect you. You—and Jenny."

"But—you kept telling me I wasn't to blame." I said. "What was I supposed to believe?"

"I guess I thought you knew what I was trying to do," Kurt replied. "I could already see the heartbreak you were facing. What was the point of you feeling guilty on top of all that? Being arrested, maybe? Destroying your reputation? As far as I was concerned, you'd been punished enough already. Just let it go, I thought. I wanted to make sure that you and Jenny had a real shot at moving on with your lives. I thought you understood. Since when do I have to spell something like that out for you?"

"So what's going on with you now? You're suddenly changing your story here? You're going to tell them I was drunk or something?"

Kurt didn't say anything. He just looked at me.

"I don't believe this!" I said. "You're really planning to fuck this up for me?"

"I don't want to do that," he replied. "But—I want you to know—this is costing me, Cal. It's costing me a lot—and I'm still not convinced what you and Eddie are doing is right."

❦

Outwardly, nothing much changed. Kurt just stopped coming in. But as things had been so tense between us toward the end anyway, I told myself it was actually for the best. It also meant I could keep the hours I wanted. I started leaving early, hitting the Cove on my way over to Lori's place. Kurt and I agreed that we'd split the take on the Ravitch job, though I'd oversee the rest of the construction. At this point, we had everything done but the kitchen and bath interiors, straightforward inside work that the crew should have finished by the end of February. Any new projects coming in would be mine, but I wasn't beating down any doors looking for prospects. It wasn't just that the economy was so bad; I was already beginning to factor that enormous Gannon payout into my future.

"What the hell are you going to do with all that money?" Edmund had asked me on the way back from our last trip to Albany.

"I'm not counting any chickens," I told him. "I don't want to jinx the whole deal." But I realized that I was no longer claiming the money didn't matter to me. Slowly, it had stopped being a sideshow in the Gannon proceedings—and had taken center stage. Every discussion we had now with Lester, Janet, and the others seemed to involve the underlying equation of Betsy's death and my financial gain: from the actual pain and suffering of my daughter's loss, to its effect on my ability to concentrate and work, to the pressure it might be putting on my marriage.

"Jenny feeling any better?" Lester asked me. He'd told me to drop by his private office at the end of my most recent session with Janet. It was the first time I'd been invited into the inner sanctum—an enormous corner slice of the building with expansive views of downtown Albany.

"I don't think so," I told him. I never fudge the facts with Lester. I believe he has a kind of X-ray vision when it comes to people—that he could probably see straight through the walls of my heart. I also sense that he'd be merciless if he caught me lying. I'm beginning to understand that it's his job to manipulate reality, and he needs to know exactly where things stand in order to do so convincingly.

"She seeking therapy?"

"No. She hardly leaves the house these days. She's cut herself off from just about everybody." Though I had heard her on the phone when I got home around midnight a few nights ago, her tone surprisingly intimate and confiding. When I'd asked her who she'd been talking to, she looked upset that I'd been listening but then told me it was Jude. I remember feeling jealous that she would still be so open with Jude—and closed tight to me.

"I think you should encourage her to get some help," Lester said. For a moment or two I was touched by his concern. Lester often projects a certain benevolent, almost fatherly, aura.

"If she remains determined not to get involved with this," he continued, "then we'll need a valid reason for her absence. If there's evidence that she's become agoraphobic, say, that could work. We could make the case that this tragedy has severely damaged her emotional equilibrium. But getting her into some kind of treatment program—one that could allow us to document her fragile state from outside sources—would be extremely helpful."

"I see your point," I told him. What does it say about my own state of mind that I'd never thought of suggesting Jenny get counseling until Lester planted the seed? "I'll try to talk to her about it."

"I apologize in advance for prying," he went on as he ran his right index finger along the bottom ridge of his mustache.

"But this is actually a relevant legal question. Has your sex life with Jenny been disturbed by Betsy's death?"

"How is that of any legal interest?" I demanded, my face flushing.

"If you're being denied marital relations—well, that's one more offense we can add to the others we're heaping onto the Gannon damages pile."

"I see," I said, looking past him to the snow-shrouded city below. I tried to remember the last time Jenny and I had made love before Betsy died but could come up with no clear mental picture of it. Instead, the many hundreds of times we'd done so came back to me in a rush—all rolled into one wild, joyful, heart-leaping memory. Jenny, slim and lovely, shimmying out of her nightgown and tossing it over her head. Laughing as she collapsed into my arms. The smell of her skin, her breath tickling my ear. I shut my eyes for a moment, remembering her touch, her lips moving across my body.

"If you consider this too private," I heard Lester say, "don't worry about it. I'm just trying to muster all the ammunition I can. And it plays into the question of her non-participation—if she's not functioning in normal ways, well, we can turn that into a positive, I think."

"Right," I said, opening my eyes again to register the dull afternoon that was already giving way to night. The whole world seemed composed of shades of gray. Kurt had walked out on me more than a week ago. And, though outwardly nothing much had changed, inwardly it had. Kurt had been my rudder. I'd always known that, but now I began to realize what it meant to have him gone. How quickly a person could drift. How swiftly I'd left my usual markers behind and—

vaguely against my will, but not protesting—let myself be sucked up into the fast-moving currents of the Gannon lawsuit.

I'd given myself over to it entirely, I realized. I'd given up the people I loved most in my life—Jenny and Kurt—for this. For what? I asked myself again. For justice? Revenge? The hard, bright moments of certainty were gone now. I was being pulled along in the powerful slipstream of need and desire. I'd made my mind up a long time ago, I realized. But it was only now that I was beginning to understand the pathway I had chosen. Ribbons of streetlights blinked on below me in the dusk.

"Sure," I told Lester, looking up and meeting his watchful, discerning gaze. "Why not? Go ahead and pile it on."

18

Jenny

❦

I've always prided myself on the way I managed to
build my own life—free of my father's strictures and
the long shadows cast by my mother's departure. I thought
I'd constructed this existence—as the New Testament
advised—on rock. Primarily on the bedrock of my marriage
to Cal. Though from time to time I've felt tremors—especially
after Betsy was born—I considered them for the most part
just the normal doubts many new mothers must feel. I tried
hard not to let Betsy or Cal pick up on any of my misgivings.
I did my best to ignore them myself: that queasy sense of
uncertainty. The feeling that the earth was shifting under my
feet. The truth that I've come to recognize only now: I've
built on sand.

Daniel and I were together twice more before he left for
Manhattan. We met at his apartment in Northridge, where
he was in the middle of packing. I hated seeing all those open
boxes. I felt sick when he talked so enthusiastically about the
sublet he'd found on the Upper West Side. He'd told me it

had a spectacular view of the Hudson River and the George Washington Bridge.

"But you'll be coming back to visit, right?" I asked him again the final afternoon we were together in Northridge. We'd made love on the floor, as his furniture was already en route to the new place. At one point, he'd pulled me on top of him. My knees were scraped raw by the floorboards. "You promised."

"No," he said, "I never promise. And, to be honest, I doubt I'll be back. There's no work for me up here now."

"Don't say that!" I told him, then immediately regretted my tone. I didn't want him to realize what a hold he had on me. How desperate I felt at the thought of him being a hundred miles away. But I tried to sound playful when I added: "I bet you're going to miss me more than you think."

"Oh, I already know I'm going to miss you," he said, propping his head on his elbow as he turned to look down at me. He ran his right index finger around my breasts, lazily sketching a figure eight. "Why don't you consider coming down to the city for a while? The place I'm subletting has a king-sized bed. Think what we could find to do with each other on that."

Daniel promised to call me the day he moved. I carried my cell phone around with me the whole time, checking every half hour or so to make sure it was still charged. Just before dark, feeling restless and edgy, I went outside to the garden, hoping to find something of his presence—and the solace it brings me—there. In winters past, I'd always enjoyed spending time outside, taking my notebooks and catalogs, starting to plan for next summer. Which seeds to buy, how soon I can start pruning and planting. Like nature itself, it seems to me that a gardener does a lot of maintenance work in the winter months. But I was too anxious that afternoon to take any pleasure in the prospect of a new season, the next cycle of growth. And what was the point? Daniel's garden was essentially a finished thing—each shrub and perennial placed just so. It would start the spring ready-made and in perfect shape. It would never really need me.

By eleven that night, I couldn't stand it anymore. I called him. He apologized, saying he'd actually intended to phone much earlier but had fallen asleep, exhausted. His voice did sound muffled, as though he was lying down. But I'd worked myself up into such a state, I imagined him with another woman. I closed my eyes, light-headed with jealousy.

"Are you alone?" I asked him.

"I'm flattered you think I have that kind of stamina," he said, laughing. Then, the laughter fading, he said, "I want to be inside you." I pictured him on the bed. I imagined floor-to-ceiling windows and the way the bridge lights might look against the night sky. It was then that I realized I had already made up my mind.

"I was thinking of taking you up on your offer," I said. "Do you still want me to come down for a visit?"

"Of course I do. Could you manage it?"

"Yes," I told him. "I'll find a way."

❦

It was Cal, ironically, who gave me the idea.

"I think you should consider getting some help," he'd told me earlier in the week. "Someone you can talk to about what you're going through. You just can't stay holed up in the house like this forever. I know your dad is pretty useless. And I guess at this point, as far as you're concerned, I'm a big part of the problem."

He was standing just outside Betsy's room, dressed for work. He knew enough to knock and wait for my okay before opening the door. He knew enough not to cross the threshold. This was the first time in quite a while that I'd seen him in the unforgiving light of morning. He needed a haircut. He'd lost weight. His expression was both sad and sheepish. Someone had put him up to this suggestion, I realized. Kurt? No, probably Tessa.

"Okay, I'll think about it," I told him, my thoughts already leaping ahead to Daniel. I spent the next few days on the Internet, making phone calls, weighing the possibilities. I decided to call Cal at work rather than lie to his face. No one picked up, and I was surprised when I left a message that it was Cal's voice on the answering machine. For years now, I'd been used to hearing Kurt's: "You've reached Horigan Builders. We're not here right now, but . . ." The new greeting was simply "Hi, it's Cal. Leave a message."

He called me back about an hour later on his cell.

"Is everything okay?" he asked. The cell phone service in our area is often patchy. I could hardly hear him; his voice was almost a whisper.

"I think I found something that I want to try. It's this meditation center in Westchester where you can go—and sort of retreat from the world. It's for a month. But you need to stay cut off from your regular life the whole time you're there—no phone calls or e-mail."

"This sounds good, Jenny. Let's talk about it some more tonight."

I was prepared for his questions and concerns by the time he got home around nine, unusually early for him these days. I'd thought through my whole improvised scenario with care. It seemed perfect, though perhaps that's because it gave me exactly what I wanted: Daniel, free and clear. I didn't even consider telling Cal the truth. I don't think I actually know what it is anymore. But now that the door has been opened, I can't wait to escape—from my husband, Gannon, the last lingering scent of Betsy on the baby pillow that I've been sleeping with all these months.

"But how will I get in touch with you if something happens?" Cal asked me. He was so amenable to all my fabrications. I hated how gullible he was. How willing. How could he be so blind to who I really was?

"I'll leave the number with Jude," I told him.

❦

Telling Cal had been easy. I assumed Jude, who tends to zone out on discussions that don't relate directly to her, would be the same. But something in my tone must have alerted her.

"Where in Westchester? For a whole month? I don't get it. This sounds so sort of woo-woo. Not like you at all."

I was sitting on the chair by the vanity, Jude sprawled across one of the twin beds, in the upstairs bedroom the two of us had shared growing up. Since moving back in with my dad, Jude has tried to liven things up with her brightly patterned hand-sewn quilts and throw pillows, but they're no match for the residue of unhappy memories that seem embedded in the very walls. Out of long habit, we were whispering, though our father, half-deaf anyway, was downstairs in his study behind closed doors.

"In case you haven't noticed, I actually haven't been myself for quite a while now."

Jude's eyes narrowed. She sat up on the bed, studying me.

230 ぎ LIZA GYLLENHAAL

"What's going on? And don't give me this bullshit. You're not going to any monastery or whatever."

"I don't know why—"

"Jenny! Hello? It's *me* you're talking to, okay? *You don't have to be afraid. I'm here.* Remember?"

It's what I used to tell her when we were kids and things got really bad. It's what I used to say to her after she left Covington, and she'd call me collect long-distance, drunk or stoned, begging for my forgiveness. Something gave way inside me.

"I'm leaving Cal," I told her.

"Oh, fuck—no!" she said, swinging her legs around to the floor. "Don't do it! So he didn't listen to you about Gannon? So he has to play the martyred hero? There are a lot worse things than that, Jen. A lot worse people. Far, far worse. Believe me."

"It's not the lawsuit," I said, looking out the window, unable to meet her gaze. I doubt it's an actual memory. More something pieced together from fragmented facts and overheard conversations. But I have this vision of my mother—red haired, long legged, her smile bright with lipstick—waving to me from the back of a motorcycle. She's waving with one arm, while the other is wrapped around the waist of a man whose face I cannot see.

For the first time in my life, I think I'm beginning to understand what must have driven her to abandon Jude and me. I always believed it was because she simply didn't care enough about us. But now I know that you can love someone deeply—the way I do Cal—and need something else. If "need" is even the word. "Crave" is closer. Is this how an addict feels? Nothing much matters to me now except being with Daniel. His body pounding into mine. Rules, caution, guilt—my old life's been swept away. I can no longer remember the person I tried to be for so long.

"What, then? I know it's been rough, Jen. I can't imagine what you've been going through. But you guys have just got to hang in there for a while longer. Just get through this lawsuit. It'll work out."

"I don't think so."

"Jesus," Jude said, shaking her head. "I hate this. You and Cal have, like, one of the few marriages in the whole world I actually have some real faith in."

"Is that why you tried to wreck it before it even began?" I said. Even now, more than six years later, my anger's still raw. That's one reason I've tried my best to put the damned memory in a lockbox and throw the key away. It was the cause of so much heartache and misunderstanding—none of which has ever really been resolved.

It happened the Christmas that Cal and I had announced our engagement. Cal's folks had invited me, Jude, and my father to the annual Horigan Christmas dinner at the farmhouse that, a year later, Cal and I would be given as a wedding present. The dinner was the same noisy, rambunctious affair that I'd soon become accustomed to. But if I'd known then how much drinking would be involved, I would never have encouraged my father to come. I watched him sit in judgment through the entire meal, his dour half smile doing little to conceal his disapproval. Jude, on the other hand, took full advantage of the Horigans' liberal approach to teenage drinking. Out of sight of our father, I saw her chug down at least three beers over the course of the night—and who knows how many more when I wasn't looking?

232   LIZA GYLLENHAAL

After helping Cal's mother and aunts with the dishes, I'd gone upstairs to use the bathroom, and, as I passed a closed bedroom door, I heard Jude talking to someone. I stopped to listen.

"I don't think you understand," I heard her say.

"That's because you . . . ," Cal replied. I leaned in closer but could still make out only snippets of their conversation.

"Why is it that . . . I never . . . Well, I think you do . . . ," Jude continued, her voice rising.

I couldn't hear Cal's response, but then I heard Jude cry out:

"No! I don't want to—"

Alarmed, I pulled the door open and saw Cal holding Jude by her wrists, my sister's face damp with tears. Why did I jump to the conclusion I did? I think it's because, though I was desperately in love with Cal, I still wasn't able to believe in him—in us. Experience told me that it was just a matter of time before my happiness came crashing down. And here was the proof! I'd almost willed it to happen. That he would betray me was bad enough, but that he'd do so with my younger sister, whom I'd spent my life protecting, was unforgivable.

But the truly unforgivable thing turned out to be Jude allowing me to believe for almost a full week that Cal had made the first move. Or that he'd shown the least amount of interest. When in fact he'd been horrified. When, in fact, Jude's "No! I don't want to—" had been brought on by Cal telling her she was being stupid and irresponsible and that "she should try to grow up."

"Aren't you ever going to get over that?" Jude asked me now. "I've explained it to you about a thousand times: I was just jealous. I was desperate. I still am, honestly. But I'll be the first person to tell you that you're making a huge mistake."

"I can forgive what you did," I told her. "But I'll never get over you letting me believe it was Cal's fault for so long. That nearly wrecked us, you know. Letting me think—"

"But you know what?" she said. "I never lied to you about what happened. You told me you didn't want to talk about it. That you never wanted to talk about it. You did one of your suffering-in-silence routines and just shut me out. Like you're doing now! Like you do every time anything really painful happens. Well, I'm fed up with you playing the big martyrish sister role. I want to know what the fuck is going on with you. Now."

"Okay," I told her. I think I wanted to see her shocked. I wanted to see her painful belief in my marriage shattered. "I'm not going to a retreat in Westchester. I'm moving down to the city to be with Daniel."

"Who?"

"Daniel Brandt. The landscape architect who redid our garden. We're— We've been—"

"You? You and Brandt? When the hell did this start?"

"It's been—"

"I don't believe this. That guy? You're leaving Cal for him? Are you crazy? He's a player. I know the type. I knew as soon as I saw him. I mean, yeah, sure, he's pretty hot. I understand the draw. But let me tell you, there's only one thing he's interested in. You can't be doing this. It's just totally unlike you."

"I've changed, then. Or I've finally faced who I really

am. Because I can't *not* be doing it. I don't feel like I have a choice. I can't go on the way I have been—without him."

"Oh no—don't do it!" Jude said. "I'm telling you— you're making a terrible, terrible mistake."

I stared at her. Who was she to tell me what to do? How to behave? As I got up from the chair, I said, "You know, I think this is the first time in my life—I mean the only damn time I can remember—that I've actually asked for your support and understanding. And this is how you respond? Thanks a lot!"

I turned to leave the room, but she jumped off the bed and grabbed my arm.

"No, listen. I'm sorry. I'm really, really sorry. You've kept me alive, Jen, kept me sane for a long time. I owe you so much. So I just have to tell you again that what you and Cal have is special. I know. Do you know why I know? Because I watch other couples, trying to figure out if they're happy, if they're close—and, if they seem to be, what the big secret is. What the hell's wrong with me—and the guys I choose—that I can't seem to find that kind of happiness, too? I've been watching the two of you from the very beginning—watching and wanting what you had—"

"Okay! Enough!" I wrenched my arm free. "This isn't about you, okay? For once in your life, why don't you try to think about *me* for a change! Think about what I might need—not what you want. For once in your life, think about someone besides your own pathetic little self!"

❦

She would call and apologize later that day, and I would give her Daniel's number for safekeeping. But when I left the bedroom we'd shared for so many years, I knew that my sister and I had never been further apart.

❦

My father must have heard Jude and me upstairs. The door to his study was open when I came back down, and he called out to me:

"Is that you, Jennifer? Come say hello, at least."

"Yes, Daddy," I said, walking down the hall toward him. He was sitting in his usual spot behind his cluttered desk, the late afternoon sun haloing the back of his head. I'd been hoping to avoid this. Not that I hadn't lied to the Reverend Honegger about a hundred times before in my life.

"I was planning to drop in to see you," I told him for starters. "I have some news."

"Yes?" His magnified gaze took me in from behind his rimless glasses. I've often wondered how he saw me. I know I don't look much like my mom. Did he imagine that I took after him? We do share the same delicate features and slender build. But, more than that, I think we're both similarly strong willed and long-suffering. I went through such hell growing up. But I did not let it break me. I did not even bend. At least, that's how I used to always think of myself. Unmovable. It's only now that I've lost so much—and am throwing away so much more—that I realize that what I've really been all these years is not unmovable, but unmoved. Not strong, but hard.

"I'm going away for a while," I said, before reciting the same story I'd told Cal. A spiritual retreat. Cutting myself off from my old life for a time. Trying to recoup some sense of direction and well-being.

"Well, I think it's a mistake," my father told me when I'd finished.

"I'm sorry?" I said. "I think it's just what I need, actually."

"No. You've been trying to escape from the world ever since Betsy died. What you should be doing now is trying to reenter life—not retreating from it further."

"I think I know what I need to do a whole lot better than you do."

"You're allowing yourself to drown in your own self-pity, Jennifer," my father said. He took off his glasses, pulled a tissue from a box on his desk, and started to clean them, saying, "You've managed to convince yourself that your pain and suffering are unique. That you deserve special consideration because of Betsy's death. It's time you started to understand that you don't. God gives us all challenges—each according to his or her ability to meet them."

He put his glasses back on, but then, as if to emphasize his point, he pushed them up onto his forehead and continued in great earnestness: "You have to begin to accept that, for whatever reason, what happened is part of his plan for you. You have to try your best to learn from it. To grow from it."

"My daughter's death was a total, horrible aberration against nature. How dare you try to tell me it's some kind of life lesson?"

"Everything that happens under heaven is for a purpose, Jennifer. Even those things that seem the most reprehensible, that seem the most cruel."

"Okay, sure. Whatever you say." We'd hit a brick wall. I

knew there was no point in continuing the conversation. We'd just go over and over the same ground, our positions hardening with each round. "Anyway—I thought you might want to know that I'll be away for a while."

"What you and Cal need to start thinking about," my father said, as though he hadn't heard me, "is having another child. That's what I would advise. Have another child."

Several people had told me the same thing. As if Betsy could be replaced. As if children were interchangeable. As if all I needed was a shiny new baby—like a toy or a pet— something to play with, something to hold. I shrank inside each time I heard this. How thoughtless people could be. Well-meaning, but clueless. That my own father would make such an insensitive suggestion seemed unconscionable to me. I could stand his holier-than-thou lectures. I had learned to tolerate his moralizing. But this went beyond that. This time he'd blundered into the darkest and most painful recesses of my sorrow. What I wanted was *Betsy* back. All I wanted was my happy, beautiful, perfect child restored to me.

"You know *nothing* about what I need!" I said, my voice shaking with anger. We'd had our fights before this, but I think my vehemence stunned him a little. His eyes widened and he sat up in his chair.

"That's not true," he began. "I like to think—"

"That's just it. You *think*, but you don't *feel*. You have absolutely no empathy. Aren't you supposed to understand how to counsel and comfort people? Isn't that supposed to be your *job*? All you know how to do is drive them away. No wonder Lilly walked out on you."

There. I'd said it. I'd mentioned my mother's name. For the first time in my life I'd said the one word that was absolutely forbidden in our household. Though Jude and I had always been rebellious and difficult, neither one of us had dared cross this particular line before. What had actually happened between my parents—why she left, why she never tried to get in touch with us again—we were never told. Yes, there'd been another man—but who he really was and where they might have gone . . . we'd been too afraid to ask. It was a subject covered over with such shame and hurt and misery that Jude and I were careful never to talk about it with anyone but each other. The few times I had the courage to broach it with my father, his face would go blank, and he'd say, almost invariably:

"She's gone. That's all you need to know."

But her name was Lilly. And Jude and I carried her genes within us. And lately I'd felt what I believed to be her blood—her restless and perhaps unstable nature—rising up within me for the first time.

"Your mother," my father said now, blinking rapidly. "Your mother—and I. What happened is between us." I waited for him to say something more. To explain. But he just sat there, his hands folded in front of him on the desk. He'd always seemed so powerful to me. He'd seemed to loom above Jude and me, all knowing. The ultimate authority—and, therefore, for unruly girls like Jude and myself, the clear enemy. I was expecting a tirade from him now. One of his damning, definitive attacks. After all, I'd thrown down the gauntlet; I'd brought the battle right into his camp. But he seemed not to notice. Or to care. He looked shrunken. Diminished. I stood there, waiting for him to continue, but he was obviously lost in his own thoughts. I began to think he'd forgotten that I was there.

"Daddy?" I said. I realized that I blamed him for everything that had gone wrong in my life. "I'm leaving now."

He looked up at that. He nodded.

"Right," he said. "Now, remember what I told you." But whether he was referring to Cal and me having another baby—or to my mother's departure not being any of my business—I couldn't say. I stood there a little longer, watching as he began to search around the top of his desk for something. Lifting up a book here. A sheaf of papers there. I turned and walked away. But, though I knew nothing about the contents of his heart, I knew his habits perfectly. I knew that eventually his right hand would graze the top of his head where he'd left his glasses. He'd finger them briefly. And he'd pull them back down onto the bridge of his nose. But by then I'd be gone.

19

Cal

I don't remember when it started exactly. At some point, I guess a few days after Jenny left for her retreat, I woke up hungover one morning and decided to have a beer for breakfast. It was late February. The ground was still frozen rock solid under an inch or two of snow. Nothing doing work-wise. I'd sort of decided to stop going into the office until the weather warmed up a little; the place was costing a fortune to keep even halfway warm. I don't know what the hell Kurt and I were thinking when we opted for electric heat. Except that we'd put the place up in the summer—when I guess a whole big oil-burner installation seemed like overkill. Our entire crew helped out with the foundation and framing. We had a big party when it was done. *We're having an office warming*, I remember telling Jenny.

"So what kind of gift am I supposed to get for that? A box of paper clips? Or a stapler, maybe?"

It's weird how much I miss talking to her. How much I

miss *all* of her, considering how little we've actually seen of each other over the last couple of months. But there was something about knowing she was here. Even if we didn't communicate all that much. For some reason, Jenny not being here makes Betsy not being here—and Betsy not ever coming back—seem all that much more real and horrible to me. It still feels so crazy and wrong. Every once in a while the whole thing just hits me all over again—like a blow to the heart.

So there I was at ten o'clock in the morning, literally crying into my beer, though the old hair of the dog was already taking a little edge off things. I gazed out the French doors where the snow-covered shrubs in Daniel's garden looked like a bunch of kids playing under the blankets. Kurt and I used to do that when we were boys. Make this whole underground world out of my mom's sheets and pillows. The two of us never needed much in the way of toys to have fun. Thinking about Kurt reminded me of what had happened the night before.

I'd been at the Cove. Lori had hooked up with me there after she was done at work. Denny and I had started a game of pool, and a group of us were hanging out in the back alcove. Someone ordered one of the Cove's pizzas—those god-awful microwaved jobs that are edible only if you're really hammered—and another round of beer. Denny and I won two games each, but I beat him double or nothing on the fifth. I pulled Lori to me, grabbing her backside, and planted a big kiss on her mouth.

I don't know how long Kurt had been watching us from the bar, but he obviously caught that much. He just looked over at me and shook his head. When I saw him pay up and leave a few minutes later, I told Lori to wait there and I followed him outside.

"What's with you anyway?" I called after him as he walked toward his car. He turned around. "I'm not even allowed to have a good time anymore?"

"Is that what that was?"

"Jesus, Kurt. What are you now? Like, my babysitter?"

"I've been hearing things. I know Jenny's away. And I'm thinking that maybe you should consider being a little more selective about who you're seen with right now."

"Oh, wait, no, I get it—you're, like, my chaperone."

"I'm, like, your brother. And I know what this Gannon thing means to you. I'm betting it means a little something to the Gannon folks, too. You think they're not looking pretty carefully into what kind of guy you are—how you live? Maybe who you're hanging out with? Don't be an asshole, okay? I don't want to see you any more fucked up than you are already."

"Whatever you say, *coach*," I told him, giving that last word a nasty little spin. It used to be Eddie who pushed my buttons. But just seeing Kurt, just hearing that slow and steady voice of fucking reason—burned the hell out of me.

"Okay," Kurt said, sighing. "I think maybe I better tell you. I think maybe you should know what's going on: they've been asking around."

"They? Who they? What are you talking about?"

"Gannon. They've been asking questions. They hired an investigator who talked to Denny and Mark on the EMS. He's called me a couple of times, too. I've been putting him off. But listen—the truth is? I'm not sure what I want to say anymore."

"What do you mean? You say just what you said to Stephens, Stokes when they talked to you. Just what you've been saying since the Jeep turned over, for chrissakes! What's all this pussyfooting? You need to be strong. You need to be clear. Stay on message. Mark and Denny will do the same."

"Stay on message?" Kurt kicked at the ground, scattering gravel. "You realize, don't you, that's just another way of telling me to lie, right? And under oath? That means breaking the law."

"Whoa! Who the fuck told me that what happened wasn't my fault? Who told me that I passed the Breathalyzer with flying colors? You start wavering again, Kurt, and I say let's just get all the liars lined up in little row here."

"I thought I was doing the right thing then," he said, shaking his head.

"You still are doing the right thing."

"Oh yeah?" He turned his back to me as he walked to his car. "I'm glad you think so."

After he left I went back into the Cove, but I blew Lori off. Not because of what Kurt had told me; I just wasn't in the mood at that point. I came home angry and went to bed pissed—in more ways than one.

But now, as I sat at the kitchen counter, thinking back over what Kurt had said, I felt uneasy. The truth is, I haven't been giving any real thought to Gannon's side of things. The last time I met with Lester, he told me that everything's on track with what's called the "discovery" phase of the lawsuit. The firm's been interviewing consultants, researching similar accidents, and preparing for our first big face-to-face with Gannon.

"I like to front-load my EBTs," Lester said, referring to

the Examination Before Trial meeting that was scheduled with the Gannon team in another week or so. "We're sending them a list of expert witnesses that should, at the very least, make their blood run cold. That list, the sled-test material, public sentiment—well, put all that together and I just can't imagine they aren't quietly running some numbers for us already. My only concern at this point is Jenny, honestly. But at least we can tell them she's under doctor's supervision now."

"Well, she's not actually seeing a real doctor, remember," I told him. "She's at this spiritual retreat place. She's doing meditation and—well, therapy like that." It occurred to me that I really didn't know a damned thing about where Jenny was or what she was doing, and that was just fine by me. Let Jenny be the one to stare at her navel and reflect on our loss. Whatever helped. But the last thing I feel like doing these days is examining my conscience. *Shit happens*—that's my motto. The point is to move on, get off the dime, take back your life. Or, if you happen to have the opportunity, take on a bunch of bastards like Gannon and stick it to them.

"She's in a *facility*," Lester replied. "She's getting *help*. That should satisfy their curiosity for now, at least. But I have a feeling we're going to need to reassure them that she'll be ready to sit down and give them her statement sometime very soon. You both understand that, right?"

I'd told him *yes*. I told him *sure*. But more and more I'm just parroting back whatever Lester, Janet, and Carl seem to want me to say. The line between fact and fantasy is as blurry now as the rest of my thinking. Once again, I tried to focus on what Kurt had told me about the Gannon investigator. About him interviewing Denny and Mark. They're both friends of mine. Drinking buddies. But I felt another wave of anxiety when it occurred to me that I'd been with Denny just the night before and he hadn't told me anything about being questioned by a Gannon investigator. Did that indicate it didn't mean anything to him? Or that maybe it meant too much?

I'm not a suspicious person by nature. In fact, I've always prided myself on being open and straightforward. But lately, as Lester talks about getting ready for this run of white water with Gannon, I've been feeling kind of wired. And paranoid. I'm having a hard time knowing whom to trust. A few days after talking with Kurt, I overhead Lori telling a friend on the phone that I was spending the night with her at the trailer. Before she'd even hung the receiver up, I was yelling at her:

"What the fuck are you trying to do? Sink this whole deal for me? *Nobody*'s supposed to know we're seeing each other."

"But, Cal," she said, tears already thickening her voice, "everybody already does. What am I supposed to say?"

"That it's over," I said, pulling my shirt back on. "That it never really was." The truth is, this thing with Lori has played itself out. And I've known it for a while. I'm only seeing the down side of who she is these days, and it's really just the flip side of what attracted me to her in the first place: her fleshiness, that little-girl voice, her willingness to do anything to please me. But mostly it's that she doesn't even come close to being Jenny. And that she doesn't have a prayer of catching up.

"Oh no, Cal." She began crying in earnest. "Please, please, please don't say that! I'm sorry. I'll call Amy right back and tell her—"

"No, Lori, don't," I said, pulling her to me. "I'm sorry. You've been great. You've been wonderful. But it's not going to work long-term. And I think it's really best we end this when it's all still good. I've just got too much on my plate right now."

"It's that detective, isn't it?" she said through her tears. "But I didn't tell him anything except that we're really close friends. I promise. And that you don't have a drinking problem. No way."

❦

I remembered being upside down in the Jeep after it rolled. But that it seemed to me I was actually right-side up—and that it was the world that had upended. That's how I felt driving away from Lori's. Everything was wrong, though I was still right. I took Route 206 straight back through Covington, right past the Cove, up into the mountains. Jenny and I used to park up here when we first got together. I remember the musty smell of the Reverend Honegger's old Camry, the reckless way that Jenny used to drive back then— windows down and her hair blowing all over the place, even on chilly nights. In those days, before Betsy was born, she was more daring and impulsive, hungry to start her own life.

"Let's make a baby," she told me one night when we'd been making out for almost an hour on a secluded little dirt road off the main highway. I could kiss Jenny forever and never grow tired of it.

"Oh, we will," I'd assured her, pulling away. "But that's it for now, or we'll be sorry." She seemed so much younger than me and precious in a way that no one else in the world had ever been before. And, except for Betsy, would ever be.

As I drove east toward Northridge, those early days came rushing back at me—as though the windows were still down—as though Jenny was still sitting right there beside me. Being with Lori these past few months has helped me realize how special Jenny is. How lucky I was to find her—and win her. And it makes me more determined than ever to work things out with her. I still can't understand—I probably never will—why Jenny's been so dead set against the lawsuit, but I'm the first one to admit that grief can totally fuck you up. It can make you do some crazy stuff.

Lately, I've taken to fantasizing about what I'm going to do with the payout, how I'm going to divide things up. Eddie deserves a small cut, of course, and he'll get it. But I intend to give Kurt even more. In fact, my secret plan is to pay off the balance of his mortgage—then walk up to him with a copy of the deed in my hand and say: "Thanks, Kurt, for standing by me the way you did."

I'm taking Jenny on a trip around the world. And then, when we're back home, I'm going to pay for her to go after her certificate in landscape gardening—something she used to talk about doing a lot before Betsy came along. She has a natural instinct for gardening, I think. Who's to say that, with the right training, she couldn't become a professional? Start her own business like Daniel? In many ways that little sun garden she put in on the side of the house is just as pretty as the pricier, elaborate hillside beds Daniel designed for us.

Daniel. He'd been in the back of my mind ever since I left Lori's. And, as I hit the outskirts of Northridge, I realized that it was Daniel I was actually hoping to see there. I desperately needed a shot of his go-for-it attitude. But I didn't know how late it was—past midnight—until I walked into

Ernie's. The bar was empty, though a couple of tables in the dining area were still occupied. That good-looking waitress I remembered from my last few times there, the one Daniel seemed to have something going with, was sorting receipts at the cash register. I walked over to her.

"How're you doing? I'm wondering if you've seen Daniel Brandt around?"

She looked me over, expressionless.

"He's moved back to Manhattan."

"Really? Are you sure? I thought he said that he was just commuting back and forth for a while."

"No," she said, turning her attention back to the stack of receipts. "He's gone. And don't bother asking—he didn't exactly leave me a forwarding address."

I felt so let down by the news. Hurt that he'd moved on without a word. Though I hadn't seen him for a while—I guess the Horigan Lumber Christmas party had been the last time—I still considered him a part of my life. A big part. In many ways, it's Daniel's voice that I keep hearing these days whenever I start to feel uncertain or afraid about what I'm trying to do. I think about that aura of calm and utter self-confidence that impressed me so much when I first met him. The sense of connection I'd felt with him almost from the start. He'd arrived in my life just when I needed guidance. And he'd helped me more than anyone else get over the torment I felt those first few weeks after Betsy died. I could still remember almost word for word what he told me when I'd asked him point-blank if he thought I was responsible for what happened:

I don't buy into the idea that actions necessarily result in consequences. That way of thinking? I think it's just a very clever system for keeping people in line, holding them back.

I had his cell phone number somewhere. But I knew I'd feel awkward calling him when he hadn't even bothered to tell me he was leaving the area. I'd thought we'd become friends. I'd given him a pretty decent commission. I'd taken him out for drinks. Solicited his advice. Listened eagerly to his opinions. I remember the way I'd introduced him around to all my dad's suppliers at the party, singing his praises, hoping it'd help generate some work for him. But I realized now, thinking back on it all, how one-sided the relationship had been, really. How unequal.

As I drove back toward Covington, the moonlight gleaming on the rain-slickened roadway, it occurred to me that I still didn't have a very clear picture in my mind of who Daniel actually was. All I really knew about him for certain was what he said he believed in. What I had so eagerly taken to my heart as gospel:

As far as I'm concerned, the whole idea of guilt is probably the worst concept mankind has ever come up with.

❧

The phone was ringing when I walked into the house, and the message light on the answering machine was blinking; I had nine messages. I heard Eddie's voice before I had a chance to pick up:

"Where the fuck are you? If you don't—"

"Hey there," I said, lifting the receiver to my ear. "I just walked in."

"Where have you been? I've been trying to get through to you since late afternoon. You can't go AWOL on me like that, Cal. You can't leave me here, holding the goddamn bag."

"Whoa, take a deep breath," I told him. "I'm sorry. I guess I had my cell off. Are all these messages from you?"

"Me. Janet. Lester. The shit's really hit the fan. I can't believe it! I just can't believe it."

"Why don't you stop foaming at the mouth, and tell me what's going on."

"It's Kurt," he said.

For a panicky moment I thought something had happened to Kurt. That he'd been in an accident and was hurt. Or worse. The room swayed.

"What? What's happened to Kurt?"

"He's on Gannon's list."

"What?"

"He's on Gannon's list of witnesses! Janet's freaking out. Lester's been ripping me a second asshole. What the fuck is going on?"

"I don't understand," I said, relieved that Kurt was okay. "How could he be on Gannon's list?"

"How? You're asking me *how*? Because he's planning to testify against us. That's how."

20

Jenny

❦

I'd been down to Manhattan a couple of times before
this. Jude and I snuck down one New Year's Eve when
we were still in high school and froze our tails off in Times
Square waiting for the ball to drop. Cal and I spent the first
night of our December honeymoon at the Marriott Marquis
on our way to St. Lucia, then almost a whole day hitting the
tourist spots—Ground Zero, the Empire State Building,
Rockefeller Center—on our way back home. What I remember is a place that seemed a blur of traffic, people, noise:
windblown trash swirling beneath the Christmas-tree lights,
"Auld Lang Syne" drowned out by the whoop of police
sirens. Chaotic, unnerving, exciting.

Daniel's apartment on the Upper West Side was nothing
like that. Sublet from a couple of Columbia University ar-
chaeology professors on sabbatical in Europe, it was all wall-
to-wall bookcases and staid, upholstered furniture. The long
front hall was lined with photos of the middle-aged aca-
demics, smiling into the camera, at various ruins—Pompeii,

the Acropolis, the Roman Forum—obviously at home amid the rubble of history. In fact, their apartment felt as still and silent as an ancient tomb.

"It's prewar," Daniel explained to me the first night I was there, when I remarked how quiet the place seemed. We were standing in the kitchen, where Daniel was opening a bottle of wine for dinner. He put the corkscrew down and knocked against the decorative tile above the sink.

"You don't have to worry about hearing the neighbors in this place. These walls are probably half a foot thick."

We had Thai takeout that night from someplace in the neighborhood Daniel had already discovered and was championing. He seemed to be an expert on the cuisine, favorably comparing the take-out pad thai to versions he'd had at restaurants in Miami and San Francisco. He looked over at me between bites at one point and said, "You're not eating much."

"I'm guess I'm just exhausted," I told him. Which was true, though the train ride down to Grand Central couldn't have been easier. Jude had dropped me off at the station in Hudson. She was uncharacteristically quiet on the drive over. Long silences stretched between our short exchanges. We were both still smarting from our argument. She waited with me until the train arrived, hugged me hard, and said, "I promise not to call you—but you have to promise to call *me* if you need anything, okay? Remember: you don't have to be afraid. I'm here."

I think she must have rehearsed that last bit, but it got to me anyway. I just nodded as I climbed onto the train, my throat constricting. I remained tearful as we passed through the little picturesque Hudson River towns, the harsh winter sunlight glancing off the surface of the water. But it was more like a memory of a feeling—rather than real emotion. When I closed my eyes, I could see the ghostly imprints of leafless branches and telephone poles—glimpsed for a split second but already being sorted and stored away somewhere in my brain. Along with the millions and millions of other images—including how many of Cal and Betsy alone?—that made up the catalog of my life. That's all they seemed to me now, though: content. Bleached of color and context. Meaningless. But the burden of not caring—the effort of feeling no regret—caught up with me by the time I reached the city.

I listened and nodded as Daniel spoke. About the new project. How he'd have to get up at the crack of dawn most mornings and would generally not be back until seven or so at night. He'd leave me keys. I could explore the neighborhood. Take in the city. We'd have the weekends together. He didn't ask me how I'd squared things with Cal. Or how long I planned to stay. It struck me that Daniel always seemed to be living in the moment. *For* the moment. How easy it was to be with him, I thought. How painless this was turning out to be. It was *no problem*—just what the taxi driver at Grand Central had told me when I gave him Daniel's address. And then I don't remember much of anything. I must have nodded off at the table. I woke up alone in the king-sized bed. Sunlight flooding the room.

For the first time in months I'd actually slept through the night. Daniel had somehow gotten me into one of his T-shirts and folded my clothes on top of my suitcase, which he'd left unopened by a chest of drawers. I could tell by the intensity of the light that it was already at least late morning. He'd probably left for Westchester hours ago. I felt logy with

sleep, but still bone tired. I think that I'd been holding everything in for such a long time, that it took me until
then—when it finally felt safe to let go—to realize how exhausted I'd been. I turned my face back to the pillow. It had
a clean, slightly antiseptic smell—lavender, perhaps, mingled
with bleach.

So began my empty, drifting days. I would get up mid-
morning, make a pot of coffee, and read the papers that
Daniel left behind. The apartment was larger than I realized
that first night, with a perfectly square, book-lined study off
the living room and another half bath. The high ceilings, the
French doors connecting the various rooms, and the ornately
carved, old-fashioned furniture gave the place an air of
timeless, faded refinement. I wandered through the rooms.
Then, feeling both restless and intrigued, I looked in the
closets. I opened a few drawers. I discovered that the
apartment was owned by Drs. Jonathan and Fran Traeger. I
carefully examined their books and photo albums. They'd
been married for thirty-four years.

I filled my aimless mornings slowly piecing together the
details of the Traegers' lives. From the most recent photographs, I guessed that they were now in their early sixties—
both graying, though still fit. (I'd come upon several pairs
of running shoes in a hall closet.) He was shorter than she
was by an inch or so and was starting to bald. She'd cut her
long straight hair—it had been halfway down her back in
their wedding picture—into one of those no-nonsense short
crops. But what struck me most about them was how alike
they looked now. The same round, old-fashioned glasses.
The same down-turning, self-deprecating smiles. I guessed
that, over the years, they'd slowly taken on each other's

characteristics—until, at this point in time, it seemed to me that they could as easily be taken for siblings as for spouses.

I went out for long walks in the afternoons—down along the esplanade in Riverside Park or up to Grant's Tomb—slowly familiarizing myself with the park's long, tree-lined walkways and the small, carefully maintained flower gardens that seemed all-volunteer community efforts. The city was a few weeks ahead of Covington in terms of the growing calendar: the crocuses had already wilted and the daffodils were bursting into bud.

The flower garden just below Ninety-fifth Street was the most mature and extensive of the community plots, and I began to visit it almost daily. It was a charming hodgepodge: a rock garden in one spot, another given over to a variety of hostas, another all rosebushes. It was like a crazy quilt of the many different gardeners' enthusiasms and, even before most of it had leafed out, I was able to envision how lovely the whole would look later in the summer. Certainly not as perfect and professional as Daniel's, but boisterous with passion. I thought of my own lost garden and—despite the pleasure I'd first taken in Daniel's designs—found myself longing to have it restored to me, with its problems intact, just as it had been before Betsy died.

For the first time I began to wonder if I'd made a mistake. What had I done—letting Daniel take over and complete almost overnight a job that I had intended to work on for the rest of my life? I began to worry that I'd traded something important—maybe even essential—in my hunger to find some kind of solace.

At night, over dinner I would usually have waiting for

Daniel, we talked about his work. The plans he was drafting for the corporate park. The problems the client's new cost efficiencies were raising. I enjoyed listening to his shoptalk. In everything that had happened between us, it was easy to lose sight of his stature as a landscape architect. The fact that he was respected and well-known only added to the pull he had over me—and my inability to get him in any kind of decent perspective. He always seemed to be looming too close—or casting too distant a shadow—for me to see him in his entirety.

"How did you end up choosing this career?" I asked him the third or fourth night I was there, as we relaxed over the last of the wine.

"Oh, it chose me, really. I worked in an uncle's greenhouse when I was a boy. So I learned the business from the ground up, so to speak. It came naturally—I had most of the genuses and species down before I even started my degree—and I tend to take the easy route in life."

"Only easy because you love it, I bet," I said. For the first time in many months I remembered the feeling of digging my fingers in the cool, damp spring earth. "I'd hoped to be a professional gardener, too, someday."

"Hoped? What held you back?"

Nothing. Everything. Cal starting his business. My job at Pellani's Garden Center, which seemed to satisfy that craving during the years I was employed there. Then having Betsy. But the real answer to Daniel's question—what held me back—was, I suspect, part of larger questions about myself and my dreams that I was just now beginning to understand I'd been avoiding for years. That Betsy's death had overshadowed—but not erased.

"Oh, you know," I replied, finishing my wine, "all the usual excuses."

Out of some tacit understanding, we managed to avoid talking about anything of real substance. Anything too personal. I did my best to follow Daniel's example and live in the moment. I sealed my new self off from the past, my marriage, the tragedy—everything but the here and now. As a consequence, almost from the instant I woke up in the morning, I began looking forward to going to bed again. I longed for Daniel's hands on my body, for his mouth to close over my mine.

Each night I felt as though I was drowning in his arms. He took me deeper and deeper into a kind of subterranean sensory world. A place where pain had the power to give pleasure. Where nothing was forbidden. Sometimes I felt as though my head—my whole body, really—would explode from the intensity of such pure, undiluted sensation. As before, I let him do whatever he wanted. And, in turn, I did what I was instructed. *Turn over. Get on your knees.* I think part of me cried out to be punished—and Daniel understood and exploited that. But then, too, I discovered something I'd begun to sense about myself since Betsy's death: I've lost all sense of shame.

❧

The second week I was there I found a couple of Fran's old journals, tucked into the back of her desk drawer in the study. I hesitated, weighing the simple black leather notebooks in my hand. Reading them, I knew, would be far more of an invasion of privacy than any of the poking around that I'd done up to this point. But curiosity—and a growing compulsion on my part to know more about the Traegers' lives—got the better of me. I spent the rest of that morning reading entries that Fran had composed—more or less on a daily basis—some twenty years ago.

What I soon discovered was that it was a journal of her ongoing attempts to get pregnant. At almost forty years old. After five long years of miscarriages. Some of it was a straightforward record of her in vitro fertilization efforts. The shots. The doctors' visits. That day or two every month when she began to believe that her luck had turned. *Their* luck, because it became clear that Jonathan wanted a child as much as she did. He'd been adopted as a baby and had never known—or apparently wanted to know—his birth mother. Other sections were more personal and revealing:

> *Period started in the middle of the night. Soon as I crawled back into bed, J. took me in his arms. I didn't have to say a word. We cried together. Sometimes I think he needs this even more than I do. I believe that our having a child—his child—would somehow help him solve the riddle of his own identity. More than solve, actually, salve it. I feel so strongly that giving J. a child would help heal the pain and anger he insists on dealing with on his own. It's probably all these damned hormone shots, but I also secretly—no doubt delusionally—feel that having a baby would help heal the world. With each new life there's new hope. Another chance. But I'm beginning to fear that our chances are running out.*

The journal ended two months after that. The entries

had been getting shorter, more perfunctory. Then they stopped altogether, midpage, almost half the notebook left blank. There were no further insights or reflections. The last entry read:

On the downtown #1 this morning. Hope ended.

It was just a matter of time, I suppose. If not the journal, something else would have triggered it. But it happened to be Fran's words and the Traegers' decades-old heartbreak— that broke through whatever flimsy barricades I imagined that I'd constructed. *Hope ended.* Just like that. It was the finality that got to me. The courage to face it. And then, obviously, to go on. To find another way forward.

That night, as I was helping Daniel clean up after dinner, I found myself asking him:

"Did you ever want children?"

"What?" he said. He was leaning over the dishwasher, but he straightened up.

"I was just curious," I replied, handing him one of the plates to load. "Did you ever want to have a child?"

"Honestly?" he asked, taking the plate from me. "No. I don't think I've ever even seriously considered it."

He finished loading the dishwasher and turned back to me and pulled me into his arms. He kissed the top of my head; then his lips traveled down my neck and he whispered in my ear: "Hey, don't go there, okay? Let's not talk—we've better things to do."

The next morning, I put Fran's journals back, carefully arranging the contents of the drawer to look just as they had when I first discovered them.

✿

I began spending most of my days away from the apartment now, visiting museums and galleries. And gardens. The ones in Central Park and Brooklyn. I began to realize that I was searching for something as I walked along the carefully groomed, formal pathways. I took the subway up to the Bronx, where the botanical garden had mounted an orchid exhibit. I wandered through the conservatory filled with room after room of exotic bromeliads. At first, the warm, heavily humid air felt inviting. How flawless the orchids seemed! After a while, though, I started to feel slightly claustrophobic. It was getting hard to breathe. I began to realize that there was something about the plants' waxy perfection that was unsettling to me. Everywhere I turned now I saw how futile—how essentially superficial—this time with Daniel was turning out to be. The graceful sprays seemed lifeless to me, more like effigies of flowers than real ones. I found myself automatically leaning down to breathe in their aroma. I smelled nothing. I'd forgotten that many orchids were scentless. It only added to my sense of emptiness.

✿

"I've always found Monet's work kind of cloying," Daniel said one Saturday afternoon as we wandered through MoMA. "That obsession with the cathedral in Rouen— those endless, turgid waterlilies. I visited Giverny with my wife once—years ago. It smelled like a cesspool, frankly. And it was overrun by busloads of Japanese tourists."

Because he'd said it so offhandedly, merely in passing, I

almost didn't pick up on the fact that Daniel had just mentioned a *wife*. This was the first real—unasked for—piece of personal information he'd given me. I wondered if it represented a chink in his armor, a willingness to have us go a little deeper with each other. And I wondered if our lovemaking the night before—the most intense it had ever been—had anything to do with it. He'd angled the full-length mirror on the door of the bedroom closet so that he could have a view of us on the bed. Afterward, as I lay with my head on his chest, staring up at the ceiling, he'd said:

"We make a good pair."

I didn't know what he meant by that exactly, and I wasn't sure that I liked his tone of voice. But I was still too hungry for his approval to call him on it. I closed my eyes, savoring the feeling of physical release. It was only in his presence—especially when we were making love—that I experienced that sense of oblivion I craved. It was only then that I felt truly safe.

Uncertain of his motives, I decided to let the mention of his marriage go for the time being. Later, though, toward the end of an early dinner at a Northern Italian place he liked on upper Madison Avenue, I leaned across the table and said, simply:

"Wife?"

"So you were paying attention," he replied. "Yes. Two, actually. Both exes now. You're not surprised, I hope?"

"No," I said. "Curious, though." In fact, I'd been having a hard time trying to imagine Daniel in the role of anybody's husband.

"It was before I realized that I didn't have to play by other people's rules. Life is far more pleasurable if you make up your own."

"I don't know," I said. "That sounds a little lonely somehow."

"Better than a little suffocating," he said. "No, scratch that. A lot suffocating."

"Which is how you feel about marriage?"

He gave me a half smile as he took me in across the table.

"It's how I feel about any relationship that comes with strings attached. That's why I think we get on so well. We both want one thing from each other—and I think we both want it pretty intensely."

"But when you decided to get married, didn't you know—"

"Hey, now, stop that," he said, reaching across the table and touching his right index finger to my lips. "Digging around in the past is a waste of time. You know how I feel: life is meant to be enjoyed . . . reveled in . . . savored. It's been wonderful watching you let go of your inhibitions these past few weeks. I feel that I've been witnessing you come into your own—physically, sexually—as I think you've never allowed yourself to do before. Don't ruin it all by trying to analyze it—or me."

But it was Daniel who reveled. I was only trying to hide. Surely he knew that. He was savoring life, and I was doing everything I could to run from it. I realized now that he'd told me about his marriages, not to bring us closer, but to make sure I understood that, emotionally, at least, he intended us to remain at arm's length. He still exerted an almost narcotic effect on me, but—like all drugs, I suppose—the potency began to wear off.

I hardly noticed it at first. Just the slightest wave of irritation when he suggested a new position. Or a ripple of distaste when he asked me to do something that suddenly seemed a little demeaning. But soon I found myself having to actively work to respond to his probing fingers, his tongue, the length of his body arching over mine. Finally, one night, when he insisted we leave the lights on, I was able to see him for what he was for the first time: a middle-aged man, intent on his pleasure, admiring our reflection in a full-length mirror.

21

Cal

❧

"Let Lester handle him," Eddie told me as we were driving up to Albany for the EBT with Gannon. The meeting was going to be held at the Stephens, Stokes offices in the big conference room where I first met Lester and his team. "Him" was Kurt, our brother, whom Eddie has been calling every name in the book except his given one since we learned that Gannon would be deposing him as a nonparty witness in that morning's proceedings.

"The son of a bitch," Eddie went on. He'd been ranting on and off since he picked me up earlier. "What does he think he's going to gain by this? I still can't figure it out. I hope Lester has it nailed."

I was only half listening to what Eddie was saying. It sounded to me like the same old vitriol he's been spewing out for the last few days now: our brother is a traitor. A spoiler. A holier-than-thou horse's ass. Eddie really *is* furious, I know, but I also sense he's trying to fire me up. Get me back on the bandwagon. Because I think he must suspect that I'm starting to slip off. Eddie sees Kurt's decision as a betrayal, a complete turnabout. But I know better, and I tried to tell him so the night we first heard the news.

"It's that he covered for me," I told Eddie. "It's because he wouldn't let the chief do a Breathalyzer at the scene—otherwise I probably would have been arrested on a DUI. And everyone would have automatically held me responsible for what happened to Betsy. Kurt saved me from that."

"Bullshit," Eddie replied. "You don't know what went on. You had a concussion. You were in shock."

"Don't you remember after the game—when you and I had that fight?" I asked him. "And you accused me of putting away the 'old brewskies'? You were right. We'd been drinking beer all afternoon."

"So everyone had a few beers, right? That means Kurt and Denny, too. Practically the whole EMS, for chrissakes. It's like the pot calling the kettle black."

This was the line of attack that Lester decided he was going to use when he cross-examined my brother: *How many beers had Kurt himself consumed? Did he make a habit of going out on emergency medical calls under the influence? Did he know he could lose his certification—and worse—for that? And wasn't that actually the reason he was so against the idea of the lawsuit from the beginning? Wasn't it that he'd been worried that the scrutiny might expose his own questionable behavior that night? In fact, wasn't that concern really motivating Kurt all along? Not the truth about my sobriety level—but about his own?*

"Lester will make it work," Eddie said, glancing sideways at me. I felt that I'd done a pretty good job of pulling myself together. I'd gotten up early and taken a cold shower and shaved. I'd put on a jacket and tie. Only I knew how much booze was still sloshing around in my stomach. That the fumes were stinging behind my eyelids and fogging my brain. I'd managed to get down some black coffee before Eddie picked me up, but now I wished I hadn't. Every time Eddie switched lanes, I felt queasy.

"I'm not so sure," I said, noticing how the eighteen-wheeler in front of us swayed sideways under its weight. I had to look away, out across the fields that had been beaten flat by winter. Now the last of the snow had melted away, and the horizon seemed to shimmer with a greenish haze.

"Lester will do his number on Kurt," I told Eddie. "But it still won't really explain why he decided to speak up now. Because if he'd just kept quiet, he wouldn't have to worry about his reputation—or any of this."

"Then why *won't* he keep his mouth shut?" Eddie demanded. "That's my question. What's he up to? What the hell's he trying to prove?"

"It's like I said: he won't break the law. He bent it pretty hard for me the night Betsy was killed. He bent it, thinking no one would ever have to know what he'd done. But he's not going to break it—for me, for anyone—by lying under oath. He's just not made that way."

"Well, he's a fool! You realize that, don't you? He's never going to get anywhere in life."

"Yeah," I said, "he probably won't."

"Hey—are you going to be okay?" Eddie asked, turning quickly to give me a closer look. "You're not wavering again, are you? Because I hope you realize how much everything today really depends on you. We've gotten this far, Cal, and we're so incredibly close right now. You just need to stay focused for the next few hours. You just need to keep your eyes on the prize."

"I'm fine," I told him, because I know it's what he wants to hear. But that's about as much as I feel capable of doing these days: going with the flow, following the path of least resistance. The sense of outrage and purpose that drove me to pursue Gannon at all is basically gone now. I don't know why. Kurt's decision has something to do with it. But I think that it has more to do with how I've changed. I've lost my way somehow. In fact, I no longer even remember what it was I thought I needed so badly. What was the point of it all? I'm just living on impulse now: moment to moment, drink to drink. Eddie continued to mouth off, but I didn't pay him much attention until we were crossing the bridge into the city.

"So anyway, I think you have to admit that you owe me," he said.

"Sure," I replied, pulling down the visor to block the sun that kept glancing off the cars in front of us.

"And, the thing is: I could use a little help right now. A cash infusion. I'm hardly alone in this, but I've been getting really hammered in the market."

"You're in the stock market?" I asked. It wasn't that I was particularly surprised by the news. Edmund has always been more interested in money than the rest of my family. It was more that, in all the time we've spent together since Betsy died, he's never mentioned it. I've never heard him on his cell with a broker, or even caught him reading the business pages. But, then, my older brother does tend to have a secretive side. Even in terms of the family, he treats a lot of things on a need-to-know basis. He was already engaged to Kristin before he decided to introduce her to the rest of us.

"Of course I am," he said. "It's the only way to make any real dough. Don't get scared off by all the crap they're putting out there. The market's not about to collapse. If anything, this is actually the best time to buy in decades. There are some incredible deals to be had."

"So?" I asked, looking over at him. His tone seemed off-handed, but he was gripping the wheel like he was driving through a storm. "What exactly did you have in mind?"

"Just what I think you'll agree is my fair share," he told me. "I've been checking into this. We can get an advance on the settlement once we've reached an agreement with Gannon. A number of lending institutions are already interested."

"What's the big hurry?" I asked, on the alert now. Something wasn't right. Eddie rarely showed his hand. But his tone had turned wheedling.

"We might have to wait months for the payout," he said. "Considering current market conditions, that means I could end up really missing out. I'd prefer to take advantage of some of these buying opportunities right now."

I knew him well enough to realize that he was lying. He needed the money—and he needed it bad. The queasiness I felt before washed over me in a wave.

"And how much were you thinking was your fair share?"

"Well, let's be honest: you wouldn't be here without me. At first, you didn't even want to go ahead with any of this—I was the one who really showed you how important the lawsuit could be. And it was me who did all the research to find us the best—"

"Eddie," I said, shaking my head. "Just cut to the chase, okay? How much are we talking about here?"

"I think I'm being reasonable when I ask for a quarter of our take. Last time I talked to Lester, he told me he's projecting that we'll be offered at least three million, and he'll get a third. So that means about half a million for me."

"You need *five hundred thousand* dollars?" The nausea hit me so hard, I had to close my eyes.

"No," he said, slowing down for the exit ramp. "I don't need it. I *deserve* it. At least that much. But I'm not asking for more. Just my fair share."

"And how long have you been planning this?"

"What?"

"I'm just curious," I said, swallowing hard to keep down the bile. "When did you start working all this out in your head? Before or after Betsy's funeral?"

"That's just plain—"

"Pull over," I told him.

"What?"

"Just pull the fuck over. *Now!*" I barely got the door open before I vomited onto the side of the highway. The contents of my stomach—a brackish liquid—splattered against the concrete shoulder, splashing back up onto Eddie's upholstery and my pants. There wasn't all that much to throw up, but I kept heaving anyway. Until there was nothing left but a sour aftertaste—and an awful aching in my throat and rib cage. I leaned back against the headrest, closing my eyes against the pain. Against the day ahead. The speed with which—as jarring as whiplash—I was being forced to face my own stupidity.

"Jesus Christ," Eddie muttered. "What a mess."

"Yeah," I agreed, but I knew he had no idea what had just happened. "You can say that again."

&

I cleaned up in the private bathroom attached to Lester's office. I used the mouthwash in the medicine cabinet and combed my hair. I leaned over with a wet paper towel to try and do something about my pants, but the movement made me feel dizzy. I had to hold on to the sink as I straightened back up. *Fuck it*, I decided, balling up the paper towel and tossing it into the trash. I felt so sick and exhausted, I wondered if I was going to be able to make it. I looked at my reflection in the mirror. The expensive lighting was designed to flatter, but it couldn't hide the circles under my eyes, the spot on my chin where I'd nicked myself earlier. I looked like hell, no question. My eyes were totally bloodshot—but it was the first times in months that I'd been able to really look at myself. That was a start.

&

The conference room was filled with people, some of whom I recognized from Stephens, Stokes—Janet and Carl among them—and at least half a dozen others I figured were a part of Gannon's legal team. The two groups had migrated to opposite sides of the conference table, though all were still standing when Eddie and I walked in. Except for Lester, who was sporting his signature bright suspenders and a polka-dot bow tie, dark suits predominated on both women and men. A side table was set up buffet-style with urns of coffee and tea, coolers of soft drinks and water, platters of bagels and fruit. Though everyone was speaking in hushed tones, the air felt charged. I glanced around for Kurt, but he wasn't there. Perhaps he'd had a change of heart, I thought. Perhaps he'd decided to let things ride after all.

"Okay, here's our man!" Lester announced as we walked in. I'd seen him earlier, and he knew I wasn't feeling well. He hadn't asked me any questions, just told me to take my time pulling myself together. He'd patted me on the shoulder.

"Remember, it's all just a big show," he'd said. "We've rehearsed your part more than enough times. Just stick to the script, and you'll be fine. And don't let this business with Kurt rattle you. Trust me—I have the whole thing under control."

Lester made me take the seat near the center of the conference table to his right. Eddie, who had no official role in the proceedings, went around to the other side of the room and took a chair against the wall, facing me. When everyone was settled, Lester—ever the master of ceremonies—suggested we go around the table and introduce ourselves. A tall, fit man with a brush cut seated across from me announced that he was William McCarthy, of Whiting, McCarthy and Freed, defense counsel for Gannon Baby Products. There were two other younger male lawyers from Whiting as well as an older woman named Sylvia Lansing who introduced herself as Gannon's general corporate counsel.

I hadn't noticed the court reporter at the end of the table until Lester suggested we "get the ball rolling" and a pudgy, balding man began quietly typing on the black stenotype machine in front of him.

Leaning across the table, William McCarthy looked at me and began the questioning:

"Gannon Baby Products is terribly sorry for your loss,

Mr. Horigan. I know those words probably sound a little hollow to you at this point, but they are offered with the utmost sincerity. Gannon does not think—and, in fact, will prove in court, if necessary—that the company's Lodestar Baby Safety Seat Model 13401 failed in any way to do its job. Gannon firmly believes that other factors were in play. In order to reach a better understanding of this tragedy, we need to thoroughly review the series of events that led up to the accident last April. So let me start by asking you . . ."

I'd been over this ground so many times with Janet that I was able to answer his questions about the warmth of the day, the decision to play ball, the game itself, without much thought. Instead, I found my gaze drifting again and again to the court reporter at the end of the table. There was something about the fluid movement of his fingers over the raised keyboard, documenting my responses, that I found disconcerting. There was no escaping it now: what I said really counted—and could no longer be changed or retracted. All those long months of discussion, planning, testing, and research had come down to this: my word. Eddie was right—everything depended on me.

About five minutes into McCarthy's questioning, a side door behind the court reporter opened and Kurt slipped into the room. I noticed him because I happened to be glancing in that direction, but the others had been looking back and forth between McCarthy and myself. I'm not sure if anyone besides me saw Kurt quietly take a seat at the far end of the row of chairs where Eddie was sitting. His sudden appearance must have distracted me, because the next thing I knew, McCarthy was asking:

"Mr. Horigan? Do you need me to repeat the question?"

"I guess so."

"There was a keg of beer at this game, was there not?"

"No," I said. "There was a cooler of beer. Actually, two. Both sides are expected to bring their own. It was a hot day."

"Yes, you've mentioned that. How many beers did you have?"

"I don't remember exactly."

"Give me a guess. How many beers do you estimate you consumed across the course of the afternoon?"

I'd discussed this particular question with both Lester and Janet. We'd circled around the problem several times on different occasions and had settled on "a couple." Meaning, at most, two. But, like so much else about that day, the beer count remains a gray area for me. And, because I couldn't be sure, I've somehow let myself be persuaded that, yes, I might have had just one or two. It might have been a couple. But the few times I've allowed myself to really consider the question on my own, I've had to admit that it was more than a couple. More like four or five possibly. One every other inning or so. Definitely one after I hit the homer. Thinking about that particular moment again, I clearly remembered the worn-down playing field. The way the sun burst through a cloud bank. *Make it happen,* I remember telling myself. *Just go ahead and make it happen.* And I knew the second my bat connected with the ball that I'd gotten my wish.

"Mr. Horigan?" McCarthy asked again. "An estimate please."

I was taking too long, I realized. And yet, it came to me that this was the central question. No, this was the only question. The turning point for me. How could I have convinced myself I'd made a stand when I took on Gannon? In fact, I'd simply turned my back on the real fight—and had been running from it ever since. Jenny tried to tell me. Again and again. But she never came right out and said it. She refused to blame me. My heart ached just thinking about that. And her.

"More than a couple . . . ," I began. Then I said, "I had too many."

"Mr. Horigan?" McCarthy asked. "Is that really your—"

"Hold on a second here," Lester said, turning to me.

I saw Eddie start to get up from his chair.

"I can't say I was drunk exactly," I said, sitting back and looking up at the ceiling. The overhead lights glittered above me, and I felt faint. I bowed my head. "But I can tell you for sure that I'd had too much to drink. I should never have gotten behind that wheel."

Everyone started talking at once. Lester called for a break. I just sat there looking down at the table. I half heard Lester, Janet, and Eddie conferring behind me, their words overlapping: "clearly not well . . . flu-like symptoms . . . tossed his cookies on the way up here . . . shouldn't have allowed . . . obviously we'll postpone . . ."

I felt a hand on my shoulder. I knew who it was without looking up.

❧

The double doors closed, and Eddie, Kurt, and I were alone together.

"Oh, boy, did you fuck up," Eddie said. "You really fucked up!" He was pacing back and forth. I was still seated, Kurt standing behind me.

"I know," I said.

278   LIZA GYLLENHAAL

"Lester thinks we can still pull this out. He's trying to feed McCarthy the line that you're sick. Walked in here sick. That he never should have let you—"

"No, it's over, Eddie," I said. "It's not going to happen."

"What?" he turned, staring from me to Kurt. "Because of what *this* asshole claims? You're really going to take that to heart? What kind of a pussy—"

"It's bullshit. This whole thing is bullshit. I was drinking, and I rolled the Jeep and—"

"You walked away without a scratch," Eddie said. "And your daughter was killed. Why? Because the goddamn seat was defective! Isn't that the whole reason we're here, Cal?"

"You tell me, Eddie," I said. "I don't give a damn anymore."

"Well, you better," Eddie said. He stopped moving. He stood across the table from Kurt and me, hands on hips. "Or the business is fucked."

"What business?" Kurt asked.

"Horigan Lumber and Hardware. I've—I made some bad moves in the market. I had to take out some loans to cover for it. And I used the business as collateral. Unless we win this suit, we're screwed."

22

Cal

॰

$\mathcal{E}$ddie told us in the parking garage under the Stephens, Stokes office building that he needed to get away for a while. He was thinking of heading north to a hunting cabin he sometimes rented with some of his old college buddies.

"I have to work out what I'm going to do next," he said, looking from me to Kurt. "I don't believe either of you really understands what you just kissed good-bye back there. We're looking into the eye of a fucking financial hurricane."

"No," Kurt said, "not *we*. You're out of Horigan Lumber. You take one step back into those offices, and I'll personally call Chief Tyler and have you arrested."

"You wouldn't—"

"Or maybe we should just make the call right now," I told Kurt. "What's the point of waiting? This asshole already admitted that he's been robbing the old man blind."

"Hold on, Cal," Eddie began. "I think that after all I tried to do for you—"

"Oh, just shut the fuck up," I said, turning to face him.

I'd been too stunned to look him in the eye after the EBT conference. Or during the awful postmortem in Lester's office when I had to tell the lawyer that I'd been lying—to myself as much as to anybody. But I think Lester must have known what was coming, because he took the news with what seemed to me surprising calm. He wasn't happy about it, and he told me there were some legal matters we still had to deal with, but it was clear the litigation was a no-go without my support. We hadn't told him what had happened with Edmund, but Lester made an interesting comment as we were leaving:

"I should always know something's wrong when it isn't the actual plaintiff who makes that first inquiry."

I should have known, too, of course. After all the bad blood between Eddie and myself over the years, I should have suspected that whatever my older brother was up to, it would be primarily to his advantage. Edmund's always been a me-first kind of guy. Why should Betsy's death have changed him in any real way? After all, it hadn't changed me—her own father. I went right on taking the easy way out, doing what made me feel better. Just as Eddie probably knew I would. All I'd needed was a little prodding on his part. And I hated myself for that almost as much as I hated him for knowing how easily I could be played.

"You tried to rob me, too," I told him. "You saw an opportunity to use the situation—and you went for it. You knew I was vulnerable. Hell, you knew I was a mess. But, then, you were counting on that, weren't you? You were able to push me in whatever direction you needed. You don't give a damn that my life's a total disaster right now. You don't give a fuck that this whole fiasco has maybe cost me my marriage. But you know what burns me the most? You know what forces me to think that my own flesh and blood is the scum of the earth?"

He looked at me blandly, though I noticed he'd balled his hands into fists. He was waiting for me to make some kind of a move.

"You don't even know, do you?"

"No, but I'm sure you're going to enlighten me. You seem to be in a very confessional mood today."

I tried to move forward, but Kurt grabbed my arm.

"Don't give him the satisfaction," he said. "If he doesn't get it, there's really no hope."

Eddie shrugged and took a few steps back before he turned and started toward his car. I was going to leave it at that. Kurt was right—there was no hope. But when Eddie nonchalantly clicked his key fob and the lights flashed on the Beamer, I lost it for some reason.

"You used Betsy!" I cried, my voice ricocheting off the low cement ceiling of the parking garage. "Betsy, Betsy, Betsy!"

❦

Kurt and I drove back down to Covington in his car. We didn't say anything for a while.

"Jesus," Kurt muttered once we'd hit the highway, shaking his head.

"Yeah," I replied. "It's just unbelievable."

"What the fuck?" he said after another mile or so. "What are we going to do?"

"I guess it's up to us to tell the old man," I said.

"You think he doesn't know already?" Kurt asked.

"No way. I just can't see him letting Eddie get away with it. Dad wouldn't put up with that kind of crap for a minute."

"Unless he'd just turned a blind eye for so long he had no other choice. But no, I can't really see that happening. You've got to be right. He doesn't know."

But as we drove on in silence, I started to rethink my first reaction. And I began to piece together a scenario that would have Jay Horigan caught right in the middle of his oldest son's schemes and lies.

During the thirty or so years my father had built up Horigan Lumber and Hardware from the single-floor storefront his father had left him to the biggest hardware supplier in the tricounty region, the financial end of the business had been handled by Alan Sheer, a reliable, reserved, old-fashioned accountant. By the time he retired and my father offered the position to Eddie, a newly minted MBA, Jay Horigan had lost all interest in that side of the business, if he'd ever really had any. In my dad's mind, the success of Horigan Lumber was due to salesmanship, goodwill, and personal relationships built over the course of a lifetime.

"A loyal customer," he was fond of saying, "is money in the bank." As far as he was concerned, only Jay Horigan knew how to keep a customer truly loyal—while almost anybody could handle the money. So he hadn't noticed when Eddie began his double-dealing. He barely glanced at the spreadsheets his oldest son insisted on printing out for him every week. Even if he did sense something was a little off, he couldn't begin to guess where to look for it. He'd never even learned how to turn on a computer.

Who knows how bad things already were when my father went in for his bypass surgery that summer? But the timing couldn't have been worse: the markets in free fall and Eddie suddenly in charge of making all the business decisions. That's probably when it began to really roll downhill—picking up steam as the construction industry tanked and lending dried up.

Suddenly, I flashed on the lunch Eddie, my dad, and that banker were having at Deer Creek Bistro the day Betsy died. How, afterward, Eddie had driven out to the ball game to assure Kurt and me that "he didn't want us to worry"—the meeting had been the banker's idea. It was the conversation that led to my fight with Eddie—and all the terrible things that followed.

"Actually, I'm pretty sure he *does* know," I told Kurt.

"You think?" Kurt asked, looking over at me, but his expression told me that he wasn't far from drawing the same conclusion.

"Yeah, he knows," I said again, "and it's probably been breaking his heart."

"What are we going to do?"

"Step in," I said without even thinking about it. "Take over. Meet with the creditors. Cut some deal with the bank. Sit down with the big clients. Make it clear we can be trusted."

"Yeah," Kurt said, his tone doubtful. "But you know how these things work. Word spreads so fast. People will be talking about this before we even wake up tomorrow morning. The nasty gossip alone could sink us."

"Okay, so we get out in front of it," I told him, trying to think the thing through. "We do what we can to spin the story. We could even try to finesse Eddie's role—I don't know, make it seem like Dad gave Eddie the money to invest or something. And everyone's been taking a beating in the market, right? Maybe we could find some smart PR guy to help us out there. Then we hire a real pro to clean up the accounting systems. Do whatever needs to be done. But I'm telling you right now, I'm not letting this ship go down."

❦

I tried to get through to Jude—the only person to have Jenny's number—on my cell on the drive back down, but, as usual, the reception was shitty.

"Listen, let me deal with Dad," Kurt said as I slapped the phone against my thigh in frustration. "I'm going to drop you at the Honeggers' on my way. That's more important."

"Yeah, that'd be great," I said. "I really need to reach her. Oh man, I hope it's not too late."

"Don't worry. It's going to be fine," Kurt told me.

"Thanks," I said as we pulled up in front of the old white gingerbread colonial. "I'll find you after I talk to Jenny. Tell the old man not to worry. Tell him we've got his back."

I rang the doorbell, but nobody came. I banged on the front door, but still no answer. I walked around the house to peer in the window of the reverend's study, but no one was there. I tried Jude's cell again, and this time the call went through. When she answered, I told her where I was.

"I'm in the basement," she said. "What are you doing here? I read in the paper that you and Gannon were having a big meeting today. Whoa—wait—did they settle?"

"I've been trying to call you. I need Jenny's number."

"I can't— No, hold on. I'll be right up. Come around back to the kitchen."

I could tell that she knew something was wrong as soon as she opened the door.

"What? You lost? So what's going on?"

"I need to talk to my wife," I told her, leaving the door half-open behind me. Jude's flip, flirty attitude has always irritated me.

"I'm sorry, but she told me I could only give out the number if there was some kind of emergency."

"It's an emergency, Jude. Okay? I need to talk to her—so please let's stop playing around here. I'm really not in the mood."

"And I'm not in the mood to be talked to like I'm a three-year-old. I promised Jenny that I wouldn't give out the number unless—"

"It's a fucking emergency!" I said, slamming the kitchen door shut behind me. "And I'm not going to let you try to get in between the two of us again. I want that number, and I want it now."

Her eyes widened, then filled with tears.

"I'm sorry. I never meant for that to happen. I was going through a really bad time then and—" But she saw my expression and swallowed hard. She pulled her cell phone from the pocket of her jeans and scrolled through the listings. She wrote a number with a 212 area code down for me and handed it over.

"Just please tell her you forced me to give it to you, okay? Against my will. I'm not responsible for what happens."

"Fine," I said. I was so used to Jude's histrionics I didn't think twice about her ominous tone. I turned to the door.

"And, just for your information," she said to my back, "I

tried to be your champion. You can hardly blame me for coming between the two of you this time."

❧

I didn't want my damn cell phone dying on me in the middle of the most important conversation of my life. I decided I'd make the call on the landline at my folks' place, which was just a couple of blocks away from the Honeggers'. I'd been using Jenny's car while she was away, but Eddie had driven me up to Albany that morning, so I had to cover the distance on foot. I jogged through town, the streetlights outside the Public Market and Covington Wine and Liquor starting to sputter on as the afternoon faded. Kurt was right: no matter what we did, this sleepy town would be buzzing with news of our misfortune by morning.

Kurt's Subaru was parked in my parents' driveway. My mother and Kurt were sitting together at the kitchen table.

"Oh, honey!" my mom said when I walked in. She stood up and hugged me. "Kurt's told us. I don't believe it. I just don't believe it."

"I'm really sorry, Mom," I said, looking across the table at Kurt. "How's he taking it?"

"Hard," Kurt said. "Though I think we were right about—what we said. Anyway, he told us he felt tired—and went downstairs a few minutes ago."

My hands were itching to grab a phone, but I asked my mother:

"Should I go down and talk to him, do you think?"

"No, let him be for now. I thought he looked exhausted."

"I'm going to call Jenny, okay? Can I use the phone in the front hall?"

"Of course. Tell her it's time to come home."

"I will," I said, wishing to hell it could be that simple.

The old black dial-up phone my parents have had for as long as I can remember sat on a mahogany side table at the foot of the stairs. I pulled the chain on the lamp beside it so that I could read the number Jude had jotted down. My fingers shook a little as I dialed—each rotation seeming to take forever. I breathed in deeply when the phone began to ring at the other end, rehearsing the first thing I would say to her: *I'm sorry, Jenny. I've never been more sorry in my life . . .*

The phone rang four times before a message machine kicked in:

"Hello, you've reached Daniel Brandt. I can't take your call right now, but please leave . . ."

I dropped the receiver back into the cradle. I just stood there, staring stupidly at the thing. The familiar voice kept repeating in my ear: *Hello, you've reached Daniel Brandt.* My mind was trying to make sense of what I'd heard, but my body already understood. I slumped into a chair next to the table. *Hello, you've reached Daniel Brandt.*

The pieces tumbled together in my head. Jenny telling me that she didn't much like him when they first met. *I don't know, there's just something about him . . .* Fighting me every step of the way on the garden. Until she didn't. Until they had that lunch together. I remember Daniel asking me: *Did Jenny tell you I took her out the day the garden went in? That we had a long talk?*

I know how these things work. And, of course, I know how Daniel worked. How he felt. He'd told me so more than once. He'd as good as warned me: *I believe life simply unfolds—as mysteriously and inevitably as a flower. And, if you have any sense at all, you'll do everything in your power to enjoy the process.*

And then there was Jenny. Whom I'd refused to listen to. Whom I'd turned my back on. The heart of Jenny's life had been ripped out of her. And I'd left her all alone—facing that bottomless void. And who was right there to fill it? Just as he'd been there for me when I felt so guilty and confused. What drew us to him? I wondered. And he to the two of us? Did he sense how damaged we both were? How vulnerable? And to think that I was the one who brought him so eagerly into our lives! I remembered the night of Jenny's birthday party when Daniel gave her those roses and the plans for the garden. He'd called her "Mrs. Horigan," and I'd said: *Honestly! Aren't you two up to first names yet? Here, let me introduce you: Jenny, this is Daniel.*

When I walked back into the kitchen, my mother and Kurt were still talking quietly across the table. I knew I had to appear to be calm.

"Hey, Mom. I'm going to borrow the Olds, okay?" A plan was starting to form in my head, though I had only the vaguest sense of its final shape.

"You get through to her?" Kurt asked.

"No. I need to check the number Jude gave me. I think I'll just shoot back over there."

"Wouldn't it be easier to call?" Kurt asked.

"I tried," I said, "but the line's busy." I didn't like lying to Kurt, but I knew that what I needed to do couldn't wait. The urge to move, to make something happen, propelled me across the room. "I just want to get this done."

"Sure," Kurt said as I opened the door. "But give me a

call after you talk to her, okay? I think I'm just going to hang out here for a while—and check back in on Dad."

"Yeah," I said. I wasn't listening. I wasn't thinking. I still had the key to my father's Olds on my chain. I sensed Kurt knew something was up, so I drove slowly down the drive. But I picked up speed, heading north. By the time I pulled into the parking lot behind Kurt's place, evening had settled in.

I pushed open the side door to the garage where Kurt and I store our heavy equipment. When I hit the switch, the overhead doors rolled up and the ceiling lights blinked on. By then I had a better sense of what I was going to do. I found the key on the rack inside the door, walked past our trucks, and climbed up into the cab of the Deere Excavator. We use it for lighter jobs: site development, garage foundations. It's a small but powerful machine—with a swing boom and reduced tail swing—easy to maneuver in tight spaces. I hadn't been behind the levers in more than a year. As the motor kicked in, it occurred to me that this might be the last time I'd be driving it. My work life would be revolving around a sales office from now on.

At top speed, the Excavator can average a little more than three miles an hour. With the lights flashing and the bucket stowed, I crawled along the side of the road. I felt oddly at peace as I drove. I felt as though my mind had cleared at last. I could see now where I had come from—all those wrong turns and dead ends—and where I was heading. I felt confident I could reclaim my life—I could win Jenny back—if I could just make this one thing right. It was about thirty minutes before I made the turn off Route 32.

The Excavator bumped along our driveway until I veered off onto the grass and down the incline along the side of the house. A new moon had risen over the fields. Daniel's garden was bathed in silvery light. I shifted into park and took one last look at the stone walls and sloping pathways. The bare branches of the pricey specimen trees just starting to thicken with new growth, the carefully arranged groupings of shrubs, the mounded contours of the perennial beds. I felt no regret as I rotated the lever and watched the bucket stretch above me into the sky. I felt only relief as I shifted into gear and guided the Excavator down the hillside.

❦

I'd been at it for more than an hour when I heard the sirens. I'll probably never be able to hear that sound again without thinking of Betsy. Despite the chill night air, I felt sweaty and a little feverish. It seemed like years had passed since Eddie had picked me up for the EBT meeting that morning. The sirens sobbed over the noise from the Excavator for a time—somewhere to the west, probably heading up the Taconic—and then bled away into the night.

23

Jenny

൙

The Traegers' kitchen faces east toward Broadway and is bathed in sunlight on mornings when the weather is clear. At the start of my fourth week there, I walked into the kitchen to make coffee and felt dazed by the light. It was late March; the sun dominated a cloudless sky. The panes of glass in the old wooden cupboards and the wineglasses drying in the drainer by the sink were shimmering in a way that seemed almost otherworldly. I slept a little later than usual that morning and woke up with a throbbing headache. Now I felt the dull, steady pain start to sharpen. It became something I could almost hear—a kind of muffled keening— like someone crying in a distant room.

My eyes hadn't adjusted to the brightness when I picked up one of the wineglasses in the drainer and turned around to put it away in the cupboard. I felt it slip through my fingers.

It cracked against a metal drawer pull as it fell—and smashed onto the tiled floor. Several large shards—along with a dusting of pulverized glass—glinted up at me. My shadow fell across the floor as I leaned over to start cleaning things up, and a piece of glass I hadn't noticed sliced into the tip of my right middle finger. Blood dribbled onto the tile. As I raised the fingertip to my lips, the noise in my head started to swell. Dizzy and frightened, I closed my eyes, sucking on my finger to try to stanch the bleeding.

And then, in that instant, my thoughts flashed back to Betsy's last day. To that moment when I was strapping her into the safety seat. But unlike all the other times I'd tried to recall what I'd done, the memory was no longer clouded or confused. I could see it clearly now:

It's almost as though I'm living it over again. As if no time at all has passed. The late afternoon sun warms my shoulders as I lean into the backseat. I feel the cool metal buckle in my fingers. I sense Tessa nearby—she's bouncing Jamie in the BabyBjörn and the rhythmic movement rocks the Jeep a little. Then I feel my heart about to burst—there's Betsy! I'm weak with joy. I breathe in her sweet, musty smell as I fit the two parts of the bottom buckle together—and hear a little *click*.

It's funny how the mind works. It's only now that I realize how I've come to blame Tessa for making me interrupt what I'm doing. How much I resent Jude because she makes me turn to Tessa and say:

"I haven't gotten a chance to tell Cal yet. About Jude coming back."

And why am I so afraid to tell him? Is it because I don't really trust him? Because I don't trust Jude? No, I see now that it's because I simply can't believe my own good fortune. My amazing luck. A loving husband. A beautiful child.

Everything I could hope for in this world—but also everything that I know in my heart I can't really count on. And that I probably don't deserve. Because any minute now, everything I love could be snatched away. Just as on an otherwise normal day, my own mother walked out the door, climbed onto the back of a stranger's motorcycle, and rode out of my life forever.

"Enough said," Tessa tells me as Cal approaches. I know something's happened between him and Edmund. He's looking at the ground as he walks, and he's not moving with his usual swagger. I can tell his mind is elsewhere. He's lost some of his cockiness since his dad had his surgery. And, with business so down these days, I know he's beginning to worry. I fell in love with such an easygoing, fun-loving guy. But I've come to admire and am slightly in awe of the way Cal's growing up, stepping up, becoming a man. As I lean back into the Jeep, I'm thinking how much I hate having to tell him about Jude—and dredge up that whole awful period in our lives.

That's what I'm thinking about when I buckle the strap that goes across Betsy's chest—or when I forget to. My husband. Someone I love too much for my own good. And I want to tell him so. That he's my whole life. But I can't now, because of this damned business with my sister. The timing's off. I feel the moment slipping away. I realize how much I've been keeping from Cal since Betsy's birth. And I know it isn't right. Soon I'm going to have to tell him the truth: how vulnerable I've been feeling, how uncertain. How my mother's shadow so often seems to fall between me and my own daughter. I kiss Betsy on her forehead.

"She seems a lot better," I tell Cal. "Maybe it was just the heat after all." I'm stepping back from the car seat and Betsy when I feel the incredible gentleness of her baby fingers, wrapping around my thumb. Her eyes are that Horigan hazel, shifting—like sunlight across pond water—from brown to green, from wary to warm. I feel a sharp tug of mother love. She smiles sleepily up at me.

"See you later, little gator," I tell her as I pull my hand away.

❦

I don't know how long I stood there in the sunlight in the middle of the kitchen. When I came to, I realized that I was rubbing the bloody fingertips of my right hand together—index, middle finger, thumb.

I was able to cry for only the first few hours after Betsy was killed. And I was still in shock then—swinging wildly between a feverish disbelief and the abyss of reality. After Chief Tyler called on me early the next morning to tell me about the car seat, I was never really able to cry for her again. I would squeeze my eyes shut to try to block out the anguish. But soon I could no longer access my real feelings—it felt as though my heart had frozen over. I remember seeing Tessa weeping at the funeral, her body rocking back and forth. I longed for the same release. I remember wondering if people would think it strange that I seemed so composed. How many months have I spent seeing myself through other people's eyes? Judging my actions through them. Awaiting a verdict. Knowing the whole time what it would turn out to be.

I leaned over the sink to wash the blood away. I watched the water sluice between my open fingers—and felt my body begin to shudder. I choked on my sobs—harsh gasps that burned in my throat. I could hardly breathe. Then I heard that high keening sound again—like an animal in terrible pain—and realized it was me. From some vast source of unending sorrow, I wept, tears rolling down my cheeks, down my neck, down the length of my body.

I cried until I couldn't anymore. Until I simply didn't have the strength to go on. Exhausted, I went into the living room and curled up on the Traegers' formal-looking couch. I realized that I could never again sleep in the bed I'd been sharing with Daniel. Just the thought of him made me feel sick—in an immediate and physical way—as though I'd ingested something that had gone bad. The memory of his smell, the rough texture of his skin, the slight oiliness of his hair—everything about him now made my stomach turn. I rested my head on a scratchy roll pillow. But it was too hard, so I pulled it to me, wrapping my arms around it for comfort. It was the first time in almost a year that I could let myself believe I actually had the right to be comforted.

❦

"Dad?" I said. The voice that answered the phone didn't sound like his, and I wondered briefly if I'd dialed a wrong number.

"I told Judith you'd call," he said. "Shall I get her for you? I'm sorry about what happened."

I thought he was referring to our last argument, when I'd become so enraged because he suggested I needed to move on with my life. When he told me that Cal and I should have another child.

"No, not yet. I wanted to tell you something." I hadn't prepared myself for any of this. I was still a little groggy from having slept straight through for nearly eight hours. It was seven o'clock in the evening. I remembered hearing the phone ringing at some point. Daniel took most of his calls on his cell, but he'd changed the Traegers' message to one of his, and for some time the sound of his voice rippled through my dreams. As soon as I woke up, though, I knew I had to get out of there—and away from him. I needed to get back to Covington. To Cal. I wanted to go home.

"Yes?" I could hear the quaver in my father's voice.

"Remember when you told me that I should stop believing that—if I could only find a way—I might somehow be able to hold Betsy again? You said thinking like that could only make things worse?"

"I was too blunt, I know," he said. "I'm sorry. I'm aware that I don't have a very sympathetic bedside manner."

"No, you don't," I said. But I'd resented him so deeply and for so long that I hadn't allowed myself to realize that in his own way, he'd tried to reach out to me. He'd tried to help. "But it doesn't mean you were wrong. In fact, I want you to know that almost everything you told me since Betsy died turns out to be true. I only wish I'd been able to listen to you sooner."

"Oh. Well. Thank you," he said, pausing a moment before he added: "You're telling me this because of what's been happening in Cal's family?"

"No, I'm telling you— What do you mean?"

"I mean what's going on with the Horigans."

"What are you talking about?"

"You haven't heard? Isn't that why you called?"

"No." The room darkened. I could tell by his tone of voice that whatever had happened was bad.

"Is Cal okay?"

"Yes. Yes, I think so," he said. "But his dad is up at Albany Medical. He's had a massive heart attack."

"Oh no," I said. "Oh, Daddy. I'm coming back right now."

"And that's not all, I'm afraid."

❦

I packed my things as soon as I hung up from talking with my father, and I left Daniel a note that said simply "I'm going home—for good." But I missed the last train out of Grand Central, and I was forced to spend a sleepless night at a nearby Marriott.

I called Jude before I left the next morning, and she was waiting for me at the station in Hudson. I felt as though I hadn't seen her in years. She even looked different to me. She was sporting a new haircut. I started crying as soon as I saw her. We both stood there on the train platform, arms around each other, sobbing like children. She finally pulled away to dig in her shoulder bag for a Kleenex.

"Mascara!" she said, dabbing at her eyes. "Can you believe it? I got a makeover last week and spent about a hundred dollars on a bunch of damned stuff that just keeps coming off all over the place!"

"Why the makeup?" I asked her. I was stalling, and I think she knew it. It wasn't only my father who had been right about things. There was so much that I needed to learn from her—but also so much I wanted to tell her.

"Why else?" she said with a shrug. "I'm so unliberated it's totally pathetic."

"You've met someone!"

"Yeah. Sure. Maybe." As we climbed into her beat-up

old Chevy van, she said, "He's the stage manager at the Warwick Summer Theatre Festival. Did I happen to mention that I landed the role of Titania in *A Midsummer Night's Dream*?"

"Oh, Jude! That's so great!" I said, turning to hug her again. "I feel like Rip Van Winkle, coming back down from the mountain after twenty years. The whole world seems to have changed."

"Yeah," she said, letting out a long sigh as she backed out of the parking spot. "It sure has."

"Okay," I said. "Dad gave me the bare bones. I need you to start fleshing things out."

"So you and Cal haven't talked yet?" she asked, glancing over at me.

"No."

"He didn't call? Because I'm really, really sorry, but he made me give him the number."

"No—," I began. And then I remembered the ringing phone at the Traegers' the day before. Whoever called had hung up when Daniel's message came on. Oh God, had it been Cal?

"No," I told her again, fighting back panic. I had to get back to him. I had to try to explain. But first, I knew I needed to calm down. Sort things out. I looked out the window at the rolling fields and farmland. The area around Hudson greens out a week or two earlier than our more northern Covington. Could it be that another spring was arriving without Betsy in the world? She'd be talking in sentences now. She'd be a little girl. I could imagine her, reaching up to hold my hand. The two of us walking through these fields together.

"Tell me what's happened," I said.

"Before we go into that, I'd like to know what—"

"It's over," I said, sensing what she was going to ask. "You were right. One hundred percent. I was so wrong—I really can't tell you what I saw in him. I can only plead temporary insanity. And tell you that I'm so sorry about some of the things I said."

"Well, you were right about me, at least," Jude said. "It really is time for me to grow up. And I want you to know that I've been trying."

"Oh, Jude—I'm so sorry—"

"Yeah. I know," she said, glancing over at me with her mischievous smile that reminds me so much of Betsy. "I just needed to milk that a little. And you've already apologized twice now. So, okay, where do I start? I saw Cal yesterday—but, like I say, all he wanted was your number; he didn't tell me anything. There were just so many wild rumors floating around! I decided to call Tessa. We talked before I left to pick you up, and she filled me in as much as she could. It turns out Edmund's been cooking the books at Horigan Lumber. He's been doing it for years, evidently. Nobody really understands yet how it happened—but it looks really bad for the business right now. The bank's probably going to have to get involved."

"And nobody knew?" I asked, trying to remember if there'd been any warning signs. But Edmund has always been so buttoned-up and businesslike, he'd be the last person I'd pick to do something like this. And he'd probably been counting on that.

"Tessa thinks that the old man might have suspected. Apparently he didn't seem all that shocked when he learned the news. He just said he felt tired and went down to his basement office to take a nap. When Kurt went down to check on him later, he found him on the floor."

"How bad is it?"

"Bad. He's still unconscious. And he's on a ventilator. But apparently he left instructions in his living will that he doesn't want to be hooked up to the thing longer than seventy-two hours. The family's taking turns being with him in Albany. Cal and his mother are there now."

"Oh, poor Jay," I said. He'd always been so proud of the business. If he had any sense of what Edmund had been up to, it must have been eating away at him. His own son undermining the work of a lifetime. The Horigans had to be reeling.

"And Dad told me Cal's pulled out of the Gannon suit."

"Yeah. When he found out why Eddie had been pushing so hard for it—that he needed the money to keep himself and the business afloat—Cal killed the whole deal. Tessa thinks he's really sorry that he ever got sucked into it in the first place. That he's sorry about a lot of things."

"He's not alone," I said, looking down. My hands were clenched together in my lap. I felt Jude's gaze on me, but when I glanced over at her she was looking straight ahead.

"I've never cheated on Cal," I told her. "I've never done anything even remotely like this before. I don't know what to say. I don't know how I'm ever going to be able to explain it to him."

"Well—news flash!" Jude said. "Cal's been screwing Lori Swinson for the past three months or something. So don't beat yourself up too much."

"What? Lori? That big dumb bottle—"

"That's the one. I think it's been over for a little while now. Not that anybody but Lori seriously believed that it could last for very long. But I think you should know: I hear Cal's not been in the best of shape."

"Drinking?"

"Yeah. And I think it's gotten worse since you left. Apparently, he went kind of ballistic last night—I guess when he heard about his dad. Tessa said you should prepare yourself. That he's really not himself right now."

But then, of course, neither of us was. Whoever we'd once been, we weren't anymore. We were just as broken and useless as Cal's Jeep. As Betsy's car seat. And there was no chance that we could put our old selves back together again. We'd both sustained too much damage. What did I have in common now with the confident, sunny boy I'd married? Or even the cocksure, party-loving man who'd taken off in the Jeep with our daughter almost a year ago? And, for my part, I must be even more of a stranger to him. I lied to him. I cheated on him. I let him believe I thought he was responsible for Betsy's death. He'd been headstrong and obstinate, but I'd done unforgivable things. Would he ever again be able to look at me with love?

I was thinking so hard about Cal, I didn't realize Jude had turned onto North Branch. I hadn't driven along this road since the accident. In fact, I'd made a point of avoiding it. Though I slept in Betsy's room for months, though I've visited her grave, I just haven't been able to face seeing the place where her life actually ended. We hit those familiar little roller-coaster hills before I had a chance to think or object. We were approaching the stretch of roadway where I imagined the Jeep had rolled—up on the left, across from the

Odhners' old dairy farm. I remember Cal telling me that the last time he saw Betsy—in the rearview mirror, just before the fox ran across their path—she'd been laughing.

I've imagined the final seconds of her life so many times. Praying she hadn't been afraid. Hoping she'd felt only a brief, wild joy—because, in fact, she'd been flying. The last of the sunlight glinted off the top of a silo and blazed across the surface of an old cow pond. Was this the last thing she saw? Sunlight—slanting through a gap in the trees—like a door, opening in welcome?

We passed the spot before I could be certain it was the place I'd had in my mind for so long. I'd imagined it differently somehow. Darker, steeper. More than just another bank along a quiet country road. I turned to look back. Had that really been it? I still wasn't sure. I faced forward again as we drove on.

24

Cal and Jenny

⚜

"Drop me off here," she told Jude just before the turn into the driveway. "I think I need to walk the rest of the way."

"Okay," Jude said, pulling off to the side of the road. "Call me later?"

"Sure," she said, climbing out of the van. But she held the door open, leaning in to look at her sister. Jude's new haircut made her look older, more pulled together.

"Thanks for saying you believed in us—Cal and me," she said, thinking how badly she'd reacted when Jude had actually told her that. How frantic she'd been to leave for the city and Daniel then. It had been the last thing she wanted to hear. But that morning on the train ride home she'd remembered what Jude said—*You and Cal have one of the few marriages in the whole world I actually have some real faith in*—and the words had come back to her like a kind of blessing. If her sister could believe in the two of them, then who knew? Maybe they had a chance, after all.

But, as she walked up the curving driveway and caught her first glimpse of the house through the trees, all her doubts came flooding back. She knew she had to tell Cal what she'd done. The terrible mistakes she had made. Starting with the first and most unforgivable. The lies she'd told. Ending with the one that could force even the most stable of marriages to founder. She knew she had to tell him. There could be no way forward if she didn't. But she also knew that, when she did, she might very well end up destroying the thing that mattered to her most in the world.

It helped that Cal would be in Albany with his dad, and that she'd have the house to herself for a little while. It would give her time to unpack. Take a shower maybe. Think about all the things she needed to say. And the right words with which to say them.

She'd left at the end of winter. Now she saw patches of green on the lawn. Furry buds on the crab apple tree. Purple shoots pushing up from the peony beds that bordered the front of the house. Thank God, Daniel hadn't touched this part of the yard. It looked the same as it did every spring, and as it probably had for generations. She might have lost the big garden, but at least she still had this. That thought helped steady her as she put down her suitcase and pushed open the front door.

☞

He'd been listening for Jude's van, so he was caught off guard when Jenny walked in without warning. Jenny's father had called him at the hospital to tell him she was coming home. God only knew how he'd managed to track down Cal's cell number. But Cal had been grateful. It was the first overtly kind thing he could remember the reverend ever doing for him. He'd driven back down to Covington faster than he should have, especially considering he hadn't gotten any sleep the night before. But driving recklessly seemed like nothing compared to everything he had already risked.

She stopped when she saw him.

"You're here," she said. He looked so wiped out, she wanted to cry. For the first time it really registered with her what he'd been going through while she'd been away. The lawsuit falling apart. Horigan Lumber collapsing. His dad in bad shape. "I thought you were up in—"

"I was," he told her, wondering what it meant that she hadn't expected him. Didn't she want to see him? Why had she returned exactly? He'd gotten his hopes up when the reverend called, but now he was no longer at all sure of his ground. It occurred to him that she might have come back just as a courtesy to him. Out of concern for his family. Maybe she had no intention of staying. Could she have actually fallen in love with Daniel Brandt? Was she still blind to what Daniel really was? But, then, it had taken him long enough to figure it out himself—too long. He'd have to tread very gently. He'd have to play the few cards he still held very carefully.

"Your dad called to tell me Jude was picking you up," he told her. "I wanted to get back here—to see you. Let me have your bag."

When he moved toward her, she took a step forward, dropped the suitcase, then retreated again. She couldn't risk him touching her. She had to keep herself together, steeled, or she would never be able to get through it all. But the look that crossed his face—a combination of sadness and

306   LIZA GYLLENHAAL

resignation—broke her heart. Could she believe that he still loved her? Suddenly, she lost her resolve. Did he have to know what she had done? Couldn't she find a way to live with it somehow—and let him keep on believing in her?

"How's Jay doing?" she asked, thinking about how much he had to deal with right now. What she had to tell him could wait. No, should wait.

"Not good," he said. His breath had been knocked out of him when he saw her step back. She didn't want to be near him. She still blamed him for everything. It was hopeless. "Not good at all. I was up there most of the night and he was unconscious the whole time. He's hooked up to all those machines. Tubes everywhere. He looks— He doesn't look like himself. The doctors aren't really saying anything yet—but I'm beginning to think the news is pretty bad."

"Tessa told Jude about the living will," she said, crossing her arms on her chest. He'd lost more weight, she noticed, but he'd cut his hair. Probably for the lawsuit. His ears stuck out a little. She used to think that haircuts made him look like a kid again. But he didn't look like that now. He looked older, actually. There was something different about his stance.

"Yeah, Dad left instructions to pull the plug after seventy-two hours," he said. "It's like a ticking time bomb. The big question now is whether we should tell Eddie what's happened. I mean, if it really is the end, then—"

"But wasn't it the news about what Eddie did that—"

"Who knows for sure?" he told her, picking up the suitcase and starting down the hall to the kitchen. "Listen, I've got to sit down before I fall down." His abruptness threw her off a little. He seemed to be carrying something a lot heavier than the bag. She could feel him weighing whatever it was in his mind. Perhaps he'd already decided that they should go their separate ways. Maybe he'd put two and two together when he called the Traegers' number, and he couldn't forgive her.

"The cupboard's kind of bare, I'm afraid," he told her, reaching into the refrigerator and pulling out a Diet Coke.

"I don't want anything," she said, watching him flip the top and drink. Easing himself onto one of the stools, he moved as if his whole body ached. It hurt her just looking at him. If only she could touch him: touch his shoulders, run her hands down his back. Instead, she made herself ask:

"What's going to happen with Horigan Lumber? Is the bank really going to take over? That's what Tessa told Jude."

"I don't know," he said. "It will all work itself out one way or the other. But that's not what I'm thinking about now. That's not what's on my mind." He swung toward her, put the can on the countertop, and said: "I need to tell you something."

This was it. She'd been right. It was Daniel. Or Lori. But he was ending it—ending the idea of *them*.

"Yes," she said. Apparently, her heart had healed enough for her to feel it breaking all over again. She closed her eyes.

"No, look at me," he said. Her face was so dear to him: soft featured and kind. He'd always particularly loved her eyes—that seemingly innocent gray-blue, offset by the arch of her brows. "I want you to look at me when I tell you this."

"Yes," she said again.

"I'm sorry, Jenny," he said. "I've never been more sorry about anything in my life."

She just stared at him, bracing for what was coming next.

He looked at her, trying to judge her reaction, but her expression seemed noncommittal. Closed off. Perhaps she actively hated him. He'd understand that. He hated himself, or the person who'd done what he had done—and then refused to take responsibility for any of it. Let her hate him. But even if she intended to leave him, he knew he couldn't let her go back to Daniel. Whatever happened, he would never allow her to throw her life away on Daniel—on someone like that.

"It wasn't just what Eddie did that made me drop the lawsuit," he told her. "Even before I knew how bad things were with the business—well, I finally had to face up to something I think you've been trying to tell me from the beginning."

"You did?" she asked. "You have?" So he knew, then. He understood she was responsible. That he had no chance of beating Gannon.

"Yes. And I finally told them the truth at the hearing."

"You *told* them?" It was as though he'd hit her. She felt tears well up, sting along her eyelids. Did he really believe she deserved that? She felt something give way within her: maybe he was right, maybe she did. Deserve it.

"I told them that I'd been drinking that afternoon," he went on, despite the stricken look on her face. He hated forcing her to live it all over again, but he had to get it out. "That I'd had too much to drink. That I should never have been driving. If anyone was responsible for Betsy's—"

"No," she said.

"And I kept right on drinking, right through her funeral. Right through everything, telling myself it was okay. Bullshitting myself." He paused, looking down at the floor. "Well, it's not okay. It's never been okay. And I'm changing that. I'm stopping, Jenny."

"All right," she said, "that's good. That's good—but you're wrong about what happened." If he hadn't taken on this burden, she might—just might—have been able to keep her secret. But she couldn't stand by and let him do this to himself.

"Listen, I think that maybe—," she began. She stopped and took a breath before she was able to go on: "I'm pretty sure I didn't finish strapping Betsy into the car seat. I know I fastened the bottom buckle. I remember that very clearly. I heard it—the click. But then I stopped for a second to say something to Tessa—and I don't know if I ever actually went back and fastened the top one. I don't know if I did, Cal. I don't think I did."

He rose from the stool. He just stood there, staring at her. She'd put her hands over her mouth, as though the terrible words had leapt out against her will. But why hadn't she told him right away? Why hadn't she shared this with him? He couldn't imagine what she'd been putting herself through all these months. She'd always been such a cautious mom, worrying about every little thing. And even if she *had* forgotten . . . But then, it was so like her to shoulder all the responsibility—to tell no one. He'd learned over the years about her outsized sense of guilt, which, he suspected, she'd been carrying with her since childhood. Only now did he realize how deeply it had damaged her.

"That's why you didn't want the lawsuit? Because of . . . what you thought you might have done?"

"I was her *mother*," she told him. "I should have been more careful."

"Come here," he said, holding out his arms.

She didn't want his pity. She could see it in his eyes. She wanted his love, even if she knew she no longer deserved it.

"And I was her dad," he said, closing the space between them and pulling her to him. "I was her *dad*. And I lost control of the Jeep—with my little girl in the back. I think I deserve to be blamed, too. I have to accept my share."

She breathed in his smell—sweat, soap, and something ineffably masculine. She couldn't believe how good it felt to be in his arms again. He picked her up then and swung her around in a circle. The kitchen—the great room—the French windows—the world outside—all passed in a delirious blur.

"Cal!" she cried. "Put me down."

He saw what had caught her attention. He set her back on her feet, facing the bank of windows. Without a word, she crossed the floor and opened the double doors. A damp breeze swept into the room. She walked out onto the terrace, and he followed her. Together, they looked out over the sloping yard where Daniel had installed the garden.

It was rubble now. Stone walls toppled. Trees and shrubs uprooted. The perennial beds pulverized. The artfully designed series of steps and pathways crushed beyond recognition. At the bottom of the hill where he had left it the night before, the Deere Excavator, silent now, oversaw her husband's handiwork.

"You know about it, then," Jenny said as she surveyed the desolate hillside. He knew, she thought, but he had still held her in his arms.

"I figured it out," he told her. She was standing in front of him so he couldn't see her expression, but her arms were folded defensively across her chest. He felt his heart turn over. This was the moment.

"I should never have let him into our lives, Jenny. He's not a good person. I should never have let him anywhere near us—near you. I was a fool. I was in such a bad place that I just couldn't see—"

"I couldn't either. But I do now. And it's over, Cal. I shouldn't have let it happen. It was so crazy and stupid of me."

"I've been stupid, too," he said.

"I know. Jude told me."

"She would have," Cal said, but she heard laughter in his voice. She felt his arms go around her again. He pulled her back against him. He was tall enough that he could rest his chin on the top of her head. They used to stand this way for minutes at a time when they were first given this house as a wedding gift. When they first had this view to look at. When they couldn't believe their own amazing luck. When they had no idea how truly lucky they were. He leaned over and whispered in her ear:

"I'm sorry about the mess."

"No, I think it's beautiful," she told him.

As they stood there together, Jenny let her gaze travel from the ruined garden up through the field to the north of the house, to the crest of the hill where she'd once thought of putting the gazebo. Where she'd imagined Betsy playing. Where one day, if their luck held, other children might play. She thought again of the path she'd once intended to put in, winding up through the wildflowers. The last of the sunlight blazed across the gray winter-weary grass, and the hillside shimmered for just a moment, backlit with a golden glow. That's how she'd start rebuilding the garden, she decided, laying in a pathway to the top of the hill.

Liza Gyllenhaal spent many years in advertising and publishing. She lives with her husband in New York City and western Massachusetts.

So Near

LIZA GYLLENHAAL

This Conversation Guide is intended to enrich the
individual reading experience, as well as encourage us
to explore these topics together—because books,
and life, are meant for sharing.

A CONVERSATION WITH LIZA GYLLENHAAL

Q. What made you want to write this novel? Did you know somebody who lost a child?

A. The story was actually sparked by a "This I Believe" piece that I heard on NPR a couple of years ago. It was about the "pathways of desire" that Daniel describes to Jenny when they first meet: "the tracks and paths we create naturally in our day-to-day lives. How we really get from place to place—from car to house, say, or across a vacant lot—rather than following the prescribed routes." The NPR essay went on to extrapolate on that idea, pointing out the necessity of boundaries and how certain "pathways" can lead to real danger—in this case the author's horse, who leapt across a cattle guard to get at some apples and broke a hip.

    The concept stayed with me and, when my mother died a few months later, I found myself longing for some sort of emotional shortcut, some quick way around the pain, something like a pathway of desire. The proscribed stages of grief just seemed too onerous—and time-consuming. My mother had died after a long, productive life, and I had many months to prepare myself for her passing and to say good-bye. If I felt this badly, I wondered, what must it be like to lose someone under truly adverse conditions? The most painful possibility I could imagine was losing a child—in a split second, without warning—and then believing you might actually be responsible for that death.

The novel grew out of that premise: how a couple copes with the worst possible scenario. I'm always drawn to writing about marriage and family, and it seemed to me that such an extreme situation would offer a lot of insight into both subjects. The rest of the story follows the divergent "pathways" they take to deal with their grief and guilt.

I've known several couples who have lost children, but, as with most fiction, Cal and Jenny are broad composites of real and imagined people. Though the novel deals specifically with a child's accidental death, I hope that it also sheds light on the journey we all are forced to take after a loved one dies.

Q. You wrote all but the final chapter in the first person point of view, but alternating between Jenny and Cal. Why?

A. I knew that I wanted to have both Cal and Jenny tell the story, sometimes even repeating the same scenes and conversations but from their differing viewpoints. How better to show them misreading each other—and growing further and further apart? Writing in the first person gave me (and, I hope, will give the reader) immediate access to their deepest emotions. Without this, I think some people might find their decisions unconscionable. They both behave in highly irrational and irresponsible ways. But, as Cal says at one point, grief "can make you do some crazy stuff." I hope that putting the reader inside Jenny's and Cal's heads helps make both characters more sympathetic and understandable.

At first, I didn't know why I wanted to cast the last chapter in the third person. But even before I wrote a word of the novel I knew that's how I wanted the story to end. It took me until I was actually working on the final scene to realize that, by using the third person, I was able to describe what Cal and Jenny were both feeling more or less simultaneously, which, I think, heightened the emotion and the immediacy at a critical point.

Q. *How did you conceive of Daniel? What do you want the reader to make of him?*

A. Initially, I thought of Daniel as just this amoral, narcissistic type of guy. Both Cal and Jenny are drawn to him, obviously, because he makes it clear that he believes the "whole idea of guilt is probably the worst concept mankind has ever come up with."

This is a comforting philosophy, of course, to two people weighed down by remorse. However, as the stor developed, I started to take a much darker view of hi And I began to understand that he was like a black hc essentially empty but also extremely powerful and gerous. Cal and Jenny were able to project their own needs and desires onto him and to believe he was offering them solace and guidance. But he was really leading them astray—down dangerous pathways—while interested only in his own pleasure and self-aggrandizement.

In the end, I think the character of Daniel is the closest I've ever come to writing about evil.

Q. The novel explores a number of sibling relationships. What was your own upbringing like?

A. I was raised in a small, close-knit community where large families were the norm. I'm one of six kids—third in the lineup and the oldest girl. There was a five-year gap between me and my younger brother, so I had very little experience of sibling rivalry and unhappiness (unless you count being tickled to the point of hysteria by older brothers). However, as a high-performing and ambitious group, we were not without drama and dysfunction. Probably because of that, I've always been fascinated by family dynamics. Jealousy, neediness, envy, loyalty, hero worship—all the great emotions are the everyday stuff of most sibling relationships. Even now so many of the habits and roles we established in our childhoods are still at play.

Q. Where exactly is So Near *set—and why?*

My husband and I have owned a weekend cottage in
rn Massachusetts for nearly twenty years. We spend

about half our time there, commuting back and forth from New York City. Our place is close to a small town that still retains a lovely New England rural feel, though a good percentage of its population are second-home owners like ourselves.

I loved writing about this beautiful part of the world in my first novel, *Local Knowledge*. I didn't want to reprise the same characters (though I do have Maddie and Paul put in a brief appearance), but I find that writing about a fictionalized version of this area is deeply satisfying. In many ways, it reminds me of the rolling hills of Pennsylvania and the community where I was raised.

Q. What sort of research did you do in writing the novel?

A. I had drafted a rough outline and was just starting to write the book when I was asked to talk to a reading group in my hometown. At the end of a terrific discussion, one of the women in the group asked what I was working on next and I briefly described the story that became *So Near*. "That's quite a coincidence," another woman said, "because my husband is a lawyer who has handled several such lawsuits." It wasn't just a coincidence; it was a real godsend. I was able to get firsthand, deeply knowledgeable advice about product liability litigation. These insights made me rethink some important details and, I believe, helped lend the story a sense of verisimilitude that secondhand research (from books, articles, the Internet, etc.) just can't duplicate.

Q. What authors do you like, and did any of them influence you in writing this book?

A. I read a lot of fiction and poetry, and my list of favorite writers is long, lowbrow, highfalutin, all over the place, and always growing. In no particular order, I love the fiction of Iris Murdoch, P. D. James, John Fowles, F. Scott and Penelope Fitzgerald, Jane Smiley, Susan Isaacs, and Alan Furst, and the poetry of Richard Wilbur, Elizabeth Bishop, Theodore Roethke, and Kay Ryan, to name just a very quick and beloved few. Over the past year or so, I've been particularly taken with—and no doubt influenced by—Jim Lynch's *Border Songs*, Allegra Goodman's *The Cookbook Collector*, and Curtis Sittenfeld's *American Wife*.

Q. Do you have a set writing routine?

A. I usually wake up early and reread whatever I've been working on. I revise constantly on the computer. (It continues to amaze me how Tolstoy could have written *War and Peace* in longhand!) Then I let the demands of daily life intervene for several hours and pick up again in the afternoon. Most days, I don't hit my stride until three o'clock or so, and then if I'm lucky get two or three good, productive hours in. I think a lot about what I'm working on when I'm not actually writing; when I'm running, for instance, or driving in the car back and forth between the city and Massachusetts. I try to work out problems—a scene I can't get off the ground, a character who refuses to behave—during that two-and-a-half-hour stretch.

Q. Are you working on something new?

A. Yes, and again, it takes place in a small town not far from Red River in *Local Knowledge* and Covington in *So Near*. It is about a married couple with two children who move from New York City back to the husband's small hometown after being traumatized by 9/11. The story is told from several points of view—one being that of the son, now in prep school, who gets caught in the middle of a drinking scandal at the couple's home, involving a classmate of his and a girl from the small town. The novel will explore questions of parental responsibility, identity, acceptance, and—of course—family.

QUESTIONS FOR DISCUSSION

1. In the beginning of the novel, Cal looks up to Kurt, just as he looks *to* him for direction in life. But after the accident, he begins to shift his allegiance and respect to Edmund. Did you sense he might be making a mistake?

2. Even before Betsy's death, Jenny seems to be troubled. Though the accident sweeps aside many other concerns, it also exposes some of Jenny's underlying problems. What are they—and how do they feed into some of her later decisions?

3. Sanctimonious and judgmental, Jenny's father is not a particularly sympathetic character. And yet, in the end, Jenny says to him, "I want you to know that almost everything you told me since Betsy died turns out to be true. I only wish I'd been able to listen to you sooner." What did you think of his advice?

4. Have you ever experienced the recurring presence of someone you loved after he or she has died?

5. Jenny's garden, especially as the story progresses, is intended to be a metaphor for her life. Did you sense that—and did that concept work for you?

6. When Cal first meets Daniel, he tells Jenny that "I felt that I knew him from somewhere. That we had this kind of *connection*." Why do you think he feels that way?

7. Do you think Kurt did the right thing when he decided to act as a witness against his own brother?

8. Unlike Cal and Jenny, Daniel never lies or alters his belief system. In fact, he doesn't change in any way throughout the story. What do you think this says about his character?

9. Grief "can make you do some crazy stuff," Cal says at one point. Do you think that excuses his actions—or Jenny's?

10. We never really learn why Jenny's mother left her husband and family. At one point, Jenny's father says, "What happened is between us." Do you think it's fair of him—or any parent—to keep such important information a secret?

11. Early on, Jenny says that there's something "creepy about demanding payment for someone's death" and calls product liability lawyers "vultures." Do you agree with that assessment when it comes to Lester Stokes and how he handled Cal's case?

12. Many marriages would fall apart after what Cal and Jenny experience. What do you think is going to happen to them in the future? Do they have a shot at happiness?